PUMPKIN SPICE

By the Author

Visiting Hours

Bird on a Wire

Across the Dark Horizon

And Then There Was Her

Queen of Humboldt

Swipe Right

Two Knights Tango

Almost Perfect

When It Feels Right

Pumpkin Spice

PUMPKIN SPICE

by

Tagan Shepard

2023

PUMPKIN SPICE

© 2023 BY TAGAN SHEPARD. ALL RIGHTS RESERVED.

ISBN 13: 978-1-63679-388-7

THIS TRADE PAPERBACK ORIGINAL IS PUBLISHED BY
BOLD STROKES BOOKS, INC.
P.O. BOX 249
VALLEY FALLS, NY 12185

FIRST EDITION: OCTOBER 2023

CREDITS
EDITORS: ASHLEY TILLMAN AND CINDY CRESAP
PRODUCTION DESIGN: SUSAN RAMUNDO
COVER DESIGN BY INK SPIRAL DESIGN

Acknowledgments

It still shocks me to say it out loud, but this is my tenth published book. What an incredible ride this has been and continues to be!

I used to talk about how writing was such a solitary endeavor. Just me typing away alone in my office or lonely in a coffee shop watching the world walk by while the words pour out of my heart. I've found recently, however, that I don't feel so alone in writing anymore. I have found my community and it has made all the difference.

My GCLS family and my Sapphic Lit Pop Up Bookstore family have given me a chance to discover my favorite part of being a writer: cheerleading my friends and telling the world about their books! These are two big families, but there are a few particularly precious gems amongst a sea of wealth. Finn and August, Patrice, Ash, Bridget, and Dunkley from GCLS. Cade, Louise, Bird, Rita, Cheri, Jennifer, and Serena are rockstars beyond measure.

Thanks, Kris Bryant, for the great title and help navigating my new publishing home.

My editor Ashley Bartlett is probably the best thing that ever happened to my writing.

Sandy, Rad, Cindy, and Ruth at BSB make everything I do possible and I am so very grateful.

And then there's Cris. My alpha reader, my cover advisor, my sounding board, my biggest fan. How can I possibly put into words what it has meant every day for the last twenty-two years that you love me? The way our relationship has grown and matured—it's more than I could have ever dreamed possible. I love you with every fiber of my being, but still—not a pumpkin.

Dedication

For Cris—my one and only, my now and forever.
Thanks for bringing so much spice into my life.

CHAPTER ONE

"Y ou can do this. It's just like riding a bike, right? You never really forget how, no matter how long it's been." I raised the axe and the setting sun glinted off the gleaming edge. "Just like riding a bike."

It was not like riding a bike.

I swung the axe, suppressing the urge to roar like Xena smiting my enemies.

I missed.

The wedge of dried pine wobbled, fell against the axe head stuck in the chopping block, then plopped unceremoniously to the earth. I sighed for what felt like the hundredth time and slumped against the axe handle.

"This is hopeless."

Somehow this task had been a lot easier when I was a teenager helping my dad. When I was sixteen, I'd spend hours in the backyard, perfect triangles of wood piling up with Dad grinning like a fool and cheering me on. I could cut a whole winter's worth of firewood in a single afternoon and still do all my homework on time.

Okay, not a whole winter's worth, but pretty close. The homework part was totally true.

I was about to ask myself what exactly happened in the last twenty-four years to make me worthless with physical tasks like this, but bending down to pick up the still too big wedge of firewood made my knees ache so I didn't have the energy. After examining the stubborn chunk of wood, I decided it would still burn despite its massive size and carried it to the wood shelter behind my cottage.

The sweat I had worked up chopping—or attempting to chop—wood cooled on my skin. September had started off warm as summer but had chilled rapidly. While it wasn't quite cold yet, autumn was descending and it could come on in a hurry this close to the mountains. It was that threat that had me out here in the limited daylight after work, desperately trying to stock enough firewood.

The store wasn't quite bare, but the pile of firewood looked awfully pitiful there in the bottom corner of my massive firewood shelter. Maybe I should check into converting the fireplace to gas again. Maybe I'd saved enough to take the leap? If I just went with an insert rather than doing a full conversion, I could save some cash.

"That would only put the cost slightly out of reach rather than completely out of reach," I said to myself.

Rather than drop the new log into the shelter, I filled my arms with a few other unevenly sized pieces and trudged inside. After kicking off my hiking boots on the stoop, I pushed through the door and kicked it shut behind me. I trod the familiar path through the mudroom, past the little kitchen tucked into one corner, and into my wide-open, lofted living room.

I knelt in front of the shelf built into the stone fireplace and carefully tucked the wood inside. It was an interesting fit, given the varied shapes and sizes, but I made it work. As I arranged the last piece, I reached out and braced myself against one of the stones that made up the hearth and chimney piece. All the stones were massive, rounded smooth, and ranging in color from blue-gray to rich tan. I traced the outline of the stone, the rough, pale gray mortar scratching my palm. I let my eye travel up from that stone to the next and the next, all the way to the vaulted ceiling.

The chimney was the centerpiece of this room, both architecturally and aesthetically. I'd designed the whole cottage around it, pulling colors from the individual stones to decorate floor, furniture, and walls. I couldn't possibly mar the effect by slapping a gas insert into it. The whole room would feel cheap and garish with fake logs. The scent of wood smoke was the crowning feature. The cottage wouldn't be the same without a roaring wood fire on snowy winter nights.

I sighed and pushed up onto my feet. "Then you have to get better at this wood chopping thing."

The sun was significantly lower in the sky when I made it back to my firewood chopping setup and it was dropping fast. I didn't have much time, but I had to give it another go. For the thousandth time, I chastised myself for not being better at this. I grumbled as I reached for the axe. "A good lesbian would be able to chop mountains of firewood."

A familiar laugh rang out across the yard, and I turned to see my sister, Rachel, walking toward me, a pair of wineglasses in her hands. "Truer words were never spoken. I'm shocked your rainbow card hasn't been revoked."

I stuck my tongue out at her and earned another of her musical laughs. Rachel was two years older than me, but she was lightyears ahead in every other category. She was six inches taller and had the sort of slim-in-all-the-right-places look that made her the prettiest one in every room. The way she could pull off skinny jeans with an oversized cardigan annoyed the hell out of me. Of course, that's what she was wearing tonight while I was making a fool of myself trying to chop wood.

In contrast to my stylish sister, I looked like the sort of plain, forgettable woman generations past would have referred to as a dowdy spinster. They weren't entirely wrong. I'd never been interested in the latest trends, but wore whatever clothing was comfortable. Plus, most of the clothing I found in the stores Rachel shopped in were far too feminine for me. Thus, my wardrobe consisted mainly of blue jeans, khakis, and whatever was on sale at L.L. Bean.

It wasn't just our styles that were polar opposites. She had the elegance and grace of a movie star, whereas I had the sort of small, understated features that had people mistaking me for a teenager even now that I was over the hill. I had a button nose and round cheeks that, when combined with my slightly prominent ears gave me an elf-like appearance that was cute when I was a kid but wasn't going to win me any modeling contracts. My mousey brown hair was the same dull shade as my eyes and left me fading into the background. When Rachel forced me to say something nice about myself, I admitted that my mouth was pretty. It was wide and easy to shape into a smile with a prominent bow. If it weren't for my charming smile, most people wouldn't even notice me when they passed me on the sidewalk.

Rachel sipped her glass of wine as she teased me. "You're too femme for firewood and too butch for spike heels. Once the Gay Authorities find out that you don't fit into either lesbian type they'll come after you for sure."

"Um, excuse me, there are more than two types of lesbian." I swiped the wineglass she held out to me and took a long sip. "I've been trying to tell you that for years."

Rachel's smile grew slowly. "Maybe you should tell yourself that, then you won't beat yourself up over this."

I waved my wineglass to indicate the pile of wood. "This is the only way I'm staying warm this winter. So I need to butch up."

I pushed the wineglass back at her and lined up my next chop. The log teetering on the chopping block was massive, wider than my shoulders by a good few inches. But I would conquer it. I had to conquer it. Not to retain my Rainbow Card, but to keep myself from freezing to death this winter.

I did not conquer it.

The axe struck home in the dead center of the log, but it wedged itself about an inch deep and stopped.

"Damn it."

Rachel threw her head back and laughed at my latest attempt. "You've lived in the cottage for five winters, how've you managed to not freeze to death?"

I struggled to free the axe from the log. "Your piece of shit, philandering ex-husband always did it for me."

The axe came free, but I immediately dropped it. In my attempts to retrieve it, my arms jerked and I knocked the log off the chopping block.

Rachel snorted into her wineglass. "At least he was good for something."

"I'm pretty sure he was just coming around in hopes of catching me with another woman."

"He's even stupider than I believed if he thought that would happen."

I stuck my tongue out at her again, but annoyance finally gave me enough strength to chop through the log. Only five or six more swings like that and I could finish breaking it down.

Rachel leaned back against the gnarled trunk of my Bradford pear. "How long's it been since you dated someone anyway?"

I shrugged and turned back to my chopping to hide the flush of embarrassment on my cheeks. If she'd forgotten how many years I'd been single, I certainly wasn't going to remind her. I also managed to channel the humiliation over my last breakup into a decent axe swing. Maybe I should have Rachel come around and nag me every night and then I could have enough firewood.

Rachel cleared her throat and took on that I-need-something-and-I'm-embarrassed-to-ask tone she'd perfected. "Speaking of my stupid ex-husband leaving me in a lurch."

"Oh God, what's he done now?"

"It's more his absence that's the problem. The kids want to go load up on pumpkins this weekend and I really need help carrying them." She'd spit out the explanation in record time, but slowed down to ask, "Want to be the kids' favorite aunt?"

I grunted as I repositioned the log. "I'm already their favorite aunt. Anyway, it's only September. Why do they want pumpkins?"

"Saturday is October first."

"That's too early for pumpkins."

"It's never too early for Lily to have pumpkins," Rachel said.

I dropped the axe and spent several minutes wheezing to catch my breath. "You see this pathetic display I'm putting on, right? Why do you think I can carry a bunch of pumpkins?"

She smiled and rushed forward, holding out the glass of wine. "Good point, but the kids don't know you're a failed lesbian. They think you're a superstar lesbian who can carry twice the pumpkins their father can."

"And you're setting me up to disappoint them."

Rachel shrugged. "Better they're disillusioned now than wait until they're teenagers."

I threw my gloves at her and took a long sip of wine. It occurred to me that this was bribery wine. I shrugged 'cause at least it was an effective bribe. "Fine. But you're buying me one of those Amish sourdough donuts and a hot apple cider."

Rachel hopped happily and leaned over to kiss my cheek. As she walked back toward her house she said over her shoulder, "Thanks, Nicki. I'll sneak in something to spike your apple cider with. You'll need it."

❖

Friday morning, I woke up three minutes before my alarm went off. This was a change because it was usually five minutes before the alarm, but I'd been so tired from my usual Thursday evening house cleaning that it didn't surprise me to be sleeping in.

I snuggled deeper into my pile of blankets and listened to the hum of the air conditioner blasting cold air into the room while I planned out my day. That didn't take long. It was a workday and I didn't have any Friday night plans. Not that I usually had Friday night plans, but every now and then I got to babysit while Rachel went on a date.

The AC cut off while I was musing over my dull day ahead and the blankets started to get uncomfortably hot. I hated being hot while I slept, but I loved being tucked under a mountain of blankets, so the AC was set ridiculously low even in the autumn. I raised my head to look for Ralph, but I knew where he'd be. Tucked into a tight, orange tabby ball at the foot of the bed on the opposite, unused side. Sure enough, he was there, snoozing away.

"Would it kill you to snuggle with me once in a while?"

He didn't even raise his head to acknowledge my rebuke.

My alarm sounded and I switched it off before it could wake Ralph. He always grumbled at me if I woke him. I pushed aside the pillow I hugged during the night, then climbed out of bed and headed for the shower.

I'd set the automatic brew on my coffee pot to start two minutes after my shower ended. Thanks to my late start this morning, it was ready before I finished flat-ironing my hair. I went with simpler makeup to make up the lost time. The coffee would get that unpleasant burned flavor if I waited too long to drink it.

I poured my first cup, then dropped my bagel in the toaster and grabbed tomorrow's from the freezer. The shelf of individually wrapped bagels was getting low and I made a mental note to make more Saturday. It wasn't until I was smearing on my tablespoon of whipped cream cheese that I remembered about the pumpkins. I checked the weather while I ate and saw that the temperature tomorrow would be in the high seventies.

I grumbled through a mouthful of sesame bagel. "Not exactly pumpkin picking weather. I wish Virginia would make up its mind about the seasons."

I could hear my grandma's voice in my head, reminding me that it was better here in the mountains than elsewhere in the state. Then my old, childhood tones bleating about how these weren't real mountains. Not like the Rockies or the Alps.

Grandma had loved the Appalachians nearly as much as she'd loved this cottage and the horse farm. Looking around my house, I could still see touches of her here. In the wheat field painting by the front door she'd bought from a friend and the old rocker she'd spent most of her days in the last year of her life. The rest of the farm was so different. It wasn't even a farm anymore. But this cottage. No matter how much I made it mine, it would always feel like Grandma lived here with me.

When I was a kid, the stable manager had squeezed his little family in here and Grandma had been in the big house with us. The whole estate had so much more energy back then. With the sounds of horses floating on the air along with the ever-present smells of hay and grass. The energy had been the first thing to go.

I was in middle school when the stable manager left and Grandma had moved in here. Everyone knew we didn't need a new manager. Everyone knew the stables weren't going to be there much longer. There hadn't been any tears or big moment, just the slow, inevitable death of the family business. In the end, I think the only one who missed the horses was me.

I washed my coffee cup and plate before filling my travel coffee mug. As always, I lamented leaving the other two cups in the pot. It just didn't taste right when I made two cups instead of the full pot's worth. I hated to waste the rest, but there was nothing I could do about it. Rachel didn't drink coffee and there was no one else to share it with. My briefcase sat, packed and ready to go, by the front door. I was driving off to the city exactly an hour after I woke up.

The drive from Bucks Mill to Charlottesville was as stunning as any drive could be. I had driven that winding route through foothills and forests more times than I could possibly count, but my heart still soared when I turned that one corner on Skyline Crest Drive and got the perfect view of Afton Mountain. The leaves were already starting to turn and soon there would be a blaze of color like nothing else up there.

The traffic got terrible when I got near work. It was more a pedestrian issue than a vehicular one. The school year had started last month, and the freshmen were still learning when and where to look out for traffic. Seeing these kids made me feel old. And poor. Most of these students were paying the ridiculously high University of Virginia tuition with their parents' money. They wouldn't have the student loan debt I'd be paying off until the day I died. I knew that better than most, since I worked in the finance department. It still blew my mind how many times we got a personal check paying a full year's tuition. The idea of writing a check that big simply did not compute.

The office was just like usual—pockets of chatter surrounded by wide swaths of silence. A few of my coworkers sent a wave my way as I neared, but most barely noticed my passing. We'd never been a particularly close bunch of colleagues, and so many of our number decided working from home was fun and hadn't come back in when the office reopened. I personally hadn't enjoyed working from home when forced. While I didn't chat much, I liked the energetic hum of people around me. Being at home too much made me antsy.

As if to prove my point that we weren't a close-knit group, not a single coworker stopped by my small office until after lunch. My boss, Fred, was just as socially awkward as me, but with a boyish face that endeared him to everyone. It probably helped that his body didn't betray him by blushing every time he did something silly the way mine tended to do.

Fred hovered in my doorway with his typical afternoon mint tea in hand. "How's Wreck-It Ralph? Destroyed the house yet?"

I forced a laugh, but it was pretty weak and Fred shook his head, looking away. Ralph was not the kind of cat with the energy to be destructive, but ever since that silly Pixar movie came out, he'd tried to make this our inside joke. I hadn't understood it until he'd accidentally left a management self-help book in the break room one day. He'd dog-eared the page that recommended inside jokes with subordinates and had notes for all of us scribbled in the margins. Everyone else had several options under their names. My cat had been the only option his brainstorming had managed.

I joked to cover the awkward moment. "He hasn't wrecked anything yet, but I'm vigilant for any signs."

He laughed and asked after a couple other tidbits about my life. Lily's soccer team and Blake's preschool classes. For all his awkwardness, he really did care about us and he remembered the slightest details of all our lives. Once he settled into the conversation, he even calmed down enough to lean against the doorframe rather than stand rigidly.

"Doing anything fun this weekend?" he asked.

I straightened my pen cup. "I don't know if it qualifies as fun, but I'm going to get pumpkins with the kids."

"That'll be nice."

I could see him searching for more to say on the matter and I was doing the same. Fred was a sweet guy, but these conversations could really be painful. It wasn't his fault or mine really. We were both just better with spreadsheets than people.

"Have any advice for the best way to carry pumpkins?" He stared blankly at my attempt to chat, so I continued, "There's a fixed price for all the pumpkins you can carry. All you have to do is take three steps with your arms loaded down and you get them all for way cheaper."

Apparently, he could blush. "I don't know if I'm the right one to ask. I could check in with Larry or Richard? Maybe even John K. Not John R, he's not that strong a guy either."

"It's okay, Fred. Really."

"Okay, well, have fun and good luck."

He bolted so quick I saw a dollop of tea splash over his mug and soak into his shirt sleeve. So much for an attempt at friendly conversation. I sighed and went back to my latest report, guessing that I'd start getting emails with pumpkin carrying advice within the hour.

The first one arrived fifteen minutes later.

CHAPTER TWO

I was truly shocked how busy Carter Farms was when we arrived early Saturday afternoon. Apparently, everyone else in town thought it was perfectly reasonable to buy Halloween pumpkins on the first day of October. We had to wait in line fifteen minutes just to get in the front gates.

"Why are there so many people here?" I asked as yet another carload of people filed into the line behind us.

Lily turned an annoyed, long-suffering look on me. "Most people in town got their pumpkins at the big opening event last weekend. We're here with the stragglers and out-of-towners."

"But that's over a month before Halloween."

"Yeah. So?"

"Pumpkins rot, Lily. No way a carved pumpkin will last that long."

"No one carves their pumpkins anymore, Aunt Nicki. You arrange them in an aesthetically pleasing display with varied heights and widths."

"Aesthetically pleasing?" I screwed up my face, trying to remember how old I was when I learned that term. Certainly I wasn't using it when I was nine years old.

"Do you even use Instagram?" Lily asked

"Do you?"

Rachel set Blake on his feet and turned to me. "Don't say it like that. I put parental locks all over her account."

I wasn't sure that made it better, but little Blake chose that moment to try bolting after someone's golden retriever. I didn't know which was worse, my niece being nine years old going on thirty or my nephew being a reckless toddler barely able to focus on one thing for longer than five minutes. Once we got inside, however, his eyes went wide as bowling balls as he took in all the sights and sounds. He held on tight to Rachel's hand and let himself be led toward the hayride that would take us into the patch to pick our own pumpkins.

Lily shouted instructions over the rumble of the tractor. "It's really important to look at the stem, not just the pumpkin itself. If the stem is all brown and icky, no way the pumpkin will last."

I nodded agreement and tried not to topple over onto anyone when the tractor drove through some deep ruts on the dirt road. The hayride was packed with excited families. I scoped out the crowd, looking for more muscular men who I could watch for notes on my pumpkin carrying technique. None of this batch looked any more prepared than me.

The hayride took us through acres and acres of fields, most of them fallow for the season. I was pretty sure Carter Farms did pick-your-own strawberries, too, but I couldn't remember if I'd been out here since the new owners took over. No doubt I'd be better at hauling pints of strawberries than pounds of pumpkins. If I crashed and burned on this outing, maybe I could redeem myself to Lily in the summer. Hopefully, the middle school Instagram craze then would be strawberry shortcake.

After another five bumpy minutes of picking sharp strands of hay out of my backside, the tractor lurched to a halt next to a sprawling field dotted with splotches of orange. I stood shakily and looked around. We'd beaten most of the crowd out here. Other families had stopped for cider and doughnuts before hitting the patch, so the field wasn't too crowded. Lily stood beside me, her hand up to shield her eyes as she glared off into the distance.

Suddenly, Lily's arm shot out, her little hand pointing to a spot in the fields at least seventy miles away. "There! That's the best spot. Let's go, Aunt Nicki."

We were the last ones on the tractor and I shot an apologetic look at the driver. He was a bulky, heavily bearded man with a round face and small, light brown eyes. I'd expected an impatient scowl, but instead his beard split into a wide grin and he waved merrily at me as I jumped off the tractor to chase after Lily.

I called to Lily and pointed frantically over my shoulder. "Your mom and Blake went that way. Don't you want to follow them?"

Lily skittered down the path between the pumpkins, hopping over vines as she ran. "They'll only slow us down. Someone else will find these if we don't get them now."

My armpits were sweaty and my shoes were a total loss by the time we got to the supposedly perfect spot. Lily had arrived before me and was tapping pumpkins.

"It should sound like a watermelon." Lily stood straight and turned on me, confusion etching a line between her pale eyebrows. "What's a watermelon supposed to sound like, Aunt Nicki?"

I shrugged and flicked mud and squishy pumpkin flesh off my Chucks. "Hollow I think."

"Then this one's perfect. Pick this one." She pointed at the pumpkin at her feet. It was bigger than her head and the rich, warm color of a perfect navel orange.

I stared at the green stem with little curlicues of vine and leaf branching off from it. The main vine was withered and browning, but the pumpkin's stem looked very much alive and very sturdy. "How do I, um, do that?"

Lily stared at me in disbelief. "You don't know how to pick a pumpkin?"

"Do you?"

She rolled her eyes and pointed to the spot where the pumpkin's stem met the main vine. "Twist it right there. Hold onto the stem so it doesn't rip out of the pumpkin." I reached for the stem and she slapped a little hand on my wrist. "Do not rip off the stem. It will ruin the pumpkin and you can't ruin this one, Aunt Nicki."

"Okay. Sheesh. Don't you trust me?"

She gave me a skeptical look and I couldn't blame her. I didn't really trust myself with this task. I rolled my shoulders, pushing the fleece vest farther back off my neck. The vest wasn't in the least bit necessary, given the high temperatures, but it made me feel like it was autumn without making me too sweaty.

I smiled over at Lily. "Here goes. Ready?"

Lily bit her bottom lip and nodded, eyes fixed on the pumpkin. She was just like me when I was a kid—focused and insistent with total disregard for the people around her. I just hoped that she kept her wide-eyed wonder at the world and comfort in social situations that I had lost over the years.

I grabbed hold of the pumpkin stem, little sharp hairs poking into my palms, and twisted. To my utter surprise, the stem snapped easily from the vine and stayed firmly attached to the pumpkin. Lily clapped and squealed with delight when I held the pumpkin out. She snatched it from me and hugged it close, smearing a little bit of dirt on her cheek.

"It's perfect. You did it," she said. I sat back on my heels, basking in the glow of being the favorite aunt, until Lily opened her eyes and pointed at another, even bigger pumpkin behind her. "Now get that one. It's perfect."

This became the theme of the morning. Each new pick was even more perfect than the last and Lily simply had to have them all to complete her display. She yanked me around our secluded patch, our pile of picked pumpkins growing by the minute. I'll admit, I got lost in the task. I was getting really good at twisting the stems off, especially after I started lifting them off the ground for better leverage. By the time Rachel and Blake found us, Lily was beside herself with glee.

Rachel gaped at us, Blake in her arms holding a mini pumpkin in each fleshy hand. "Nicki, what are you doing? That is way too many pumpkins."

My cheeks heated up as I looked at our haul. It was a lot. Like enough for three families. Lily looked up at her mother, tears filling her eyes like Rachel had told her she had to smash every one of those perfect pumpkins to pieces right then and there.

I scrambled for excuses at the sight of her tears. "They're for both of us. Some are for my house."

Lily turned her watery gaze on me and I was the Hero Aunt again. The heat fled from my cheeks and into my chest. When she looked at me like that, it made the sweaty armpits and muddy shoes worth it.

Far from looking at me like I was a hero, Rachel rolled her eyes and leaned in close to whisper, "You got played, Aunt Nicki. Played like a chump by a preteen."

I couldn't argue the fact, given that Lily's eyes had dried instantly and she was instructing us all on how to carry her prizes back to the hayride. It took all of us to get them back to the tractor. Even Blake had to carry one of the small ones along with his own minis. Halfway back he lost focus and stepped on a cracked, rotting pumpkin that had fallen into the path. He fell hard and started wailing, only slightly louder than Lily screaming about the pumpkin he carried. The only damage was to Blake's now stained jeans, but nerves were frayed to say the least by the time we loaded our prizes onto the tractor.

To my great relief, there were wagons to carry our pumpkins when we got off the hayride. This was lucky as I hadn't found anyone to copy yet and I couldn't for the life of me remember any of the tips from Fred's email. Why hadn't I memorized the list? And there was no cell service out here on the farm, so I couldn't pull up the email and check.

We were dragging two wagons full of pumpkins toward the cashiers when I noticed the carrying zone. Some of the largest, fittest men I'd ever seen were struggling to carry half as many pumpkins as we were toting. Beaming children and simpering wives were cheering them on and the staff, all dressed in flannel shirts and green vests with the Carter Farms logo on the back, seemed just as excited. I couldn't help visualizing the sad, disappointed looks they would give me when I crumpled under the combined weight of pumpkins and adolescent expectations.

"Oh no!"

I lurched to a halt at Lily's scream. "What? What's wrong?"

"Oh no. This is terrible. What am I gonna do?"

I knelt beside her to take her hands. "What's wrong, sweetie? Are you hurt?"

"It's all ruined. We might as well not get any of these. How could I have forgotten?"

Now Rachel was kneeling on her other side, looking even more distressed. "What's wrong, Lily? What happened?"

"I forgot to get a white pumpkin," Lily said.

I'll admit—I was confused by that answer. I'd been checking Lily for signs of injury or imminent danger. I rolled her words around in my head, trying to make them make sense. Her mother was much quicker off the mark. She sighed and pushed back to her feet, muttering what sounded like every syllable of Lily's first and middle names. I was starting to get annoyed, but the middle name thing had been a guerrilla tactic of the women in our family going back four generations. Hearing a middle name in public was enough to make me want to hide.

I stood up, brushing off my knees. "I don't think those are a real thing. Isn't it just paint?"

Lily gave me such a withering look that I nearly broke out her middle name, too. "Of course, they're a real thing. Tinley Bamford has two and they look amazing. I have to have one or I'll be the laughing stock of my grade. If not the whole school."

I wanted to argue, but I'd known the Bamfords for too long to doubt Lily. Her mother, Meaghan, had made my life hell when we were in school together. My family didn't have a quarter of the money hers did, even when we still had the stables, and she never let me forget it. Once she'd married into the Bamford fortune, she'd rubbed it in everyone's face. No doubt, her daughter was equally terrible. But as much as I wanted to help Lily in her fight against the school mean girl, there hadn't been any white pumpkins in the field and I didn't see any on the tables of pre-picked pumpkins for sale.

"I'm sorry, honey, but it doesn't look like they have any white pumpkins."

"Actually, we do have some."

The voice that came from over my shoulder was so smooth and smoky that I prepared myself to see a gorgeous woman when I turned around. I did not prepare enough.

To say this woman was hot was an insult to the word. She was at least a foot taller than me, so I had to look up to make eye contact, but boy was that worth it. She had the most captivating eyes. Chestnut brown with the gentleness of a kind animal. A tiny sparkle showed in them as she turned up the right side of her thin lips in a crooked half-smile.

It was a mistake to look at her lips, because dragging my eyes away from them became nearly impossible. The bow in the center was deep and her jaw was wide, creating a perfect, nearly square frame for her mouth. My mind wandered to impure thoughts before I could catch it—immediately fascinated by the way those pale lips would feel against mine.

My lips moved to say something, but I couldn't feel them and so the noise they made was not from any language codified by humans.

The crooked half-smile broadened to her full mouth and dimples popped out in her cheeks. Dimples. My Achilles' heel.

She shoved her hands in her back pockets and laughed. "Sorry? Didn't catch that."

I tried to swallow and figure out what I'd meant by that jumble of letters, but putting her hands in her back pockets had done incredible things to the fit of her flannel shirt and the peek of white undershirt beneath. They stretched across a small but very enticing chest, pushing the thin Carhartt jacket back on her shoulders. Because of our height difference, the display was far closer to my eyes than was good for my language skills.

I finally managed to clear my throat and say, "Oh really? Where?"

She shoved her thumb into the air over her right shoulder and the movement pushed back her sleeve, revealing swirling gray and black tattoos in a cuff around her wrist. "Just over behind the barn here. I can show you if you'd like."

Lily marched off in that direction without another word. I yanked at the handle of my wagon, but it took a few tugs before I could get the overburdened wheels to turn. While we trundled along in Lily's wake, I took in the rest of this mystery hottie.

She was built like someone who spent a lot of time outdoors doing all the butch things I couldn't quite manage. Chopping firewood and tossing hay bales and lifting whole houses with her pinky finger. She had wide, square shoulders and her forearms where she'd rolled up her sleeves were enough to make my face go numb. She looked like she'd recently had a haircut, the sides of her brunette hair were cut tight and faded into a neatly parted swoop on top. I could see from where the collar of her shirt pulled away from her neck that the bronze of her skin was a tan, the freshly exposed patches were pale and freckled.

I was so intent on my guide that I wasn't paying attention to the ground beneath me. When we left the area that had been trampled flat by dozens of visitors, the wagon wheels caught on the lip and sent the whole, overloaded wagon careening off track. I lost my grip on the handle and the wagon went tearing off on its own down the slight hill.

"Oh crap!"

The stranger's only reply was a muttered word much less child-friendly than mine before she bolted after the wagon. Fortunately, a rut in the field beside the barn stopped the wagon. Unfortunately, the abrupt halt sent half the cargo toppling over the side.

"Crap, crap, crap." I was getting more articulate by the minute.

When I arrived beside the stranger at the crash scene, she said, "It's okay. The ground is pretty soft from last week's rain."

Rachel hurried up with the other wagon's handle in one hand and Blake asleep on her shoulder. "Nicki? What happened?"

I kept my eyes on the ground so she couldn't see my embarrassment. "Just dropped some pumpkins. Can you go help Lily pick out a white pumpkin?"

Rachel patted me on the shoulder as she trundled off in search of her wayward daughter. I did my best to scrape up a shred of dignity as I hauled a pumpkin back to the wagon. Before I could balance it back on top, a gentle hand dropped onto my forearm. Goose pimples sprung out on my skin and I looked up into the stranger's warm, captivating eyes.

"Let me check it for cracks before you load it," she said in a low, husky voice that did nothing to dispel the prickling on my arm. "They'll rot faster if they're cracked."

"Oh. Okay. Thanks."

She took the pumpkin from my arms and turned it this way and that, caressing the orange skin. It should be illegal to be that sexy inspecting a pumpkin.

"I'd hate for you and your wife to pay for a pumpkin that'll rot. Your daughter would be so disappointed."

I blinked twice and then managed to say, "She's not my wife. She's my sister. Lily is my niece, not my daughter."

"I'm sorry. I didn't mean to assume."

"I am though. Gay. Not gay with her, just, um…"

"Unattached gay?" she asked, the half-grin back and just as devastating as before.

I blushed so hard my face felt like it was melting, but I thought there was a hint of a twinkle in her eye. "Yeah. Very unattached gay."

"Good to know."

There was definitely a twinkle in her eye now and her smile had grown full and blinding. It fit so well in her square jaw and the dimples had my knees turning to Jell-O. Her eyes seemed to be getting closer. I couldn't tell if she was leaning in or I was because I could not feel any part of my body. All I could do was stare into her eyes and soak in the warm scents of autumn on her. Dried leaves and hay mixing with a warm, spicy cologne.

Lily's squeal of delight shattered the moment, and I blinked like I was waking up from a dream. I looked over to see Lily running toward me with a pair of smallish white pumpkins tucked into her armpits. When I turned back to the stranger, she was checking the last pumpkin and settling it carefully onto the wagon.

"Look at these, Aunt Nicki. Aren't they the most beautiful white pumpkins you've ever seen?" Lily squealed.

"Totally."

I had never seen a real white pumpkin, so it wasn't a lie, but I honestly hadn't even spared them a glance. The stranger knelt down on one knee in front of Lily and leaned close.

"Now don't go telling anyone else in line where you got these. It's our little secret stash, okay?"

Lily grew serious and nodded. "I wouldn't dare tell. And I'm very good at keeping secrets. Right, Aunt Nicki?"

"Right. She's a vault."

The stranger stood and gave me one last, killer smile before strolling back toward the crowds. Yes, I definitely watched her go. Every. Incredible. Step.

"There's drool on your chin," Rachel whispered in my ear as she marched past.

CHAPTER THREE

Monday morning, I woke up my usual five minutes before the alarm. I lay in bed, staring at the slatted ceiling. I tried to plan out my day as usual, but a handsome face kept barging into my thoughts. One with a square jaw and dimples and eyes like a chestnut mare. In fact, I hadn't stopped seeing that face in my mind's eye since I'd left the pumpkin patch. It had taken me until Sunday morning to realize I had never gotten her name, so I couldn't even properly daydream about her.

My alarm blared, making me and Ralph both jump. He grumbled and settled back down while I scrambled to turn it off. It had been ages since the alarm had caught me by surprise. I leapt out of bed and scrambled to start my day, but everything was slightly off. I was low on toothpaste, but couldn't find the backup. I knew I'd started a shopping list Saturday morning, but I couldn't find the paper to add toothpaste.

The worst came when I got to the kitchen, ten minutes late, and found that I had eaten my last bagel Sunday morning. I'd meant to make more, but I'd completely forgotten while arranging pumpkins on my stoop and daydreaming about muscular forearms peeking out from rolled up flannel shirts. It was too late to make up for the oversight, so I decided to head into town for one of Sallie Bell's famous cheddar bagels. I might even swallow my pride and order one of her delicious pumpkin spice lattes, despite the social stigma I was sure to endure.

Bucks Mill was as charming and sleepy a little town as ever existed. Nestled into the Virginia foothills directly between No-Consequence and Everyone-Knows-Your-Name, barely anything had changed in the forty years I'd called it home. Mom-and-pop shops that couldn't seem to make it anywhere else in the country thrived here. I saw delivery trucks painted with the local hardware store's logo more than Amazon's fleet, and that's how I wanted it to stay. Bucks Mill staying quiet and forgotten meant I always got a parking spot outside Sallie Bell's Bakery and Café.

That was when I didn't have to fight for space with all the chalkboard signs screaming in colorful letters that "Pumpkin Spice Season Is Here." I had to weave between three sandwich board signs on way from the street to the front door. They were touting everything from the standard pumpkin spice latte to pumpkin spice bagels with pumpkin spice cream cheese. It was way over the top—just like Sallie Bell herself.

Sallie scurried around the counter to wrap me in a cinnamon-scented hug. "Well, look who's darkening my doorstep. If it isn't my favorite customer."

I gave an embarrassed wave to Becky Sanderson, who had been dictating her order to Sallie before I'd distracted her. "I'm sure you say that to all your customers."

Sallie leaned over and kissed my forehead before she hurried back to Becky. She called over her shoulder, "Of course I do. But with you I really mean it."

I got into line behind Becky, who leaned back and whispered, "She says that to all her customers, too."

I gave Becky a nervous laugh, but she didn't look too upset about me interrupting her order. Sallie turned her attention back to business, giving me a chance to look around.

This place always reminded me of my grandma. Sallie Bell's mother had been her best friend and the original owner of the bakery. I'd spent hours in here with Grandma and Granny Bell when I was a kid, scarfing down cookies and slurping my hot chocolate like it was the strong black coffee Grandma drank. I'd been Lily's age when Sallie had come back to Bucks Mill, two failed marriages behind her and her maiden name back on her driver's license. Then our gossiping trio had turned into a quartet and Sallie had taken a motherly interest in me. The gossiping was a Bell woman trademark, but, as far as I could tell, I was the only one in town Sallie treated like an orphaned puppy. Apart from the nagging about finding a nice woman and settling down, I didn't mind it one bit.

"Run out of bagels again?" Sallie asked after she'd sent Becky off with a decaf coffee and cheese Danish.

"Yeah, I forgot to bake more yesterday," I said, scanning the pastry case for a replacement breakfast.

"I've told you a hundred times you don't have to make your own. Let me send you home with a dozen or two?"

"No, thanks, Sallie. I like to make my own." Realizing too late how that sounded, I scrambled to continue, "Yours are great, but I love kneading dough. It's therapeutic."

Sallie waggled her knobbly fingers. "It's therapeutic until it's arthritic. I'd barely be able to move these if I hand mixed everything like Momma did, rest her soul."

The door clanked open behind me, distracting Sallie and giving me a chance to look back at the case. Everything was either shaped like a pumpkin, colored like a pumpkin, or flavored with pumpkin. I loved autumn as much as the next girl, and pumpkin spice season even more. There was something unbeatable about cinnamon, nutmeg, ginger, and cloves steeped in frothy milk and mixed with more espresso than was good for me. The moment I'd had my first PSL, I was hooked.

I usually kept a tight lid on my obsession, though. Pumpkin spice was one of those things that everyone had to have a strong opinion about. People either loved them or hated them, there wasn't any in between. While I fell hard on the love side of the equation, Rachel had planted her flag on hate. She insisted the whole thing was a gimmick and lectured me constantly. According to my cynical sister, it didn't even have anything to do with pumpkins. Anyone could throw together cinnamon, nutmeg, ginger, and cloves. There wasn't anything special about it. Her constant abuse had sent me back into the PSL-loving closet and I could only be myself around Sallie Bell.

Sallie leaned over the case next to me. "I just love this time of year. Pumpkin spice season. It's even better than eggnog and peppermint season, don't you think?"

"Hands down," I said, doing a little excited bounce on my toes.

"You have to have the pumpkin bagel special."

"As long as it's our little secret. If Rachel asks, I got the cheddar."

"I'll take it to my grave. And I'm sending you home with a dozen pumpkin spice bagels. No arguments and no refusals. In fact, I'll have them delivered to your cottage. No extra charge. Is the key still under the mat?"

I considered arguing, but really, what was the point?

"Yes. Thanks so much, Sallie. That's sweet of you."

She dropped a sliced bagel into the toaster and went to work on my latte while she talked a mile a minute. I couldn't get a word in edgewise. "Can't have you getting arthritis like me. It's hell when it gets cold. Of course, if we got snow it might make the pain worth it, but no. Not here. Just biting cold for a month or two and then back to damp and dull until May. Here's your card back, dear. And your coffee. Just wait over there and I'll bring you the bagel when it's done."

I found myself, debit card in one hand, steaming latte in the other, in the back corner of the shop. A line had formed behind me and Sallie's nephew was stuffing a big box full of Danishes and donuts, so she was on her own. I turned my eyes back to the assortment of cringeworthy pastries and lost myself in the sounds of the shop. The bell over the door tinkling along with the squeal of the hinges each time a new customer arrived. The gurgle of the espresso machine and the hiss of the pass-through toaster. The scrape of knife on bread and credit cards on leather wallets. The background hum of a coffee shop straight out of heaven.

"They have amazing pastries here, don't they?"

I thought I'd imagined the voice at first. After all, I'd been daydreaming about those rich, deep tones for two days. But the voice was accompanied this time by that smell of fallen leaves and warm cotton. I turned to look at the stranger from the pumpkin patch, just as delicious as ever, though it was a green flannel under the jacket today rather than red. The sight, scent, and sound of her had me ready to melt.

Rather than melting, I dropped my coffee. Well, almost. I caught it rather ungracefully before it had a chance to spill, but it was a close thing.

"Yeah. It's all so good." Too late I registered how my voice had faded out into a purr, almost a moan, at the end. It definitely sounded suggestive. Clearly, she thought so, too, because one of her thick eyebrows arched slightly and her half-smile grew to show another tooth.

"At first, I thought it was great that I had the job to pick up the farm's order. Now I worry about my waistline." She slapped one hand against her stomach just above a large silver belt buckle.

"Your waistline looks great to me." The words just fell out of my mouth before I could stop them. Worse, my eyes had fixed on her hand where it had rested, one thumb hooked behind her belt. My face heated again. "I'm sorry. I didn't mean to say that."

"I'm happy to hear it."

God, why did she have to smile like that? Why did her eyes have to dance and her cheeks dimple?

"I didn't get a chance to introduce myself the other day. I'm Carter," she said, holding out her hand.

"Like Carter Farms?"

"Yeah. I've always gone by my last name."

"Why's that?"

"I'll tell you if you shake my hand and tell me your name."

I was such an idiot. Fortunately, I didn't berate myself out loud. She still held her hand out for me to shake and I still fiddled with my coffee cup like an awkward idiot.

"Sorry. I didn't mean to make you wait." I grabbed her hand and tried not to memorize the feel of her warm, slightly calloused palm against mine. "I'm Nicki Russell."

She held on to my hand longer than she really had to. Or maybe it was me holding on. It was probably wishful thinking that she was as reluctant as me to release it.

"Pleasure to meet you, Nicki Russell." When I released her hand, she scrubbed it through the short hair above her ear, then stuffed it in her pocket. "You paid up, so I suppose I have to tell you now. My parents gave me a traditional family name and it doesn't suit me. Never has. So they let me go by Carter."

Interesting that she had asked permission to choose her own name. I was going to ask her about it, but Sallie Bell appeared on the other side of the counter. She thrust a clipboard at Carter, who took it and scribbled something at the bottom. Looking over her shoulder, I saw that she signed "D Carter."

Handing the clipboard back to Sallie, she shot me a sideways glance. "You didn't think it'd be that easy to find out my first name, did you?"

Sallie held out a paper bag to me, the contents bulging the sides out. "Here's your pumpkin special. Need anything else, sweetie?"

"No, thanks, Sallie. I'm good."

Sallie wandered off back to the register, and I knew that was my cue to go. But Carter would still be waiting a while and I wanted an excuse to keep talking to her. Problem was, I'd always been terrible at small talk. The last thing I wanted to bring up was the weather, for goodness sake. I looked all around for something to talk about, but all I saw was a sea of orange and the bagel in my hands. The battle over pumpkin spice supremacy seemed a logical discussion. Considering that she sold real pumpkins for a living, I was sure Carter would be as virulently anti-pumpkin spice as Rachel was.

I waved the bag and rolled my eyes. "You must think this whole pumpkin spice trend is super annoying. I mean you are into the real thing, right? Not this knockoff stuff."

Carter smiled and shrugged a little, but I couldn't stop my mouth from going on and on.

"I mean, I don't really like the pumpkin spice craze. I just let Sallie Bell give me the special because I didn't want to hurt her feelings. It'll probably be good 'cause Sallie made it, but it's still just silly pumpkin spice, right?"

"Your pumpkin spice latte." Sallie's nephew held out the massive paper cup to Carter and gave me an "I caught you but I won't mention it because I don't want to embarrass you until the perfect future moment" look. Once he was gone, Carter gave me a look that was garden variety sheepish.

Before she could speak, I blurted out, "I'm sorry. I don't know why I said all that. That was super judgey and shallow and I promise I'm not really like that. I actually really like pumpkin spice stuff. All of it. Even the Oreos."

Carter laughed and reached out, her hand resting lightly on my forearm. Sparkles of electricity tingled through my arm where her skin touched. "It's totally fine, Nicki."

"No, I was a total jerk."

"You weren't." She waved her cup around at the decorations and pastries. "All this is a little silly, honestly. And yeah, my family's into the real thing and would probably agree with you. But I love fall, Halloween, pumpkin spice, all of it. I grew up on a farm in California nestled into the mountains. It was a whole lot like this place. With the first hints of chill in the air, Halloween decorations started going up. This time of year always makes me feel like a kid again."

I felt myself leaning in, entranced by her words almost as much as the dimples and the way they made her jaw look like something out of Greek mythology.

"Now that I'm older and I'm in a magical place like this." Carter trailed off and she shrugged, meeting my eye again. "I lean into it more."

I opened my mouth to ask about that farm in California or why her family had moved here or any one of a thousand other questions her childlike enthusiasm for the season invoked, but Sallie appeared on the other side of the counter, huffing and puffing under the weight of a massive box of pastries.

Sallie said to Carter, "Here you go, dear. I put in some of those bear claws your daddy likes, too. Those are on the house as long as I get a free trip through the corn maze."

"Come as often as you like, Ms. Bell. Mom said to tell you the pumpkin butter will be out next weekend."

"Oh, what a treat. I helped her with the recipe, you know. I'll remind her how to be a proper Southern lady soon enough, mark my words."

Sallie hustled back to the register, shooing her nephew back to the espresso maker, and Carter picked at the corner of the box. She didn't quite meet my eye, but then I couldn't bring myself to meet hers, either.

"Well, I guess I should get these back to the farm."

"Yeah, I should get to work myself."

"It was very nice to officially meet you, Nicki Russell."

Chapter Four

"D o you know Lily is talking about taking ballet classes?"

"Which Lily? My Lily?"

"Yes, your Lily. How many Lilys do you know other than your daughter?" I asked.

Rachel sipped her wine then let her head fall back against the wicker chair. "I'm sure I know another Lily. I must've heard it somewhere when I was pregnant, right?"

"You got it out of a baby book. Stephen didn't like the first three options you gave him and Lily was option four," I said.

"How do you remember this and I don't?"

I raised my wine glass to my lips and tapped the globe with the ring on my pointer finger. "Because you are a lush and I am the smart one."

"I'm pretty sure that's reversed." Rachel took a long sip of wine, swallowed, then said, "Yep. You're the drunk, I'm the genius."

"Sure, sis, sure."

We giggled together at the old joke as she refilled our glasses. Truth be told, more of the now empty bottle had gone into my glass than hers, but Rachel had always been a lightweight. While she poured, I watched the sun setting behind the mountains in the distance. A conspiracy between the mountains and the season made sunset down here in the valley hit right after dinner. We'd both always loved the view from the wrap-around porch, so whenever I crossed the yard for dinner in the family house, we ended the evening here. Just the two of us and a bottle of good Virginia wine.

"How are things at work?" Rachel asked as she settled back into her chair. She sank lower into the thick cushions with every sip.

"Fine. They're raising tuition again next year. The Board of Visitors thinks we need to invest more in the baseball team and we need cash."

"Nicki, sweetie, I meant you. Not how's the school doing. UVA has stood since Jefferson powdered his wig and it will stand forever. Tell me about your work."

"Oh. It's, um, fine?"

"Has Fred been a terror?" Rachel asked.

"No, he's fine. Poor guy, he tries so hard."

"What about that woman who was a pain? What's her name? Pam? Patricia? Paula?"

"Gretchen."

"Right. Has she calmed down?"

"I don't think she'll ever calm down, but she works from home three days a week so I don't have to deal with her much," I said.

"Ugh. Y'all are so lucky getting to work from home. If I could spend just one day here I would be so happy."

"Actually, you'd have to deal with your children when they get home and wouldn't get anything accomplished."

"Right." Rachel pouted into her wine glass. "Those two. Wait. Didn't you say something about Lily?"

I laughed and watched as the last sliver of blazing orange sun slipped behind the trees. "She wants to take ballet classes."

"Why?"

"Presumably to learn how to dance ballet."

Rachel stuck her tongue out at me and I returned the gesture. "But since when does she want to learn to dance?"

"Since Tinley Bamford started ballet lessons."

Rachel groaned. "Of course it's because of Tinley Bamford. Every minute of every day is Tinley this and Tinley that. You don't think…"

"What?" I asked.

Rachel sat up and looked at me with a thoughtful expression. "Does she have a crush on that girl?"

"I don't know. I don't think so."

"She talks about her a lot. I seem to remember you talking about someone a lot when you were her age. What was her name?"

"Cara Mason."

"You do remember everything."

"I remember Cara Mason," I said, thinking back to just how pathetic a baby lesbian I'd been. "I daydreamed about her every day. She was gorgeous. Anyway, I think this is a hero worship thing for Lily, not a crush."

"How can you tell?"

"Queerness is a sixth sense. I feel a disturbance in the Force when I'm around others like me," I said.

Rachel was leaning forward now, soaking in my words. "Really?"

"No, idiot, I can just—I don't know—tell. I think she's too young to know who she likes. Just don't be obnoxious about pushing heterosexuality on her. Everyone else will do that."

"Well, how do I tell her it's okay to be gay? If she is, of course."

"I'm pretty sure she knows since you still love me. Besides, she'll tell me way before she tells you."

"Hey that's not fair!"

"I'm the cool aunt, remember?" I rarely got to use my smug smile, but I pulled it out of storage just for fun. "Cool aunts hear everything first. Especially the gay stuff."

Rachel settled in a moment, but I saw the gears working. It didn't take long for her to turn back to me and say, "Speaking of. A little birdie told me some choice gossip about you and a certain hot lumberjane."

That wiped the smug smile right off my face. I sat up straight and tried to sound aloof. "First of all, Sallie Bell is not a little birdie and second, she doesn't know anything."

"So you didn't have a long," she put down her wine so she could make air quotes around her next two words. "Cozy looking conversation with the hot new lesbian in town?"

"It wasn't cozy. It was friendly."

Rachel shrugged. "Well, you haven't been that type of friendly with anyone in a long time. I think it's about time and I think she's super cute and you should definitely hit that."

"Rachel!"

"What? Live a little. Besides, she's a farmer. That means she's good with her hands, right?"

I jumped out of my seat and was halfway down the stairs when her laughter caught up with me.

"Get back up here and finish your wine."

I almost didn't go back, but it was a really good wine. *Sure, you're staying for the wine. Keep telling yourself that, Nicki.* I sat back down and snatched up my wine. After a few moments of silence, I chanced a glance at Rachel. She was still smiling like the cat who'd swallowed the canary.

"Stop that."

"Stop what?" she asked with mock innocence.

"Stop looking smug."

"You're the one who should be smug. She's a ten," Rachel said.

"Ten what?"

"Ten out of ten. On the hotness scale, you doofus."

"Right. I knew that."

"Sure you did," Rachel said. "Anyway, I haven't even told you all the gossip I heard about your little crush."

"I do not have a crush."

She waved her hand and settled back in. "Oh please. I know that look. You can't stop thinking about her. And she looks a hell of a lot nicer and more down-to-earth than your grad student disaster."

Every muscle in my body tensed at the mention of my last, most terrible relationship. I shook the thought away so I didn't spiral. "She seems very nice, but I don't know anything about her and I don't intend to find out."

"Well, I know a lot about her. Sallie Bell told me all the juiciest gossip. Want to hear it?"

"No." When my brain screamed yes, I said with more force, "Definitely not. You know how I feel about small-town gossip. If I find out anything more about Carter, I want to find it out from Carter."

"So you do want to know more about her. I knew it."

I crossed my legs and tried not to think about how wonderful that would be. "If I become friends with someone, I want it to happen organically. Not because the local busybodies want to blab about everyone else's life."

"Sure. Friends. That's what you want to be with Carter. Don't you even want to hear the confirmation that she's gay?" Rachel asked.

"I don't need confirmation from you or anyone else for that. I have a sixth sense, remember? I'm serious. No gossip."

"Have it your way, little sis, but I have a feeling you'll be singing a different tune soon enough."

Wednesdays were my least favorite days at work. Fred asked us for a list of our delinquent accounts on Wednesdays and I always hated turning those in. It felt like tattling, and I'd had enough teachers scold me for that when I was a kid. Usually without any punishment to the person who had done the bad thing I'd told the teacher about.

Most of us in the office spent Monday and Tuesday trying to ensure our reports on Wednesday were better than the week before. Most of us failed. There were two types of folks who were delinquent on their accounts. First, and most ironically, the kids whose parents were the richest were the least likely to pay their bills on time. I'd spent a lot of time trying to figure that one out, but I just kept coming back to entitlement. The rich folks thought they were above menial tasks like paying their bills, so their bills went unpaid and racked up late fees. The second type were the folks who were struggling to pay because they wanted the best for themselves or their children and had to scrape and save and still couldn't quite make their payments.

I hated contacting either of these groups. I could have easily been in the latter. I'd dreamt of going to UVA my whole life. Growing up in a small town in UVA's shadow, I knew I'd get the best education money could buy there. Only my family would never have enough money to buy it, so I did the sensible thing and went to a smaller, cheaper, less-renowned school. I consoled myself with the knowledge that I could get a job here and then my grad school would be free. One day I'd take advantage of that. As I'd been telling myself for ten years.

Contacting the rich folks whose accounts were delinquent touched off a different facet of my fight-or-flight response. While the struggling students made me feel guilty, the rich ones scared the bejeezus out of me. There was nothing more unpleasant in life than calling a rich person to ask for the money they owed you. It wasn't the profanity, of which there was usually plenty, but the way they slyly insulted me the whole time. They never called me names outright, they just danced around the fact that they saw me as a servant begging for spare change. I suppose it was embarrassing for them, and they lashed out as a result. Still, a bully is a bully, no matter why they do it.

So Wednesday morning, I stared at my delinquent account list and pondered whether I wanted to be the recipient of insults or tears. Neither was appealing, so I let my mind wander to Monday night's conversation with Rachel. Particularly the end of it when Rachel kept pushing to give me the inside scoop on Carter. I'd had to empty my glass and march off to bed just to make her stop dropping hints and innuendos.

I really meant it when I said I didn't want to know the Carter gossip. I didn't like gossip. Never had. It felt like an invasion of privacy. But I could admit to myself that I clearly was interested in knowing more about Carter. I couldn't stop thinking about her, in fact. How had I never met her before? Surely the farm had been around long enough that we should've run into each other?

Too late I noticed that my mouse had been hovering over the internet icon on my desktop. Then my finger clicked the mouse and soon enough I was typing "Carter Farms Virginia" into the search engine.

As the computer chewed over the results, I said to myself, "Snooping is better than delinquent accounts. Besides, accessing public information isn't snooping. It's research."

Google didn't have much to offer, honestly. I found a few articles from a few years earlier about a family from California buying the land at auction. It was from our town paper, the *Bucks Mill Sentinel*, and featured an interview with Amanda Carter, the matriarch of the family. She explained that the family intended to fix up the old farm and make an interactive experience for the community. She promised a lot in that article and, as far as I could tell, she'd delivered.

The rest of the links were less helpful. The Facebook page for the farm listing the dates for pumpkin picking in autumn, strawberry picking in summer, and the promise for a new service coming soon: a Christmas tree farm.

The farm's website was sharp and clean, without any of the Comic Sans or hard to read paragraphs common to so many amateur attempts. The splash page featured a slide show of kids with face paint and piles of pumpkins. I watched the whole thing twice, hoping to see Carter featured, but I only caught a glimpse in the background of one that might've been her. It also might've been one of her siblings. The picture wasn't that great. She also wasn't listed under the "Meet the Farm Team" page. Maybe she was shy? Or she was just here for the season before heading back to wherever was home for her? The latter seemed more likely. The warm, friendly smile she'd lavished on me several times didn't seem shy at all.

"Got that report for me, Nicki?"

I jumped at the sound of Fred's voice. He looked at me apologetically, but I was keenly aware of the fact that he'd caught me doing not work during work hours.

"Sorry. Yes. It's late. I'm just finishing up."

"Not a problem," he said.

A new picture had rotated to the front of the Carter Farms webpage and it sparked a memory. "Hey, Fred?"

He'd been shuffling away but came back. "Yeah?"

"Remember that office trip we took this last summer? The team building thing?"

A massive grin split his face. "Strawberry picking. Gretchen won the prize for biggest berry and Ahmed made the tallest strawberry pyramid."

I watched the picture of the little girl with a strawberry painted on her cheek flick away. "Was that Carter Farms we went to? I feel like it was a place close to my house."

"Sure was. Gretchen suggested it because she lives right outside Bucks Mill, too."

I almost asked him if he remembered seeing Carter there, but then I realized how weird that would be. He would have no reason to remember a towering, gorgeous butch woman. I flipped through mental images of that trip but couldn't remember seeing Carter. I know I would remember her if she'd been there. No way I would've missed her.

"Is that where you went pumpkin picking? How'd that go? Did you use my tips?" Fred asked excitedly.

"I did use your tips. Thanks again. I carried a ton of pumpkins and saved a lot of money thanks to you." I didn't tell him that we'd selected so many pumpkins that I had to do the walk twice. And still had to buy a few outright because it was way too many to carry. All he needed to know was that he'd helped. That made him smile and even blush a little. It was the blush that made me feel guilty for wasting company resources researching my crush. I closed the browser page and opened up my spreadsheet of delinquent accounts. "I'll get this report for you right away."

CHAPTER FIVE

I need your help," Rachel said through my driver's side window.

"Of course, but can I turn my car off first?"

"Probably doesn't make sense, since you'll just have to turn it right back on." Rachel turned as her front door opened and Lily came sprinting out. "It's back-to-school night, but Blake is sick. Can you take Lily and meet her teachers?"

"Don't you want to meet her teachers?"

Rachel raised an eyebrow. "Sure. I'll take her and you can hold Blake while he projectile vomits. Sound good?"

"Get in, Lily."

Lily beamed as she climbed into the passenger seat and buckled herself in. It still felt weird to have her ride in the front. She'd only reached the weight where she could forgo the safety seat that summer and she now considered herself a full grown-up. She also had taken to giving me directions, even though I had gone to her elementary school more times than I could count, since I'd been a student there myself eons ago.

The parking lot was nearly full when we arrived, and Lily lamented having to park so far away. I was pretty keen on the distance, since it gave me more time to prepare for the awkwardness that would be this evening. I had no problem filling in when Rachel needed help in the parenting department, but the moms in Bucks Mill were super cliquish and, having no kids of my own, I wasn't included in their groups. Each group of parents we passed gave me a different look, depending on their level of cool. It was either dismissive, pitying, or outright disgusted. Just like it had been at Bucks Mill High. At least I knew what to expect from which group.

Lily seemed oblivious to the looks. She was young, so she'd have time to develop a deep sense of disappointment in the people of this town. Especially if she continued trying to be friends with Tinley Bamford.

Once we got inside the school, I reverted to an awkward pre-teen. The miniature furniture and brightly painted halls looked exactly the same as they had when I was a kid. At least Lily was still in elementary school. Those weren't the worst years. I still had the fresh, youthful enthusiasm that had been crushed out of me by middle school and covered in a thick layer of angst by high school.

Lily took my hand and led me toward the third-grade hallway. She smiled at a few kids, but her focus was entirely on getting to her classroom. As we passed a few teachers, mingling in groups, a terrible thought occurred to me.

"Lily, what's your teacher's name?" I asked.

"Ms. Petersen."

My stomach dropped. "Of course it is."

"She's really nice and very pretty. You'll like her."

She was nice and she was definitely pretty, but I hadn't liked her enough after our date a couple of years ago to call her back when she asked for a second one. I definitely should've taken the vomiting toddler option tonight. You'd think that someone with as few exes as I had wouldn't be in danger of running into one of them like this.

Fortunately, when we arrived at Lily's classroom, Karen Petersen was busy talking to a group of parents at her desk. I dropped into one of the student desks all the way at the back and tried to make myself invisible. It wasn't actually that hard since the desk was made for an eight-year-old and I practically had to fold myself in half to get into it. Lily gave me a withering look and hurried off toward a group of kids huddled around Tinley Bamford. I watched her go, assuming that I would see Tinley give her the same look of disgusted confusion her mother gave me any time I waved to her. To my surprise, Tinley ignored her other admirers to wrap Lily in a big hug, then grab her hand to pull her into their conversation. Maybe I was wrong about them. What I assumed had been a hero-worship style infatuation might actually be a friendship after all.

Lily stayed a few desks ahead of me with her friends when Karen started her presentation. I had a hard time arranging my notebook on the tiny desktop, but it was important to take notes so Rachel would be up to date on Lily's classes. Unfortunately, the other parents didn't seem as organized as me. As soon as Karen provided an overview of class projects and student expectations for the year, a parent asked whether the students would have any major projects. As Karen patiently repeated everything she'd already said, I let my mind wander back to our one and only date.

We'd met at a school function not long after Karen had moved to town and she asked me out that same day. I should've said no, but I've never been good at that, and she had those confident, sexy green eyes. It wasn't a bad date, but we didn't gel, so I avoided her calls for a few days until she caught me out about town. She took it well when I declined a second date, but it had been awkward. She'd messaged me a few times since, inviting me to Pride events in Charlottesville or concerts with lesbian musicians. I never responded since those sort of events weren't interesting to me. Plus, I made sure we didn't accidentally bump into each other again. I hadn't seen her in over a year and I had planned on never seeing her again until stupid Blake and his stupid stomach flu.

About halfway through Karen's presentation, she spotted me. I could tell the moment it happened, because she stumbled over a word or two and tried to cover it up with a small cough. From then on, her eyes would occasionally return to me and I would smile politely and look away. The more often this happened, the more awkward it got. A couple of parents turned to see who she was looking at and I tried to slide farther down in my desk. Unfortunately, there was no farther down to go and soon I was worried I'd never be able to extract myself from the tiny chair.

As soon as Karen finished her talk, I peeled myself out of the desk and hurried to Lily. "Ready to go home, kiddo?"

Lily and Tinley turned in unison to stare at me in horror. "You haven't met Mr. Rhodes, the art teacher, or Mrs. Jefferson, the music teacher," Lily said.

"Okay." I held out my hand to Lily. "Let's go meet them. Where are their classrooms?"

"Hi, Lily," Karen said from behind me. "Hi, Tinley."

Too late.

"Hi, Ms. Petersen. This is my aunt Nicki. My mom couldn't come tonight because my brother's sick."

In a surprisingly light tone, Karen said, "We've met actually. Good to see you again, Nicki."

I turned to find her smiling at me. I'd expected some bitterness or anger or something, but her smile was genuine if a little sad. That actually made it worse 'cause now I felt bad for disappointing her.

I hurried to say, "You too. Lily was just going to take me to meet the music teacher and art teacher."

I couldn't for the life of me remember their names. When I turned to Lily, she was gone, off chatting with Tinley and her friends again. Cringing, I turned back to Karen who had clearly realized I was trying to bolt.

She took a step toward me and lowered her voice, though there weren't any other parents or kids anywhere close to us. "You don't always have to run away from me, you know. We can just be friends. Or even comfortable acquaintances."

I tried to mirror her smile, but I couldn't think of anything scarier than being comfortable acquaintances with her. This was the problem with small towns, it was impossible to just ghost someone when you didn't mesh on a date.

Because I'm a wimp, I said, "Okay. Sure."

Lily reappeared exactly two minutes too late. "Ms. Petersen, Tinley says you're organizing the Halloween festival this year. Is that true? Please say it's true."

Karen turned away from me and her smile became far more genuine and animated when she bent over to talk to Lily. "I'm in charge of organizing volunteers, but there haven't been any yet."

"What does that mean?" Lily's eyes were wide as dinner plates and warning bells started going off in my head.

"Well, if we don't get any volunteers, we might have to cancel the Halloween festival."

Lily's bottom lip quivered and the warning bells were joined by red flags waving.

"I'll volunteer." Honestly, when I heard the words, I didn't even realize I'd said them. I just blurted them out so fast, my brain didn't have a chance to tell me to shut up.

Karen looked at me like I'd grown a second head, but I didn't pay her much attention. Lily was doing that thing again. Looking at me like I was her hero. Like I had saved her life and she would never love or respect anyone more than she respected and loved me in that moment. That look had me by the heart. It had ever since the first moment she looked at me in the hospital nursery. I was a sucker and a half, but I always would be for this kid.

"Aunt Nicki, you're the best." Lily squealed and ran off back to Tinley.

It would've been nice to get a hug or something, but she was an excited kid, so I made allowances. Once she was gone, however, the full weight of what I'd done crashed over me. I turned to Karen, who was still staring at me open-mouthed.

I couldn't take it back now, not with Tinley and Lily holding hands and jumping up and down across the room. I shrugged and said to Karen, "I guess we'll get to work on that comfortable acquaintances thing now."

"It's really great of you to volunteer, but I'm not actually going to be working on the Halloween festival. I'm just getting volunteers. I'm swamped with the winter talent show," Karen said.

"Oh."

"But not to worry. The festival is being held off site this year and the business owner running it will do most of the work."

"That's good."

Karen pointed over to the spot where Lily and Tinley had brought Meaghan Bamford and a couple other moms into their conversation. "Plus, it looks like they're working on signing up a few other volunteers."

Great. Just what I needed. I wouldn't be working with Karen, but with Meaghan and her cronies. At least I'd have the business owner to help. I wondered who would be hosting. Sallie Bell's was too small for an event like this, but there was always the hardware store or maybe the pharmacy? The school had done a Christmas play in the banquet room at Main Street Café one year. Maybe it was a whole downtown thing. That would make it bearable.

Lily looked over her shoulder at me, a radiant smile on her cheeks. My heart did that little pitter-patter it did every time I made Lily's day. I could do this. Whatever I'd gotten myself into, I was Lily's hero at least until Halloween.

❖

"I really think I'm getting the hang of this," I said as a pair of perfectly split logs toppled off the chopping block.

"That was much better than the last five attempts."

Lily's backhanded compliment didn't dampen my spirits. I'd only been working on my firewood stash for a half hour and I already had a respectable stack of chopped wood. They were much more even than my last attempt. It might even be enough to start a fire one day soon.

"I think it's all in the wrists," I said, lining up my next shot.

It was not all in the wrists. I missed the log and gave the chopping block itself a glancing blow that sent my gleaming axe blade deep into muddy soil. Lily did a passable job of holding back her laughter, but her body was shaking with silent giggles. I ignored her and dug my axe out of the dirt.

Lily was sitting on the wide base of the tree I was in the process of chopping. A neighbor with a chain saw and a great deal more tree knowledge than me had chopped it into manageable pieces after it fell during a spring rain. Ideally, I would have chopped it then so it could properly season before the autumn, but Rachel had been going through her divorce then and I didn't have the time. Fortunately, the tree had dried relatively well in its larger pieces, so Lily's jeans didn't get wet.

"Why are you cutting firewood when it's so warm, anyway?" she asked as I cleaned the axe blade.

My next chop hit the center of the log, but only went about a quarter of the way through. "Because it'll be cold before you know it, and it takes me so long to do this that I need an early start."

Wiggling and tugging freed the axe for me to give another swing. I missed the spot I'd already hit, but this chop got a little farther through. Enough for me to pick up the log with the axe and bang it onto the chopping block. That forced it through enough that I could peel it apart with satisfying ripping noise.

"My daddy used to chop wood for you, didn't he?" Lily's voice had gone quiet and a little strained. The change was so abrupt I stopped mid-swing to look over at her. She wasn't looking at me. She was looking at the toes of her now very dirty pink Converse. She held her feet out in front of her, rubbing the toes together and a little too focused on them.

I put down my axe and dropped onto the log next to her. She still didn't look over at me. I laced my fingers together and stared at them, giving her privacy from prying eyes.

"How are you doing with your daddy living somewhere else?"

Lily shrugged, her little shoulders snapping up and down while she tapped her toes together. I knew if I gave her time, she'd find the words she needed to say, and eventually she did.

"I don't really understand," she mumbled.

The watery sting of sadness in those words broke my heart. I wished I could tell her I did understand. That it was totally normal to be sad and confused and maybe even mad, but she knew me and I knew her. She knew my parents—her grandparents—had been high school sweethearts who spent their whole lives together. Even when Dad passed, Mom wasn't far behind, passing six months later. I didn't know what it was like to have divorced parents, and Lily didn't want empty platitudes.

"I don't really understand either, but I know it was the right thing for both your mommy and your daddy. Sometimes we have to trust other people to know what's best for them," I said.

She was still intent on her toes, but her tone was a little lighter. "Some of my classmates have parents that live separately, too. We talk about it sometimes."

"Does that help?"

"Yeah."

"What do you talk about?" I asked.

Lily finally looked up at me. "Mostly about how we get double presents on birthdays. Do you think Santa will come to both Mommy's house and Daddy's house? Will I get four sets of presents? Mommy, Daddy, and two sets from Santa?"

I laughed and pulled her into a sideways hug, making a mental note to make sure Rachel and Stephen came through on quadruple presents. "Maybe so. I guess we'll have to send him an extra list this year, just to be safe. One from your daddy's address and one from your mommy's."

Her eyes sparkled. "Is that how it works? Can I send one from your house, too? We can split the presents."

Shoot. Now I'd have to buy her Santa presents, too.

"We might not want to push our luck," I said.

"Don't worry, I can write the letter with my left hand so Santa won't be able to tell."

"That's a neat trick. Where'd you learn that?"

"Come on, Aunt Nicki." She dragged out the "on" to cover several syllables and accompanied it with an epic eye roll. "Everyone knows that trick."

"I don't. You'll have to show me sometime."

Lily got quiet again and went back to staring at her toes. The little nibs on the side of her shoes made the shoes skitter and jump as she rubbed.

"Do Mommy and Daddy still like each other?" Lily asked.

"They do. They always will. Just in a different way now."

"They never fought before. Will they start fighting now?"

Part of my heart soared to know she didn't know how much Rachel and Stephen had fought, especially toward the end of their marriage. Part of it broke for the inevitable day she would discover how much they'd worked to hide it from her. They hadn't worked so hard to hide it from me. I'd heard them yelling at each other plenty of times. When Stephen came home late and didn't explain where he'd been. When Rachel pushed and pushed until he snapped. They'd had those fights in the driveway and the yard between our houses. Rachel would come over to me crying sometimes. Stephen usually left again. At least they'd protected the kids from the worst of it.

"I don't know, Lily, but you know what? It's normal for people to fight. Sometimes things are so important to people that they get too loud. Yelling is okay sometimes, as long as you don't say mean things. No matter how much you care about someone, sometimes they make you mad. Haven't you had fights with your brother?"

"Yeah, but he's dumb."

"See that's the kind of thing it's not okay to say. That's a mean thing, isn't it?"

"Yeah. I guess." She shrugged again and scrunched up her face.

"He isn't dumb, he's just younger than you and he doesn't understand some things are important to you that aren't important to me."

"Like my rock collection. He lost one of my rocks last week. I'd found a pretty pink rock by the creek and he lost it."

"And that made you mad, right?" As if I had to ask. That lost rock had led to a meltdown the likes of which I'd rarely seen in my niece.

A hint of her anger still showed in Lily's scowl. "So mad."

"And you yelled at him."

"Yeah."

"So you had a fight," I said.

"Yeah."

"But that doesn't mean you're bad or he's bad or you don't love him."

Lily said in a rush, "Yeah, but I really want him to go live with Daddy sometimes. He messes up stuff all the time."

"But even if he did, you'd still care about him, right?"

She rolled her eyes again, but all the sadness was gone from her voice. "Yeah. I get it. It's just like Mommy and Daddy."

No, your daddy is a lying, cheating jerk, but close enough. "Exactly."

"Hey, Aunt Nicki?"

"Yeah?"

"You know they have videos on YouTube about how to chop wood, right?"

Chapter Six

Instead of driving home after work on Friday evening, I headed to Bucks Hill Elementary School for the first Halloween festival volunteer meeting. The kids had long since left, but there were still a few cars dotting the parking lot, no doubt belonging to teachers working on lesson plans and grading. I just prayed Karen wasn't one of those teachers. I was not prepared to have any more conversations with her quite yet.

As I suspected, Lily and Tinley had bullied the other popular moms into helping with the festival. Meaghan Bamford had elected herself leader and arranged for this meeting in the school cafeteria. I was the only adult in the group who worked full time, but I was also the first one to arrive. I even had time to collect a coffee from Sallie Bell's in anticipation of a long, tedious meeting.

Stepping into the cafeteria was even more of a blast from the past than walking through the halls on back-to-school night. I'd been a shy kid and lunch time had always been a struggle for me. I sat with Rachel before she moved on to middle school. By that time I'd acquired a few friends who were just as quiet and awkward as I was, so we muddled through. Still, we were always a little group separated from the other kids by several rows of empty chairs.

I selected a seat at the table closest to the door and tried to fold myself into another tiny seat. The cafeteria was full of stools attached to the sort of tables that folded up and could be stacked against the wall to make room for cleaning and other activities, and they were probably the least comfortable tables for human beings. I wasn't even a tall person, but my knees banged into the stool beside me, the metal arm attaching it to the table, and the bottom of the tabletop in quick succession.

Fortunately, the only person to witness this stunning display of grace was the elderly janitor. He entered through a door on the far wall and scowled at me. I gave him a smile and even a little wave, but he turned his back on me and started folding up the tables at the other end of the room, slamming their sides together in what felt like an overly aggressive manner before rolling them over to the far wall. Clearly, I was disrupting his routine and he wasn't thrilled about it.

This seemed like a good time to fall back on the "ignore them until they go away" strategy I usually employed. Turning away from the janitor, I peeled the top off my pumpkin spice latte and held it up to my nose with both hands. Cinnamon and nutmeg and the rich aroma of steamed milk filled my senses. I closed my eyes, taking it all in. I knew it was clichéd and overdone, but I couldn't help it. There was nothing like a pumpkin spice latte to get me into the Halloween mood. Heck, to get me into the autumn mood. I took a big sip, letting the creaminess carry my worries away. I could survive this meeting. Even the snide comments Meaghan Bamford and her cronies were likely to lob my way would bounce off if I set my mind to it.

"Fancy meeting you here."

Oh God. I turned as slowly as I could, expecting to wake up from this nightmare any moment. Okay, not nightmare. No nightmare looked that good in flannel and a fleece vest with a silly pumpkin logo on the chest. No, Carter fit squarely in the dream category. A very good dream. But what on earth was she doing here?

Realizing that I'd been silent too long, I tried to set down my coffee and unfold myself from the tiny cafeteria stool in the same movement. Predictably, I accomplished neither task. I banged my knee on the underside of the table again and tipped my coffee too far. Fortunately, there wasn't much latte left. Unfortunately, what was left sloshed across the lip of the cup and splattered onto the tabletop.

"Oh shoot," I said, finally managing to get to my feet.

Carter sprang into action, catching the cup before it fell completely over and setting it upright. Then she grabbed a bandana out of her back pocket and ran it through the mess.

"I'll go get some paper towels," I said, bolting off toward the janitor.

He was holding out a damp, dingy rag when I got to him. His expression was firmly disgruntled and didn't shift a hair when I thanked him and apologized. By the time I got back to the table, Carter had most of it cleaned up, but I was able to wipe away most of the stickiness.

"Sorry about your bandana. I'll get you a new one," I said.

She smiled and leaned close. "Don't worry about it. I nabbed this one from my brother. He'll never know."

Her smile and proximity squeezed all the air out of my lungs. How could she possibly have eyes that devastating shade of brown? It should be illegal. Or at the very least come with a warning label.

"I'm still really sorry. I'm such a klutz."

At that moment, Meaghan Bamford crashed through the cafeteria door, laughing into her cell phone like some sort of minor celebrity performing for the paparazzi. Her ability to move with superhuman grace only highlighted my status as the most awkward thing in the world apart from a newborn deer. Meaghan gave Carter a cheery wave and I used the distraction to escape back to the janitor to return his rag.

By the time I got back to the group, two other mothers had arrived. I recognized Becky Sanderson, but the other was only familiar as a member of Meaghan's inner circle. Predictably, Meaghan was holding court, having drawn Carter into the group.

"Oh good, you made it, Nicki," Meaghan said as though I was the last to arrive rather than the first. She wrapped her hands around Carter's bicep and leaned close with one of her simpering smiles. "Everyone, meet Carter. She's here as the representative of our hosts. This year the school Halloween festival will be held offsite at Carter Farms. Isn't that wonderful?"

The other moms clapped and traded excited gasps and laughter. I was too terrified to join in. I'd thought volunteering would force me to spend time with Karen. The reality was so much worse. The only option for my sanity was to avoid Carter until she moved back to wherever she came from after the season. Now I'd be spending who knew how much time with her organizing the festival.

I suppose I should have expected this when Karen said the festival was being held offsite. I mean, the pumpkin patch made far more sense for a Halloween festival than the hardware store or Main Street Café. If I hadn't been so worried about being Lily's hero, I would have figured it out on back-to-school night. Then I would've been able to gracefully back out of volunteering and leave it up to Meaghan and her cronies instead of subjecting myself to the very real possibility of embarrassing myself in front of Carter. Kind of like I'd already done tonight.

Meaghan didn't give me too much time to freak out—not that she noticed I was. She selected a table at random and immediately began a discussion of logistics. The other moms were too busy sucking up to Meaghan or checking their phones to pay too much attention, but I was prepared. I grabbed my notebook and pen and scrambled to keep up, taking notes on everything Meaghan and Carter suggested.

"We have a spare barn." Carter glanced over at me as she spoke, and I tried to make less noise with my note taking. "I think that would be the best place for games."

Carolyn Henley gushed and put her hand on Carter's forearm. I couldn't help notice she did that a lot. "What a great idea. That would also give us a warm place to be if the weather's bad."

Apart from Carolyn's googly-eyed addition, Meaghan ran the show. The more time passed, the more this whole thing felt like me taking notes on a personal conversation between Carter and Meaghan. Meaghan made a lot of suggestions that seemed to put most of the work on Carter's shoulders, but she must not have minded because she accepted all the work with no hesitation. Carter kept glancing around, her eyes falling on me enough to make me really self-conscious. The first time it happened, I assumed she was just being polite by looking at each of us, since Meaghan wasn't making any effort to involve us in the planning.

As time passed, I wasn't so sure. Her eyes flicked to me more and more often, once or twice accompanied by a soft smile. Each time her eyes settled on me, a jolt shot through me. I started to crave the feeling, my body humming with mingled anticipation and worry. Was she looking over because I was annoying her? Or did she feel the same vibration that shook through me when our eyes met? I knew it was impossible, but it was a fun daydream.

The problem was, when daydreams started in my head, they were immediately followed by panic. I hadn't had the best track record when it came to romance. It wasn't that I'd never dated, more that the dating had never gone well. Honestly, that's why I'd avoided Karen and a small handful of women who'd approached me in the past few years.

The thing was, if I did more than avoid them, I would probably fall in love with them. I did that way too fast and way too often. I would meet a woman and I'd like her. She'd distract me the way Carter distracted me tonight, and I'd confuse that distraction for chemistry. We'd go out a few times and, before I knew it, I'd think I was in love. Problem was, for them it was still a distraction. A pretty girl to have a good time with for a little while until the real thing came along. And by the time I figured out they'd only seen me as a distraction, I was heartbroken. My last big breakup had finally convinced me that love wasn't in the cards for me. I just had to make sure my proclivity for falling hard for a pair of enchanting eyes and a charming grin didn't get me into trouble again. And it hadn't for a long time. But then I hadn't had a test nearly as tempting as Carter in a long, long time.

"Well, I think this was a great start, don't you, girls?" Meaghan beamed at the other moms, soaking in their praise.

"How about you all come out to the farm tomorrow night to look around?" Carter looked over at me with a smile that was equal parts mesmerizing and terrifying.

Meaghan hummed. "Not sure that timing would work for me. Ladies, is there a good night for a field trip one evening this week?"

"We've got ballet on Tuesdays," Carolyn said.

"And tee ball Wednesday and Friday," Becky said.

The mothers debated amongst themselves while I packed away my notebook. I'd never considered how many extracurricular activities elementary school aged kids could have, but maybe I should have. The good news was that packed schedules meant fewer meetings and fewer chances for me to embarrass myself in front of Carter.

"How about you, Nicki?" Carter asked. "What's a good evening for your schedule?"

The whole group went quiet and looked at me. Carter was smiling, the rest looked shocked to see me there. I couldn't blame them. I melted into most crowds even without someone as compelling as Carter or commanding as Meaghan in the group. Meaghan glared at Carter as though she'd said a four-letter word in front of a child.

"Oh, I can do whenever. My schedule's open in the evenings," I said.

After a beat of uncomfortable silence, Meaghan said, "Okay, then let's plan on Thursday at six."

Carter didn't take her smiling eyes off me when she said, "Thursday at six. Can't wait."

CHAPTER SEVEN

M y cell phone rang as I was finishing lunch on Thursday. Normally I wouldn't dream of answering my cell at work, but I was technically off the clock, so I made an exception.

"Hey, Nicki, it's Meaghan. Listen, I'm going to be late to the Halloween festival meeting tonight." Before I could reply or even take a breath, she continued, "Tinley has a recital coming up and she needs more practice time. Tonight's the only free time the dance studio has, so you see I don't have any choice."

I swallowed hard, trying not to think about how much more one-on-one time with Carter this meant for me. "Of course. Not a problem. Carolyn and Becky will be there. We can catch you up when you arrive."

"Oh, Becky isn't coming," Meaghan said flippantly. "Her husband's away for work this week."

Panic flared in me again, but I told myself it was okay. Carolyn would still be there. I'd still have a buffer, even if she was a hopeless flirt. I did wonder why Becky didn't mention the conflict during scheduling, but it was too late to worry about that now.

"No problem. I can email notes to her so she's prepared for next time."

"Sure. Fine. Thanks for taking lead on this, Nicki. You're a peach. Bye."

She hung up before I had time to ask what she meant by me taking the lead, but my timer went off, indicating my lunch half hour was over. I shook the nerves off so I could be present for the second half of my workday and told myself to worry about the trip to the pumpkin patch after I clocked out. It was easier said than done, but I managed.

Driving across the mountain back to Bucks Mill after work, all that suppressed nervousness washed over me to the point that I almost gave up and drove home instead. In fact, I turned on my blinker to do just that, but I couldn't go through with it. I was sure Carter would forgive me. So would Meaghan and Carolyn and Becky. Lily wouldn't. I had a sneaking suspicion this Halloween festival would be very much like the group projects I'd done in high school with Meaghan. Without me doing all the work, there'd be nothing to turn in. This festival meant so much to Lily and I just couldn't let her down. No matter how awkward it was. No matter how much I wanted to avoid the gorgeous farmer.

"Do it for Lily," I said to my reflection in the rearview mirror.

Five minutes later, I climbed out of my car in the gravel parking lot at Carter Farms. I squeezed my notebook to my chest and practiced breathing normally. That ended abruptly when a familiar form, clad in dark washed jeans and a radiant smile walked toward me across the parking lot. I forced a smile to cover the drooling and held perfectly still until she stopped in front of me. It wasn't easy considering she actually looked happy to see me.

"Nice to see you again, Nicki," Carter said.

"You too."

My voice squeaked and my eyes were starting to water. I really needed to take a full breath soon. Fortunately, Carter turned to scan the parking lot and my lungs finally started working again.

"We're open for another hour, but the rest of my family can handle the customers while we plan the festival."

"Okay. If you're sure your family won't mind?"

"Mom'll give me a hard time, but it makes her happy to give me a hard time."

"Does your whole family work here?"

After I said it, I internally berated myself for being nosy, but she didn't seemed bothered by the question at all. "Nearly. We have a sister who stayed in California to be a dentist, but we don't talk about her much. Being such an obvious disappointment and all."

Carter gave me a wink to show she was joking, and that made my lungs deflate like popped balloons again. If I spent too much more time around her, I might just pass out from lack of oxygen.

While we walked to the farm entrance, I told Carter about Meaghan being late and Becky having to cancel. Carter's wide smile never faltered, but I had to wonder if she was disappointed the school wasn't living up to our side of the bargain. I determined then and there to pull our weight, even if the moms flaked out on me. It was the least I could do for the Carters since they were being so generous with their time and space.

When we got to the gate, a sturdy woman detached herself from the small group taking tickets and walked over to us, a wide smile making her cheeks wrinkle like a happy bulldog. Her flannel shirt was more worn than Carter's and far too large for her. I wondered if she'd borrowed it from her husband. She looked like a caricature of a farmer and her features so strongly resembled Carter's that I had to assume she was her mother.

She held out a calloused hand. "You must be one of the volunteers from the school. I'm Amanda Carter, owner and proprietor. Can't tell you how happy we are to have the festival here at the farm this year."

Her shake was surprisingly gentle, though a little too enthusiastic. She prattled on sweetly about the farm and her family and how they'd wanted to host the festival last year but were too new to the area to be prepared. Her soft voice filled the evening air, sending an unexpected pang of loss through my chest. Her warmth made me miss my mother like I hadn't in ages. There was something about a farm woman that would always feel like home to me. It reminded me of my mother and grandmother, smelling of oats and horse and being happier than anyone else on earth.

Even though Amanda talked nonstop, requiring no response from me or Carter, it didn't feel insulting like when Meaghan dominated a conversation. Instead, it felt like a woman who was so proud of her family and career that she couldn't help gushing.

Before she could tell me the history of their previous farm in California, Carter interrupted. "Okay, Mom. That's enough for one day. You'll be seeing Nicki a lot between now and Halloween, I'm sure. You can bore her then."

My stomach twisted at the thought, but not altogether unpleasantly. Maybe it was just the way she said my name like she liked it. Or the way standing next to her felt warm and was more comfortable because I didn't have to look into those eyes.

"Where's the rest of your crew?" Mrs. Carter asked, looking over my head to the parking lot. "I thought there were four of you?"

"One's going to be late and another wasn't able to make it." I checked my watch to see just how late Carolyn was. "And I'm starting to worry about the last one. Let me text her to see how far out she is. Sorry to take up so much of your time."

Mrs. Carter waved off my apology, but it wasn't long before I had to apologize all over again. Carolyn immediately texted back to say she couldn't make it, but Meaghan said I was taking notes anyway, so she would catch up. The worst was looking up at Carter because she didn't seem bothered at all. In fact, there was a twinkle in her eye that seemed to say she hadn't expected the others would make it. Did she know them so well already? Maybe I was just a dope for not having guessed this would happen. It certainly tracked with everything I knew of Meaghan and her crowd.

"Why don't you and I start the tour and Mrs. Bamford can find us when she arrives," Carter said.

I didn't miss the way she called me Nicki but called Meaghan Mrs. Bamford. Was it possible that one person in the world actually preferred me to a Bamford? I suppose all the small-town power structures that had ruled my life since infancy didn't affect her, being an out-of-towner.

Mrs. Carter gave me another one of those enveloping handshakes and then I followed Carter off into the farm. My work loafers weren't as adept at traversing the uneven ground as my sneakers had been on the first visit, but that wasn't the reason I kept stumbling. It was really hard not to be distracted when Carter walked so close to me and kept up a running dialogue with that honey and gravel voice of hers.

As she took me past the lean-tos with registers and crates overflowing with pumpkins, apples, knobbly gourds, and decorative corn, I tried to take notes, but I kept getting lost in the rumble of her voice and the occasional flash of her eyes as they flicked toward me. Once or twice, she offered options of whether to remove certain displays, and sometimes I even managed to coherently defer until I could consult with the rest of the volunteers.

"Here's the barn for the main event." Carter effortlessly hauled one of the massive doors open a few feet and stepped inside. "We can move the tractor to the other barn. It's just a backup for the hayrides."

While Carter slapped a palm affectionately against one of the tractor's massive tires, I slipped into the interior of the barn. Slanting rays of sunlight came in through windows high in the loft, but most of the space was dark and cool and smelled like the outdoors. Like years of leaves piling on top of each other, old hay, and aged wood. I closed my eyes and breathed in the scents and felt relaxed for the first time in days.

"This reminds me of being a kid on my parents' horse farm," I said when I felt Carter standing beside me. "Minus the horse smells, of course, but it's close enough."

"You grew up on a farm?"

Carter leaned against a post a few feet in front of me, the last of the evening sunlight glowing against her skin.

I hugged my notebook close to my chest to keep memories of my family shame away. "I know I don't seem the type now. It was a long time ago."

"How long?"

"They started selling off acreage when I was Lily's age. It didn't really click that we were losing the farm until the horses went up for sale."

"That must've been hard," Carter said in a low voice.

I shrugged, but I don't think she bought my attempt at being flippant. "It feels like a different life."

That part at least was true. The sad part was that there wasn't a clear line when my life changed. Not like a death or an event that I could point to and say that's it. That's where I went from living on a horse farm to just living in a big house near someone else's barn. It was such a slow bleed, and we'd never been the rich breeder types. We never had the beautiful animals who competed in the steeplechases that were so famous around here. It's not like losing the farm lost us any social standing. It just meant Dad went to work in town instead of in the backyard.

I cleared my throat, trying to banish the memory of how hollow my Dad's eyes were when he put on his tie for work. "This is a great barn. Maybe we could put a haunted house in here or something? There's plenty of room."

Carter didn't push me to talk more about my family and I appreciated that. "We actually already have a haunted house. It'll be open for the festival. I was thinking games in here."

"What kind of games?"

Carter walked toward me and I forced myself not to step back. "I'm not sure. You're the kid expert, right?"

"Hardly. I'm just the aunt. The moms would probably have a better idea."

"I don't know. Don't aunts know their niblings better than their parents?"

I tried not to feel the little burst of pride in my chest, but I failed miserably. "We know them in different ways, I guess. Lily trusts me to talk about things she wouldn't talk to Rachel about."

"You're one of those people who're easy to talk to."

She said it like a statement, not a question, and I felt the heat on my cheeks in time to look away. "I don't think it's me. Like you said, everyone loves their aunts."

Carter laughed and leaned back against the barn post. "You haven't met my aunt. She could scare the paint off a Buick."

A laugh burst from my lips before I could catch it, but I slapped my fingertips over my lips as soon as I could. Carter smiled over at me and it made me feel like I was melting into the packed earth under my feet. I turned away and focused back on my notebook to recover.

Carter didn't push. She walked past me to survey the space. "I think the old standards of games and activities are the way to go. Ring toss and pin the tail on the donkey, only with a black cat. Do kids play those games these days?"

"Honestly, I have no idea," I said.

"Well, we can teach them all the classics if they don't know them."

I pointed to a few hay bales stacked in the corner. "When I was a kid there was this game at the festival. A bunch of those cheap suckers stuck into hay bales and each kid picked one. Some had the bottom of the stick marked and if you picked one, you got a prize."

"That sounds easy enough," Carter said.

"I'll do some research."

I scribbled down a note as Carter locked up the barn. The last stop on the tour was the haunted house. There was a long line outside, despite the approach of closing time.

Carter asked, "Want to go through? So you can see what it's like for the kids?"

"No, that's okay. I don't want to keep you, and I'm not really into haunted houses."

I immediately regretted my answer since Carter looked disappointed. Normally I wouldn't be interested in someone who was so obviously a kid at heart—folks who were playful like that generally got bored with me very quickly—but it was actually kind of endearing from her. It probably had to do with her baby face and gentle eyes.

"The offer stands anytime. Plus, I need to be sure it isn't too scary for the little kids. I don't have any of my own so I can't be sure," Carter said.

I found it interesting that she mentioned she didn't have any kids of her own. Was that a subtle way of telling me she was single? I discarded the thought, since plenty of partnered people didn't have children. I considered offering to bring Lily to check it out, but we were almost back to the parking lot by then and I spotted Meaghan marching in, Tinley and her older brother in tow.

Trying to keep the annoyance out of my voice, I said, "Hey there. We were just finishing up the tour."

"Good because I don't have time for a tour anyway. We need more pumpkins. That's why I'm here," Meaghan said in clipped tones.

So she hadn't had any intention of coming to help with the Halloween festival at all. I should've suspected. Carter certainly did. She shot me a quick wink while Meaghan told Tinley to hurry up and get what she wanted.

"No problem. I can send you all the notes I took," I said through gritted teeth.

Meaghan didn't even bother to answer. Her phone was in her hand and she was already marching away to follow her daughter.

"Thanks for the tour. Have a good night," I said to Carter.

Before I could hurry off to my car where I could formulate a devastating takedown of Meaghan I'd never deliver, Carter said, "Should we set up a time for you to come back? All of you, I mean. To set up the games and decorations in the barn?"

I looked around for Meaghan, but she was gone. Who was I kidding anyway? The chances weren't good that she'd show up even if we scheduled around her many parental responsibilities.

"Sure. How about this weekend?"

"Sunday afternoon?"

"Sounds great. I'll let the others know."

CHAPTER EIGHT

I found myself ensconced at a little table in the corner of Sallie Bell's on Saturday morning, a book in hand and a half-eaten bagel next to my empty coffee cup. I stared at the page, the words blurring into obscurity as I worked to convince myself I was not here in the hopes of seeing Carter. I was here because I enjoyed Sallie's cheddar bagels and she made decent coffee. I was here because Virginia had given me the first crisp day of autumn and I could see the blaze of fall foliage on the mountains from this table. I was here because my house was too quiet and I needed to be around people.

I didn't come close to convincing myself.

Barely a day had passed when I hadn't thought about Carter. It was pathetic to have such an intense crush on someone I'd only ever seen a few times, but I couldn't help it. I'd been single for five years, and not the flirty, casual sex with strangers type of single. The ghosting a pretty woman after a first date type of single. The spending too much time with my niece and nephew, mastering cooking meals for one, cat as my only sleeping companion type of single.

I just wanted to see her one more time. Maybe she'd say something rude or arrive with a girlfriend on her arm. Anything to break the spell she had over me. Anything to make the next three weeks of Halloween festival volunteering bearable.

"Want a refill, dear?" Sallie Bell asked from behind the counter.

It was a slow day. Probably too early for most folks, now that I thought about it. But it would be busy soon and I had to keep this table. It was the only one in the little dining area that had an unobstructed view of both the front door and counter. More importantly, it was the only table where anyone at both of those spots could see me. It would mean something if Carter came in but didn't come over to me, right? Of course, I'd already been here almost an hour and she hadn't shown. Maybe she wasn't getting the farm's pastries this morning. Maybe this whole exercise was for nothing.

I nodded at Sallie Bell, the wind having completely gone out of my sails, and pushed my chair back.

"You stay there. I'll bring it to you," Sallie said.

I took another bite of my bagel. I'd abandoned it ages ago when the front door had opened and my stomach had done a somersault of anticipation. It had only been Todd Bailey from the hardware store next door, coming in for his morning coffee and gossip session, but my stomach hadn't recovered. Now it was cold and a little stale, but it was still a Sallie Bell bagel, so better than most.

"What are you doing lingering?" Sallie Bell asked as she swapped my empty coffee cup for one with curls of delicious smelling steam rising from it. "It's not like you. Not that I mind of course, but this is the longest you've spent in here since your granny passed."

Would it sound stalkery to say I was hoping a certain devilishly handsome farm girl would come in for pastries and talk to me? Of course. It would also hurt Sallie Bell's feelings, so I said, "I was feeling nostalgic. Plus I've been cooped up too long this week. Wanted to get some fresh air."

"The air in here has calories, but it sure doesn't disappoint," she said with a laugh.

The tinkle of her laughter was echoed by the bell over the door. I leaned around Sallie's wide frame, and my breath caught at a flash of flannel and a very familiar Carhartt jacket. Carter was just turning to look our way when Sallie's nephew called to her.

Sallie was oblivious to my desperate need for her to go away and let Carter come over to talk. "Feeling nostalgic, huh? I suppose that's natural. You sure did spend a lot of time in here when you were a little one. Your granny and my momma were thick as thieves. Did I ever tell you about the time…"

Sallie's words faded into a gentle buzz as Carter's eyes roamed the dining room. I scooted my chair to the side and she finally saw me. My heart leapt into my throat and air couldn't quite make it through when her brown eyes settled on me.

"The two of them had told the Sanderson boys that if they ever ran through town yelling that sort of stuff again, they'd get a whoopin' like they wouldn't soon forget. Of course, my momma…"

The right side of Carter's lips twitched up and my heart was beating again, this time so loud in my ears that I thought I might be passing out. I raised my hand and gave a feeble wave. More just a twitch of my fingers than a wave. I probably looked like I was swatting a fly or calling for help. Anything other than a friendly invitation for her to join me for a few minutes or an hour or maybe the rest of my life.

Still, her smile grew and she returned the wave. Sort of. She raised a couple of fingers and made a sharp wrist movement like she was flicking a nonexistent cap brim. It was suave and oh so very butch. The exact opposite of what my twitch had been. I held out hope that she would come over to say hello, but then Sallie's nephew appeared with a latte and an enormous box of pastries. Carter signed a clipboard, said a few words of thanks, gave me one last smile, and then vanished back out onto the street.

"Darn it."

"I know," Sallie said. "They were quite the pair, those two old biddies. God rest their souls and keep them in line until we can join. Right, dear?"

"Uh, yes. Right." I stood up and gathered my things as quickly as possible. "I should really be getting home."

"You haven't finished your bagel or your coffee."

"I—um—not very hungry this morning."

"And didn't you say you'd been cooped up all week? Stay a while longer and we can visit."

"No," I said a bit too harshly. If I hurried, I might catch Carter before she left. I could casually stroll past her car. "I should be going. Thanks again, Sallie. See you soon."

"Take care, dear. Say hello to your sister. Remind her not to be a stranger, you hear?"

I waved distractedly with one hand and opened the door with the other. I practically tumbled onto the sidewalk just in time to see the battered red pickup with "Carter Farms" stenciled on the side rumble down the street.

"Double darn."

The drive home was uneventful, but I had a hard time dragging myself out of the car after I parked. I had planned my morning so meticulously, now my entire, empty weekend stretched out in front of me. It wasn't until Rachel looked up from her flower bed and waved that I finally forced myself out of the car.

Rachel wiggled her hands into garden gloves. "You're up and out early this morning. What gives?"

For about two seconds, I considered making up an excuse for being out of the house before the sun came up. But, honestly, I just wanted to unload all my pent-up frustrations from the morning. I didn't even ease into the story, just blurted out my ridiculous plan and how Sallie Bell's chattiness ruined it. I even told her about the way my stomach did flip-flops at seeing Carter again.

"You really like this woman, don't you?"

"That might be going a little far. She's interesting," I said.

"And super hot."

I sighed and slid down the banister until I was sitting on the bottom step inches from my sister's knowing grin. "Yes. She is super, unbelievably hot and I really want to talk to her even though I'm terrified."

"Then why don't you go back to the pumpkin patch?"

"The volunteers are going tomorrow. I'll see her then."

Rachel tapped my sneaker with her trowel to get it out of the way. "Meaghan and her nosy friends will be there tomorrow. Go today."

"I can't go two days in a row. That would be pathetic and obvious."

Rachel winked at me. "Sounds just like my baby sister."

"You're mean."

"And you need to put yourself out there. Take a chance. Tell Carter you like her."

"Taking chances isn't my thing," I said.

"You took a chance when you went to the coffee shop this morning."

"That was different," I said. Rachel lifted an eyebrow in response. "Okay, it was sort of taking a chance, but I did that in a flash of bravery. I get one of those per decade and Sallie ruined it."

"That's bull. You volunteered for something at the school. That's way out of character for you and your hermit ways."

"That was for Lily," I said.

"And it was sweet. Now do something brave and sweet for you and go back to the pumpkin patch."

"I want to go to the pumpkin patch," Lily said from above me on the stairs. She was still wearing her Pokemon pajamas and fuzzy slippers, but she ran down the steps to hop in front of me. "Please take me, Aunt Nicki. Please?"

"Did you set this up?" I asked Rachel.

"No, I did not and, Lily Elizabeth Hanson, we are not buying any more pumpkins."

I had noticed the porch was slightly overrun with festive displays. One or two more large pumpkins and the whole thing might collapse under the weight.

"Fine." Lily drew the word out like she'd been insulted. "But there's a haunted house. Can we do the haunted house, Mom?"

"No haunted houses. Why is everyone trying to get me to go through the haunted house?" I asked.

"Who is everyone?" Rachel had completely abandoned any pretext of gardening at this point.

"Carter showed me during the tour. She asked me to go through with her so I could tell her if it was age appropriate for the kids."

"You all act like we're babies. Haunted houses are fun," Lily said.

"They really aren't," I said. "No to the haunted house."

"Yes to the haunted house. It's a great idea. You can leap into Carter's arms when you get scared," Rachel said.

"Haunted houses don't scare me. They're all so fake."

"Then you can fake getting scared." Rachel sounded an awful lot like Lily and the two shared a look of exasperation. "All you're looking for is a reason to faint and make her catch you."

"That sounds pretty unethical," I said.

Rachel scoffed and pulled off her gardening gloves. "It's morally ambiguous at best."

"Um, sis, it's completely biguous."

"That's not a word."

"What's the opposite of ambiguous then?" Rachel shrugged and looked at Lily who shrugged back. "It doesn't matter. I'm not doing it. That's so manipulative."

"That's so romantic," Rachel said.

Lily's attention was bouncing between us like a spectator at a tennis match. She was practically quivering with anticipation. Or maybe cold. It was a chilly morning and she was only wearing pajamas.

"Okay, fine. We can go to the pumpkin patch so Lily can do the haunted house, but I won't go in with you and I won't fake being scared," I said.

"We'll talk her into it on the drive over," Rachel said to Lily.

"You will not." I jumped to my feet and glared down at her. "Besides, Carter won't have time to go through a haunted house. She'll be working."

The conspiratorial look Rachel and Lily shared chilled my blood far more effectively than the autumn morning.

CHAPTER NINE

The morning had dawned crisp and bright, with temperatures closer to the chill I expected from autumn but the sky a clear, cloudless robin's egg blue. The afternoon had warmed up, but only slightly. It was still sweater weather, my favorite kind. Rachel had asked for an hour to shower and get Lily ready, and I was more than happy to switch up my look. Something more appealing to an outdoorsy woman like Carter.

I happily pulled on a cream white sweater to go with my skinny jeans and sensible loafers. It hadn't rained in a while, so I wasn't too worried about ruining them. I spent longer getting ready than usual, curling my shoulder length hair so I could wear it down and cover my ears. They stuck out just a little too far to be cute, but my hair could cover that.

Unfortunately, my extra care with my outfit plus Rachel's perpetual disorganization meant we were later than I wanted getting into the car. By the time we made it to Carter Farms, the parking lot was jammed. With this many customers, it seemed less likely that I'd get to speak to or even see Carter. She'd probably just spot me across the crowded farm and realize I was stalking her. I rubbed my thumb along my palm as we stood in line, pressing so hard my knuckles ached as I looked around for that familiar face.

Rachel grabbed my hand to stop the fidgeting. "Stop that. Don't be such a nervous Nellie. You look great. She'll drool all over you."

I wanted to object, but I secretly hoped she was right. Having my hair down covering my ears and framing my face highlighted my best feature—large, wide eyes the dark brown of oak trees. Today of all days, I felt like I might have the looks to catch Carter's eye. All I had to do was track her down and ask about our plans for tomorrow. Keep it casual. Business related. I could do that. Maybe I could even make it through a whole conversation without embarrassing myself or tripping over something.

We were just passing through the gates when I spotted her. She'd discarded her jacket since her trip to Sallie Bell's—odd since this was the coldest day we'd had in months. But the absence highlighted how square her shoulders were and how long her neck was. Her flannel was open at the throat, exposing acres of tanned flesh and the sharp points of her collarbone.

Carter spotted us and waved. This time I forced myself to give a real wave in return, not the jerky twitch I'd managed this morning. To my surprise and delight, she turned our way and jogged over.

"Get ready to faint into her arms," Rachel whispered in my ear.

I slapped her arm just as Carter arrived in front of us. Her eyes were glued on me and I once again congratulated myself for taking extra time with my makeup.

"Welcome back. I wasn't expecting to see you until tomorrow." Carter's voice rumbled into my chest, making it hard to breathe.

All my bravery shriveled and flaked away like dead leaves abandoning a branch. She thought I was weird for showing up here today when I'd be back tomorrow. This was a terrible idea. How could I have let Rachel talk me into this?

Unaware of my internal struggle, Carter said, "The little guy isn't with you today? I'm sorry, I don't think I caught his name last time."

"Blake," I said somewhat breathlessly. I couldn't seem to make my lungs fully expand when Carter's eyes were fixed on mine.

"My brother's a big scaredy cat, and we're here for the haunted house. We left him at my daddy's house," Lily said.

"Your aunt Nicki is a big scaredy cat, too," Rachel said, her elbow digging into my side.

I elbowed her back, but then realized Carter must think we were idiots for picking at each other like teenagers. I cleared my throat and said, "I'm just here for the cider and doughnuts. I'm not going through the haunted house."

Rachel cut in, giving an exaggerated sigh. "What my sister means is that she doesn't want to be a third wheel. I'll be holding Lily's hand as we go through. There won't be anyone to hold Nicki's hand, though, so we haven't convinced her to join us yet."

My face was blazing like a forest fire at this ridiculously obvious attempt at matchmaking. I waited for Carter to stammer some excuse to run away, but her smile only grew.

She stepped forward and held out her hand. "I can't let that happen. We have the best haunted house in the area. It'd be a shame for you to miss it. Why don't you let me hold your hand?"

I honestly don't know what kept me standing at that point. Between the mischievous, knowing look in Carter's eye and the warmth of her this close, my knees turned to jelly. I couldn't help but lean forward. She was so close and so enticing. Then my brain caught up with my libido.

"Oh no, I can't. You're working. I couldn't take you away," I said.

She gave me a wink and I'm pretty sure I died. "My dad is my boss and he's too much of a pushover to fire his own daughter."

I kept leaning in like my body had a mind of its own. My eyes slipped down to settle on her thin, pale pink lips. Before I knew what was happening my hand was in hers, settled lightly between her fingers and palm.

"Plus, I told you I need to know if we should have it open during the festival. I need volunteer opinions." She moved back, settling on her heels and taking a light but insistent grip on my hand. "So it's settled."

"If you insist." I forced my eyes to the ground so I didn't do something stupid like launch myself at her lips. It had been so long since I'd kissed anyone, I wasn't sure I even knew how anymore.

Lily skipped off toward the line forming outside the haunted house. "Let's go then. What are we waiting for?"

My heart to stop racing. I couldn't say that out loud, of course, so I just kept my lips pinned together. Rachel followed Lily and

Carter gave a slight tug on my hand. We followed behind them across the yard toward the haunted house, but at a much slower pace. I couldn't really tell if it was me or Carter setting that slower pace and giving us just a hint of privacy, but I appreciated it no matter what.

"I saw you at Sallie Bell's this morning. I wanted to say hello, but I didn't want to interrupt your conversation," Carter said.

If our joined hands weren't currently swinging lazily between us, I might never forgive Sallie Bell for keeping us apart. I tried for a nonchalant tone. "Oh, you could have interrupted. Sallie was just gossiping as usual."

"I hope she wasn't gossiping about me."

"Oh God no! She would never do that." Embarrassment flooded me and all the happy feelings of talking to Carter evaporated. "She isn't that kind of gossiper. More like really chatty than anything mean-spirited."

Carter chuckled and we were so close I could almost feel the sound. "Relax. I won't tattle on you."

Our eyes met again and she winked. My whole body went numb. Unfortunately, I was still walking. My toe clipped a clump of grass and I started to fall forward, my momentum yanking my hand out of Carter's. Quick as a flash, she reached out and caught me by the elbow, her arm wrapping around my waist to stand me back up.

Carter used the heel of her boot to stomp down on the clump of grass. "Sorry about that. The ground here isn't very even."

Once the grass was settled, she looked me up and down, asking if I was okay. I squeaked a response that may or may not have included words, but she seemed satisfied. She released me slowly and that's when I realized I'd been on tiptoe, my hand wrapped around her bicep. It took all my strength to let go.

She took my hand again as we resumed our course to the haunted house. I don't know what I'd done to encourage that, but I could have squealed with delight. Glancing over at the line, I spotted Rachel and Lily waiting for us. Rachel gave me a thumbs up and I shot her a don't-you-dare-say-or-do-anything-to-embarrass-me glare.

Carter indicated the haunted house with a jerk of her chin. "This used to be the main farmhouse. When my folks bought the place they built a new house farther out. We had solar power and geothermic heat and all the green living bells and whistles out in California so they wanted them here. This place has been vacant for a few years, so it was the obvious choice for the haunted house."

I wanted to ask more about that. To learn everything about her family and why they moved from California and whether she inherited those sexy dimples from her mom or her dad. I didn't manage to articulate any of the questions before we got to the back of the haunted house line. There was a brief argument between Rachel and Carter about who would pay for Carter's ticket, but Rachel won in the end. She usually did. I tried to remind myself to give her some cash later, but I had no confidence that my brain would ever work correctly while I held Carter's slightly calloused palm against mine.

She hadn't let go after we got to the line, even though I couldn't trip standing still and there was nothing scary about a big old rickety house with a line of teenagers in front of it. But I wasn't in any state to argue. She could hold my hand until the end of time if it was up to me. The added bonus was that the hand holding required we stand close to each other. If the contact wasn't enough to do it, the warm, wood smoke and fallen leaves scent of her would soon start my palm sweating.

We didn't have to wait in line long. They were taking groups of two or four in at a time, and we got separated from Rachel and Lily. I suspected that Rachel had talked them into it while I was distracted. Carter and I went in together, just the two of us, and her hand gripped a little tighter as the lights in the foyer blinked out.

The first few rooms were a blur of screaming and flickering lights. Each room was set up to be spooky or gory in a different way, and the actors herded us from room to room quickly. Not quickly enough for me to miss the little flaws that ruined the illusion, though. An obviously rubber knife here. Hinges on a trap door there. It was enough if you wanted it to work, but I had never been good at suspending my disbelief. Plus, I was bitter because the quick exits from rooms meant Carter had dropped my hand to steady herself in the second room.

A pair of zombies in torn clothes and green face paint chased us up the stairs in the kitchen just in time for me to bump into Rachel's back. She jumped and screamed, then turned and laughed. Her eyes settled on Carter, several steps behind me and trying to disentangle her sleeve from some cotton spiderwebs on the banister.

"Have you done it yet?" Rachel whispered.

"Done what?"

"Jumped into her arms, idiot."

"What? No. I'm not doing that." I checked to see Carter was still out of earshot. The blaring scary music helped.

"Do it in the next room. Lily says we go through three bedrooms up here."

"How does she know?"

Rachel rolled her eyes. "Tinley Bamford, of course. Now get ready."

"I'm not doing it."

"Having fun?" Carter roared to be heard over the music. Her wide grin displayed perfect teeth, glowing an eerie purple from the blacklight.

"Y—yeah."

I turned and Rachel gave me a last wink before she and Lily disappeared down the hall. A closed door kept us from bunching up too much and Carter stood so close behind me on the landing that her breath rustled my hair. I wanted to lean back into her. Feel her whole body against mine. Maybe get her to wrap her arms around me? I couldn't of course. We were still acquaintances. Practically strangers. That was way too intimate a move and one Rachel would fully endorse. That was all I needed to know to deem it inappropriate.

Without warning, the door burst open and hands reached through the wall to push us into the next room. The lights were low, glowing from strange angles. Red from under a dresser, green through the breaks in a closet door. Smoke poured from underneath a large, four-poster bed with sheets stained dark and gory in the low light.

The lights started to flicker and I knew the jump scare was coming. Carter's warm presence was right behind me, her hand brushed my back as she turned in place to scan the room. I should do it. I should take Rachel's advice and pretend to be terrified. Throw myself into Carter's arms and bury my face in her neck. She would catch me. I would cling to her. She would protect me and hold me tight. Our bodies would press together for a moment and I would know if her breath caught the way mine did just thinking about it.

I saw a flicker of movement from the corner of my eye. Now was my chance. I should do it. It was pathetic and silly and so obvious, but women far more ridiculous than I had certainly done silly things like this to get the one they wanted, right? What was so wrong with being silly sometimes?

The music screamed and a figure in bright white loomed beside us. They lifted their arms and they were too tall to be real. They opened their mouth and shrieked, but I could see their dirty boots beneath the torn up antique wedding dress. It ruined the illusion and I chickened out. I felt Carter tense and her arms shifted ever so slightly. Had she expected me to leap into them? Had she been anticipating my silly, transparent attempt to have a hot woman hold me? Why wasn't I letting her?

I made the decision and acted. I faked a scream and threw myself at Carter.

She wasn't there. I'd been too late because the scare had already ended by the time I chose to act. I toppled past the spot where she had been and fell hard. The last thing I saw before my skull slammed into the hardwood floor was those dirty boots that had ruined the whole thing. Then my body did me the favor of losing consciousness.

Chapter Ten

Being on the somewhat clumsy and awkward side, I'd had many embarrassing moments in my life. None of them compared with sitting on a wooden bench outside a haunted house, my sister giggling a few steps away, and my crush holding a bloody bandana to my forehead.

Carter knelt in front of me, concern pooling in her eyes as she inspected the bump on my forehead. "I just want to say again how sorry I am. This is all my fault."

"No, it isn't. I'm a klutz," I said over the throbbing inside my skull.

"Do you think she has a concussion?" Rachel asked. She'd gotten her laughter under control and now looked genuinely concerned. She sat next to me and put a tender arm around my shoulder.

"I don't have a concussion."

"I was literally there to hold your hand so something like this didn't happen. Did you lose consciousness at all? If you did it might be a concussion," Carter said.

There was no need to be completely truthful now. I probably passed out from shame, not the bump on the head, anyway.

"No. I'm fine. Really."

Carter's mother walked over and sat on my other side, the warmth I'd felt from her before radiating off her again. She massaged a chemical ice pack in her hands as she looked me over.

"I brought you an ice pack for that knot on your head," she said in a smooth, rich tone that matched the confidence she exuded. "And an offer to kick my daughter's butt for letting you get hurt in our haunted house."

"Oh no, it wasn't her fault."

"Yes, it is. But Mom couldn't kick my butt if she wanted to," Carter said.

Amanda laughed. "You forget I've got an army of sons and nephews to help."

I tripped over my words trying desperately to preserve a scrap of dignity. "Please don't call out the cavalry. I keep telling everyone it wasn't her fault. I'm not hurt, just embarrassed."

"Well, that's sweet of you, but she's still getting double work and half rations for the next week." Amanda's cheery face shifted to professional in a blink. "On a serious note, we can call for an ambulance if you want. You really should have that checked out. It'll go on the farm's insurance, of course."

Tears of embarrassment prickled my eyes. If I was taken away in an ambulance I would have to crawl into a cave in the mountains and never emerge again. "Oh, please don't do that. I really am fine."

Amanda took the bandana from Carter and wrapped the ice pack around it. She pressed it to my forehead and the sudden chill sent a shiver through my whole body. Amanda patted my knee, but I could see Carter's hands flexing until her knuckles were white.

"If you're sure," Amanda said.

"I am. Thank you. And I'm sorry."

"Nothing to be sorry for. I insist you let my daughter walk you to your car."

Before I could object, Rachel leapt to her feet. "That's a great idea. Lily and I will go bring it around." She gave me a significant look and said, "Take your time, Nicki. Walk slow."

"I'll make sure she does," Carter said, holding out her hand.

An hour ago, I would have swooned at the sight of Carter, on one knee in front of me with her hand held out and hope in her eye. But swooning was exactly what got me into this humiliating mess, so it didn't have quite the same effect.

"Will you let us know how you're feeling over the next few days? If you feel ill and need to go to the doctor, please send us the bill," Amanda said.

I had no intention of doing any such thing, but I assured her I would so there wasn't any more arguing. She gave my knee one last squeeze and left. Just like that, I was alone with Carter again. Well, alone with Carter and my goose egg of embarrassment.

"I really do feel terrible about this." Carter leaned closer and took my hands in hers.

"Please don't feel bad. Seriously."

"No promises."

A tiny laugh burst from my mouth and she gave me a quick smile. I knew it was a smile of pity, not appreciation. I had an ice pack on my forehead and spots of blood on my favorite sweater. I could not have more thoroughly embarrassed myself if that had been my goal. There wasn't the slightest chance in the world Carter would seek out my company again. The next three weeks of volunteering would be unbearable and I'd never see her again after the festival. Something about that realization finally put me at ease. It could not possibly get worse from here and that was oddly reassuring. I felt like myself—the version of me Rachel, Lily, and Blake saw—and it felt good.

"Danielle?" I asked.

Carter blinked dully. "What?"

"Is your first name Danielle?"

Carter's eyebrows scrunched together and she tilted her head, just like a confused puppy. After a moment, her forehead cleared and she smiled. "Oh, I see. You think you can guilt me into revealing my biggest secret just because I let you bang your head against an old bed?"

She stood and used both hands to help me to stand. In all honesty, I was still a little wobbly on my feet, so I let her steady me before we set off at a ridiculously slow pace, her hand on my arm to keep me balanced.

"I think I hit my head against the hope chest, not the bed."

I was sure of it. If I'd been able to time my fear reaction better, we might have both toppled onto that bed. That missed opportunity was just another reason I would be regretting this haunted house adventure for years to come.

"Either way, you're still trying to use it against me," she said.

I managed a smile. "Something like that."

"Well, the answer is no. If that had been my name I'd probably go by Dani."

"Deborah?"

"Nope."

"Give me a hint?" I asked.

"You want me to give you a hint so you can guess my deep, dark secret?"

"Yeah."

"No way."

"I guess I'll just have to keep guessing. How many women's names start with D?"

Carter laughed. "Hundreds. Even some that were popular the decade I was born. There were literally hundreds of options my parents had other than the name they gave me, family name or not."

"I better keep guessing or else I won't be able to get through them all."

People stared at me as we walked through the farm, but the joking with Carter distracted me wonderfully. Since I knew just about everyone around me, I would certainly get concerned phone calls later, but right now I let myself focus entirely on Carter and the way her hand on my arm felt both comforting and intimate.

"Darlene?"

"You aren't going to guess it," she said.

"Daphne?"

"That would be so much better than the truth."

We laughed together and it made my head pound, but I didn't care. For the first time all day, I felt comfortable talking to the woman I was so enchanted by. Maybe I could get through this volunteering gig now that I was certain she had no interest in me at all. It was a wonderful feeling, like sitting down in front of a roaring fire with a steaming mug of hot chocolate.

Unfortunately, we'd reached the parking lot and I could see Rachel waving to me from her minivan.

I reluctantly turned to Carter. "Thank you for walking with me. I think I've got it from here."

"Okay." She shoved her hands into her back pockets, her shoulders scrunching up around her ears. "Sure. You're welcome."

The high of being myself around Carter was wearing off or else I might've done something stupid like asking her on a date. I'd never been the one to ask someone on a date before, but being around Carter made me feel and do all sorts of things I'd never done before. Part of me wondered what it might be like to be around her more. What I might be like if I was around her more.

I'd told Rachel that I didn't want to learn about Carter through the rumor mill, and internet snooping hadn't done me a lick of good. But maybe if I could stay this relaxed around her we could talk more and I could learn about her the old-fashioned way. I could learn what she liked to do with her spare time and her favorite foods and maybe even whether she was planning to stay in Bucks Mill after the farm closed to guests for the winter. It wasn't like me to obsess over someone this much, but I really, really wanted to get to know Carter. I really wanted to know her first name.

Today was not the day for those questions, though. I turned to her to say good-bye, but she spoke first. "I guess we should reschedule this volunteering date." I blinked at her, replaying the words in my head but only really hearing the last one. I felt my eyes widen and a look of panic washed over Carter's face. "Day. Volunteering day. To decorate the barn. Your head will probably be pounding tomorrow, and I don't want you to feel obligated."

Disappointment flooded me. She clearly didn't want to see me so soon. After my display today, how could she? Still, no way I was going to shirk my responsibility to Lily or give Meaghan Bamford the excuse to call me a slacker. I forced a smile. "I'm sure I'll be fine for tomorrow. I'll be here at noon."

"Are you sure? What if you wake up with a migraine or something?" There was a sparkle in her eye that I didn't want to read too much into.

"I have plenty of aspirin, so don't worry about me. Besides, I can't let Lily down. I have to be the hero aunt," I said.

"I'm sure you're her hero no matter what."

"After my tumble today, I doubt it."

Carter stepped closer. "Heroes are allowed to fall down, you know. And you got back up. That's a great lesson for her," she said in a low voice.

"Technically, I was carried out of the haunted house. By you." My lips had gone numb while I got lost in her eyes, so it didn't even feel like my own mouth speaking the words.

"I remember." The two words sent a shiver through my entire body. Since I was completely incapable of speech, it was a relief when she said, "See you tomorrow, Nicki."

She actually looked pleased at the prospect, and that realization made me dizzier than the head wound. I was in a daze as I walked back to the van.

Rachel stared expectantly at me as I buckled my seat belt, but the headache had exploded in intensity in the absence of Carter's intoxicating presence. Unfortunately for me and my aching head, Rachel had seen the whole thing. She squealed and clapped, bouncing in her seat like an exuberant child. No amount of shushing or groaning in pain could get her to quiet down or leave me alone.

"I told you it would work," Rachel said.

"Nothing worked. I just confirmed I'd be back tomorrow to decorate the barn."

She leaned in so Lily couldn't hear and whispered, "I know how much you'd love to decorate her barn."

Heat flared on my cheeks and my headache throbbed. "Shut up and take me home."

Chapter Eleven

As Carter had predicted, I woke up the next morning with a blinding headache. The pain, however, was nothing compared to the idea that Meaghan, Carolyn, and Becky would gloat over my absence if I didn't show. I took a double dose of aspirin, and that made me feel just human enough to shower and get ready.

Unfortunately, that was harder than usual as I had to deal with the results of my fall. I stared at my forehead with a sort of soul deep humiliation. I applied so much makeup I was close to running out of concealer, but it didn't do much to help. It only turned it from the purple-black of a day-old shiner to a slightly lighter, slightly opaque version of it. Like an eggplant dipped in whole milk. It also didn't help that the bruise sat on top of a knot the size of a chocolate croissant. No matter how I swooped my bangs, it just wouldn't cover the evidence of the disaster.

Worse still, I arrived late for volunteering. I'd lost a good ten minutes by chickening out once I arrived at the farm and turning around to go home. Then I realized Rachel would berate me if I gave up the chance to spend time with Carter, so I turned around again and made it all the way to the farm. Carter wasn't around to greet me when I arrived, so I headed to the barn, whose main doors were slightly open.

When I peeked inside, I saw Carter in conversation with her mother. Not wanting to interrupt, I hovered by the door, waiting for them to finish. Which of course took me from creepy stalker territory to creepy eavesdropper territory. I just couldn't win. I tried not to listen, but then Amanda said something that caught my attention.

"You're a natural at this, you know. You're going to miss it."

Carter's eyes roamed over the barn, avoiding her mother. "Which part? The crowds of townies or the decorating a barn for the local school?"

"Don't act like you aren't happy as a pig in a puddle. I can see the smile on your face when you help these kids find the perfect pumpkin."

"I've always liked kids, you know that."

Amanda rubbed her palm across Carter's back in such a motherly way it made my heart ache. "Don't I know it. But mark my words, you're going to miss selling pumpkins."

I missed the rest of the conversation as my breath went out in a little burst. I'd known deep down that Carter wasn't a permanent fixture in Bucks Mill, but it was one thing to suspect she'd be gone after the season was over and another to have it confirmed. Disappointment throbbed in me like a second heartbeat, but it was something I was so used to that the discomfort passed quickly.

When I heard the back barn door squeal open, I finally crossed the threshold. Carter turned from watching her mother leave and, when she spotted me, a smile curled her lips.

"Good afternoon," I said with as much forced cheerfulness as my disappointment and my lingering head wound would allow.

"Hi there. I wasn't sure you'd make it. How are you feeling?" Carter asked, her eyes on the goose egg.

"Fine. Thanks for asking."

I looked around the barn in search of the moms. Carter seemed to guess my intent and said, "None of the moms showed."

My irritation got the better of me. "I'm not terribly shocked to hear that."

Carter smiled at me, a twinkle in her eye. "Oh, they were the popular ones in school, huh? The ones who always made you do all the work on group projects I bet."

"How did you guess?"

"I might've had a few late nights myself making up for slackers."

My eyebrows shot up in surprise—a most painful experience when one had a head wound. After biting back a groan of pain, I said, "You? I would've thought you'd be one of the cool kids who skated by."

Carter laughed and there was a hint of bitterness I knew very well in the sound. "This may shock you, but being a butch lesbian and captain of the Future Farmers of America club in California in the nineties did not earn me a seat at the popular kids' lunch table."

Suppressing a grin, I tested to see if our joke from yesterday would still land. "Plus with a name like Daisy."

Carter laughed and shoved her hands in her pockets. "I had a rabbit named Daisy once."

"That wasn't an official denial."

"I officially state, my name is not Daisy. Thank God," she said.

The joke did wonders to set both me and the mood at ease. "Shall we get to work anyway?"

Just like my first visit to the barn, I felt at home the moment I walked through the massive rolling doors. While Carter shut the door behind us to keep any curious customers from wandering into the festival zone, I clomped across the packed earth floor, occasionally scuffing over old hay, to the center of the barn. The more I surveyed the place, the more I decided it was the perfect spot for the Halloween festival.

With the backup tractor relocated, the barn felt massive. It was twice as long as the school cafeteria where the previous year's festival had been and at least as wide. The hay lofts overhung the perimeter, offering plenty of space for hanging decorations, but there were only two ladders, so less chance kids could escape up there and get hurt.

The only downside was the light. It was pretty dim inside, even on this bright Sunday afternoon, and the few bare bulbs hanging from the ceiling didn't do much to cut the gloom. Since the festival would be in the afternoon before trick-or-treating, I assumed it wouldn't be as much of a problem. The only problem was the way my mind kept spinning around the idea of fumbling around in a dark barn with Carter if we stayed too late today.

"Your friend brought by some donated decorations." Carter indicated a stack of boxes by the far wall.

"My friend?"

"Karen." My surprise at Carter being on a first-name basis with my ex must've shown on my face, because she said, "Ms. Petersen? I thought you two knew each other."

My palms started to sweat and found myself stammering. "Yeah. We—um—yes. We know each other."

"It's just that everyone else at the school calls you Lily's aunt. She called you Nicki."

I tried to come up with something witty or thoughtful to say, but all I could think about was Carter talking to Karen. Why had they talked about me? Had Karen told Carter she and I had dated, albeit briefly? How could that have come up unless it was some weird way for Karen to come out to Carter. If I'd gotten to know Karen better, either as a girlfriend or a friend, I might've discovered whether Carter would be Karen's type.

Who was I kidding? Carter was everyone's type.

My apparent lack of vocabulary didn't seem to throw Carter off. She went straight to the boxes to sort through old paper spiders and orange and black streamers. We decided I should handle the decorations and Carter could do the heavy lifting. I wanted to argue that I could handle it, but that would have meant missing the opportunity to ogle Carter's arms as she grabbed hay bale after hay bale to outline the three-legged-race track. Plus, decorating meant I spent the day in the hay loft, saving me from having to lead conversation.

After an hour or so of work, Carter called up to me, "Can I ask your opinion on something?"

I'd just hung the last honeycomb paper ghost and needed to head down for the streamers anyway. All I could do was pray she'd turn her back while I awkwardly mounted the ladder. Fortunately for my dignity, she didn't watch and I didn't fall off the thing.

Carter indicated a large sheet of plywood painted white with a grid of pencil marks all over it. "I had this idea for a Plinko-style game. Do you know what that is? Will the kids like it, you think?"

"From *Price is Right*?"

"Yeah, it was my grandma's favorite show. I watched it with her all the time when I was a kid."

Carter explained how she would partially imbed screws into the board, leaving pegs in an alternating grid pattern. The kids would drop disks from the top, which would bounce down the pegs and land in prize slots at the bottom.

"We could do candy prizes. I can make a platform for the kids to stand on behind it. It could be a lot of fun," Carter said.

"Sounds great, but isn't that a lot of work for you?"

Carter's grin was so wide and childlike, I couldn't help smiling back. "It's okay. I can keep it after and play Plinko whenever I want to think about Granny."

Carter had started working and I had taken the streamers up into the hayloft before I realized I should have asked her about her grandmother. The way Carter talked about her reminded me of how I talked about mine. They were probably really close and I missed out on a chance to bond over our mutual love of our grandmothers. I spent the rest of the afternoon twisting streamers and mentally berating myself for not picking up on social cues.

By the time I descended the ladder Carter had finished adding the pegs to her Plinko board and I was thoroughly dejected about my chances of ever having a meaningful conversation with her. We finished the day's work discussing whether bobbing for apples was sanitary and going over logistics for the next weekend's work.

"I'll let the moms know," I said.

Carter leaned in with a conspiratorial grin. "Tell them of course, but you know we'll probably be completing this group project alone."

My headache was back with a vengeance, and I was too tired to watch my words. "Yep. This group project belongs to the two of us now. Sorry for all the extra work. I'm sure you didn't plan on this when you signed up to host the festival."

Carter switched off the barn lights on our way out. "I don't mind."

"I'm sure your parents aren't thrilled to lose an employee for this long during the busiest part of the season."

"They didn't expect me to be here to help anyway, so it's not impacting them too much." Carter shoved her hands deep into her pockets as we walked toward the parking lot. "I just sort of dropped in on them in August and they put me to work."

"I'm sure they're happy to have you home." I was desperate to ask why she'd dropped in and how long she planned to stay, but the smile had left her eyes and I had no doubt there was an unhappy reason she'd come home unexpectedly. To deflect from the obviously painful topic, I checked that my bangs were still in place and said, "I, for one, am glad the moms didn't show and ask about this goose egg on my head."

Carter gave me a sheepish grin. "I wanted to ask how you're doing after all this work, but I didn't want to pry."

"Nothing a bottle of aspirin and/or a bottle of wine can't help with. But I'm still embarrassed about the whole thing," I said.

"I'm the one who should be embarrassed. I promised your sister I'd keep you safe and I failed."

We were getting close to the edge of the parking lot. Soon I would walk to my car and another week would pass without me seeing Carter. I could stalk her at the coffee shop, but each time I thought about it I worried she'd get sick of me or I'd do something else to make a fool of myself. Still, I couldn't deny that I really liked spending time with her, even if we didn't talk much.

"No one can protect me from me. You may have noticed I get into a lot of accidents," I said.

"All the more reason I should've been vigilant."

Rather than step into the gravel lot, I turned to look at Carter. The sun was setting behind her, giving her pale hair a warm, orange glow. Her face was partially in shadow, but nothing could dim the light in her eyes. I wanted to stand there and get lost in them. I wanted to make up for all the quiet moments with interesting conversation. Problem was, interesting conversation wasn't really my thing. My thing was more like spilling coffee and cracking my head on hope chests.

I turned away from her sparkling eyes. "I'm parked right over there. I should probably head home."

"Sure. Yeah."

"Bye," I said.

"Bye."

I turned away, trying to sear the memory of her into my brain. After all, there would only be a few more chances for me to see her. There were only three weeks until Halloween.

"Wait."

I whipped around faster than was advisable for someone as clumsy as me. "Yeah?"

"Can I buy you a cup of coffee some day?" She still had her hands in her pockets, and she looked nervous for the first time since I'd met her. "To make up for failing to be your protector?"

My stomach sank at the confirmation. Pity. That's all it was about and I didn't want anything to do with that. "You don't have to do that."

Carter pulled her hands from her pockets and took a step forward. "Maybe you could just let me buy you a cup of coffee then?"

My mouth fell open and I stared. I must have been breathing, but it sure didn't feel like it. It didn't feel like anything at all inside my body. I was just flashing between numb and tingling and my brain couldn't seem to make anything happen.

I waited too long to get control of my body. Carter's eyebrows shot up and she took a step back. "Oh. I'm sorry. I thought maybe you would be...I didn't mean to make you uncomfortable. I apologize."

"No!"

I shouted because she was turning to go and I definitely did not want her to go. I took a step forward but tripped over a stake marking the edge of the parking lot. I toppled forward with a detached sense of inevitability.

This time, rather than smashing my head into something very hard, I fell into Carter's waiting arms. My cheek nuzzled against her shoulder, the scent of fresh hay and clean cotton filling my senses. Her neck was inches from my lips, smooth and tan and so kissable.

"See? That's what I was supposed to do yesterday in the haunted house," she said softly. She chuckled and I felt it vibrate through me from the million places our bodies touched. Maybe Rachel had been right. This was an extremely pleasant experience.

I looked up into her eyes. "I would love a cup of coffee."

Carter set me back on my feet and her dimples were so deep and her smile so wide it took all my willpower to let her go. She grabbed a little wooden pencil from her pocket and scribbled something on a scrap of orange streamer.

"Here's my number. Is there a good day for you?"

"I—um—have tomorrow off for Indigenous Peoples' Day. Is that too soon?" I took the scrap of paper and pulled at the corner, careful not to smudge the number.

"That's perfect."

"Really?"

"Yeah." She turned to look over her shoulder and I noticed for the first time how many people were swarming around the farm. "I should check in with my folks. It's close to closing time. See you tomorrow? At Sallie Bell's?"

I tried to project confidence, like this was something I did all the time. "Sounds good. How about after the breakfast rush. Ten o'clock?"

"I look forward to it."

I held onto my carefully controlled composure with all my might and managed a nod. She smiled and jogged off into the crowd. The streamer fluttered in my hand as a gust of wind tried to grab it. I gripped it so hard it crumpled around the edges, so I shoved it into my jeans pocket to keep it safe.

Driving home, I gripped the steering wheel so tight my knuckles were white. I had a date with Carter for tomorrow morning. The thought made me equal parts giddy with anticipation and nauseous with anxiety.

CHAPTER TWELVE

I didn't tell Rachel about coffee with Carter. I couldn't stomach the idea of her cooing and exclaiming and asking if it was a date. I didn't know if it was a date, and her excitement would only make me nervous. Better to go in unsure than be aware of certain humiliation.

"You've got the humiliation covered," I mumbled to myself as I caked another layer of concealer on my forehead.

If I'd thought the bruise and goose egg was bad the day before, it was nothing compared to the mountain that greeted me in the mirror Monday morning. I'd foolishly hoped the bruise would begin to fade or at least the swelling would go down. If anything, the bruise was darker and more terrifying.

My first instinct was to cancel with Carter. After all, I wasn't sure if it was a date. If it was, I didn't want to show up looking like a newborn zombie, ready for her first rampage through town. If this wasn't a date, I didn't want to ruin any chance of ever being asked on one.

I didn't cancel, though. The more I thought about hiding out in my house to avoid Carter, the more my stomach twisted into sickening disappointment. It was a strange sensation for me. I usually panicked at the idea of spending time with someone I found attractive, not the thought of missing a potential date.

The more I thought about seeing Carter—of seeing her smile and hearing the breathy laughter she used when she told a funny story about her family—the deeper my desire to spend time with her. She had this way of making me feel completely at ease and nervous at the same time. Her eyes never looked through me like so many other people's. When she looked at me, it was like she saw me. And even better, that she liked what she saw. I couldn't give that up because of a stupid bruise.

Since I'd nearly depleted my supply of concealer Sunday, I had to get creative to make myself presentable. A little frantic Googling led me to a color correcting trick of using a peach lipstick underneath the concealer. I read the article three times before making the attempt, the nerves I'd chased away coming back in spades.

Standing there, a tube of peach lipstick hovering over my forehead and fear clouding my vision, I nearly turned back. Avoidance was my thing, after all. I could just set that lipstick down, crawl back into bed, and pretend like I'd never met Carter. Sure, I'd be sad to lose out on a chance to stare into those captivating eyes, but our entire acquaintance had been a disaster from spilling my wagon of pumpkins to cracking my skull open in her haunted house.

"It wasn't a disaster." I stared into my eyes in the mirror and gave myself the best pep talk I could manage. "You got coffee with Carter out of it, didn't you?"

I didn't respond that the coffee was as confusing as the head wound because talking to yourself in the mirror isn't what sane people do. Instead, I gritted my teeth and drew an X in lipstick across the bruise on my forehead. Coffee. That's all it was. I could drink coffee without embarrassing myself.

It wasn't until I was spreading a thin layer of foundation over the blended lipstick and concealer that I remembered dumping a pumpkin spice latte across the elementary school's cafeteria table. I didn't have time to freak out, though. After checking my watch, I gasped so loud Ralph sprung up from his normal spot on the bed. I absentmindedly patted his head as I rushed out, earning a swat of displeasure. Luckily, Bucks Mill was a small town and I only had to drive from the outskirts to get to Sallie Bell's. I arrived just as the cuckoo clock overhead chirped the hour.

Carter was already there, ensconced in the same out of the way table with good sight lines I'd used the other day. She looked up from a ratty paperback and waved, trying to hide the book behind two massive, steaming mugs of coffee. Her embarrassment at the book was so charming, my shoulders immediately relaxed and I managed a genuine smile as I walked to her side.

"Nice to see you this morning, Dakota."

Carter chuckled deep from her chest, her shoulders rolling with the subdued sound. I dropped into the chair across from her and she slid one of the mugs toward me.

"Nice try," she said.

"Dylan?"

"You keep picking names I would really lean into. I told you it's embarrassing."

"I can't imagine anything about you could be embarrassing."

Silence rang in my ears as soon as the words fell out. This is what happened when I got too comfortable. I let the stupid, embarrassing things I think fall out of my mouth.

"I'm sorry. That was too much."

"Don't apologize." Her smile widened with each word. "That was sweet. Thanks."

My face was burning too hot to drink the coffee, but I cradled it between my hands and stared into the milky depths.

"Thanks for the coffee," I said.

"I hope you're not over pumpkin spice lattes yet."

I tried to lift the mug to my lips, but I couldn't seem to control my fine motor skills. As usual when Carter was around, I'd done something embarrassing. I tapped at the mug and forced my eyes in every direction except across the table. Why did I even come here? This was such a bad idea. Maybe I could just sit quietly until she made a graceful exit.

"Is everything okay?"

Carter's voice had gone from the lively, enchantingly brusque tones to a calm, inquisitive whisper. I chanced a quick glance up at her and saw the same concern from her voice painted across her features. She deserved better than this. Better than me.

"Yes," I said while silently screaming at myself to snap out of it. "No."

I expected her to be taken aback or angry or something. Instead, she chuckled quietly. "Uh-oh. This isn't starting off well."

"See, you say things like that and I just..."

As the words burst out of me, I'd looked up without intending to. Her eyes grabbed me and my insides turned to mush. I forgot what I was saying and that I was flustered and annoyed with myself. All I could do was stare into her eyes.

"You what?"

I shook myself. "I don't get it."

"Get what?"

She knew what I was talking about. I could tell because she was still smiling even though I was sputtering like an idiot. It was like she was having fun with my discomfort and confusion, but that wasn't the kind of person she was. Maybe she just wanted me to say the things that were on my mind so we could talk about them. Rachel did that to me sometimes. She knew better than anyone that it took a lot of coaxing to get me to open up. Maybe Carter was learning that, too.

"Is this a date?" I finally asked.

After I'd said it, I noticed how quiet the room had gone. The song piping out of the speakers overhead had stopped and the espresso machine wasn't hissing. I didn't think I'd been too loud, but it was a small dining room. I turned slowly and saw two people at the counter staring at us. Sallie's nephew stood across the cash register from them, his finger hovering over a button and his mouth wide open.

I groaned as I turned back around and slapped my palm across my face. Not a wise move, given the massive bruise there. "Ow."

I opened my eyes at the rattling noise coming from the tabletop. The spoon next to Carter's mug was shaking, tapping against the ceramic mug. The table was shaking it. Carter was shaking the table as her body jerked with silent laughter. It wasn't malicious laughter, obviously. Her eyes sparkled in the same way they had when we joked about her name. This was genuine, almost self-deprecating laughter.

But it was still laughter. I grabbed my purse and tried to stand up, but Carter stopped me by laying a broad, warm palm across my hand. Her thumb stroked across my knuckle and she gave my hand the lightest of squeezes. It was so gentle and so sweet from such an imposing woman, I couldn't help but sit back down.

"Nicki." Her voice was a purr. A rumble. The solid creak of an oak tree in a winter wind. "Yes. This is a date. At least, I want it to be a date."

"Oh."

She blushed and looked away, just like I did when I was embarrassed about something. But what on earth could a woman like her have to be embarrassed about? "Is that okay? I'm a forty-year-old woman selling pumpkins on her parents' farm. Not exactly a catch."

"You're joking, right?"

"Should I be?"

"If you think you aren't a catch you clearly haven't seen your own arms recently or you haven't been out much."

She flexed her biceps under her pale blue button-up, and the self-conscious display was incredibly endearing. "Well, I haven't actually been out much for the last couple of years, but I still sell pumpkins for my mom." She grimaced and reached down by her feet and brought up a small, brown paper bag. "Speaking of my mom and things that are not sexy on a first date, she asked me to give you some pumpkin butter."

"Your mom sent me a gift?" I asked.

"Like I said, embarrassing. I told her it would be weird to bring a gift from my mom on a first date, but she insisted on giving you the first jar from this year's batch. And I'm supposed to report back to her on how you're feeling after the accident."

I touched my hair, making sure it covered the bruise. "I'm fine. Please tell her I appreciate the gift. It's very sweet."

"I'm glad you're feeling better. I probably shouldn't have dragged you out of the house today," Carter said.

"I'm glad you did." I managed a smile of my own. It wasn't as bright and sexy as hers, of course, but it was something.

"Me too," she said.

We both fiddled with our coffees then, and I realized maybe she was as nervous to be here as I was. She said she hadn't been out much in a while. Maybe she'd been single for a long time, too? I couldn't really believe it, but stranger things had happened.

"What would you be doing if you weren't selling pumpkins for your mom?" I asked to break the silence.

"I would say living in my car, but I drive my mom's truck."

I laughed and it felt normal. Not forced or awkward at all. Almost like a woman on a date. "I mean what's your dream job? If you could do anything in the world, what would it be?"

She settled back in her chair and raised an eyebrow. "That sounds like a date question. Does that mean we're on a date? You never confirmed that's what you wanted."

That was the moment I realized her hand was still on top of mine. She started running her thumb along my knuckle again, leaving a trail of warm sparks behind. My tongue was stuck to the roof of my very dry mouth, so I just nodded. Apparently, that was enough of a confirmation.

"Okay, then. That's easy." She took a sip of coffee with the obvious intent to build suspense before answering, "I'd be eradicating *Lymantria dispar*."

Not an answer I was expecting.

"Maybe I need to rethink that date thing. You want to eradicate an entire species? Are you a serial killer?" I asked.

She snorted into her coffee and took a moment to dry her lips. "Not exactly. My degree is in environmental conservation."

"Wouldn't a conservationist want to keep that species alive?"

Carter's expression turned serious, a very sexy rigidity settling into her jaw. "Not one who loves trees. *Lymantria dispar* is the European gypsy moth, and they destroy entire groves of oaks and chestnuts."

Most of the trees surrounding my house were oaks and I had a hard time imagining them all gone. I'd spent my whole childhood collecting acorns and watching the blaze of orange and red from their leaves in the fall.

"I used to work for the Bureau of Land Management. Part of my work was curbing the effects of invasive species. I work in rangeland management. Or I did. Things got a little derailed for me recently," Carter said.

Her whole manner changed when she talked about her old job. There was something like a shadow behind her eyes, but there was an energy behind her movements. She clearly loved the work, but then why had she left that job? Before I realized it, the nerves had leaked out of me. She had me completely spellbound in the matter of a few minutes.

I sat back and took a sip of my coffee. This was turning into an interesting date after all.

Chapter Thirteen

I'd just started my first wood fire of the season when Rachel showed up with a bottle of apple pie moonshine and a relieved-the-kids-were-at-their-father's expression. It turned into a gleeful smile when she weaseled out of me that I'd gone on a date with Carter.

"You have to tell me everything." She curled up on the sofa.

"I'm going to a need a drink for that," I said.

Rachel waved at the jar. "Then pour us both one. I promised Bob I'd try it."

"Bob?" I asked as I grabbed juice glasses from the cupboard.

"At work."

I gave her a knowing smile. "Cute?"

"Seventy-two."

"Out of ten?"

"Years old," she said.

"Oh. Not so much your type then."

I handed her a glass and flopped down on the rug in front of the fireplace, letting the warmth flow over me. It brought with it the familiar, calming aroma of woodsmoke and the occasional pop and hiss of slightly damp logs burning. The fire wasn't strictly necessary tonight and I'd had to use most of the wood I'd managed to chop, but it was worth it for the ambiance. The warm spice of the moonshine married perfectly with the moment.

"So." Rachel drew the word out expectantly. "Tell me about this date."

I tried not to gush, but it was hard to contain the happiness memories of chatting with Carter stoked. As I described our conversation, even the awkward parts lost their sting. All I could focus on was her devastating smile and the way she allowed herself to be vulnerable. Thinking back on it, that's what had put me at ease. The way she never tried to sugarcoat anything about herself. It wasn't exactly normal for a first date, when people usually lie through their teeth to show themselves in the best light.

When I finished, Rachel rolled onto her stomach. "I don't think I've ever seen you this interested in a woman. Even the grad student."

"Especially the grad student."

I'd avoided saying her name since the night she dumped me while all her intellectual friends watched from behind glasses of fancy wine. That humiliation hadn't started my habit of hiding in my house from hot women, but it hadn't exactly helped me deny the instinct. Normally just thinking about the grad student made me want to pull the covers over my head like there was a monster under my bed, but even thoughts of her couldn't burst this happy bubble.

"I don't think I've ever felt this way about anyone. At least not this early," I said.

Rachel took a sip of her drink and made a face. "This stuff is terrible. Do you have any wine?"

I uncorked a bottle of red. "I'm setting myself up for disaster, aren't I?"

"Stop doing that."

"Doing what?"

She accepted the wine glass with the same giddiness she greeted the news of my date. "Stop being scared. What will it take for you to finally take a chance on love?"

"I haven't been avoiding chances at love. They just haven't shown up before."

I stowed the apple pie moonshine away in my mostly bare cabinets. It wasn't terrible, but I was excited to dive into the heaviness of red wine.

Rachel raised her glass. "Well, it's here now. In flannel and a Carhartt jacket and muscles for days and that smile."

Her words trailed off in a groan and I eyed her suspiciously. "Sounds like you're interested, too."

"God no. I've never liked women and now I'm sort of over men, too. I'm happy you're ready to dive in, though."

I could see how hard she was working to maintain her smile, but I knew better than to ask about it. Rachel had to be in the right mood to talk about her divorce and in an even more specific mood to admit how much it broke her heart. Besides, I didn't hate the fact that I was the center of the romantic attention for once in our lives.

I pulled my knees to my chest, the excitement tempered by a healthy dose of fear. "I don't know about diving in. It's been a long time and, well, you know how terribly this has always gone for me in the past. Maybe it's better to be careful."

Rachel shook her head emphatically, and wine nearly sloshed out of her glass onto my rug. "Fuck that. You're nearly forty, Nicki. It's time you did something reckless like fall in love with a sweet, stable, thoughtful woman who is clearly interested in you."

"Did you miss the part where her dream job is making an entire species of moth extinct?"

"Okay, then it's time you fell in love with a sweet, unstable, thoughtful woman who is clearly interested in you."

I couldn't help but giggle along with her as we sipped our wine. Besides, wasn't she right? If I let my past ruin my future, I'd be alone forever. I was content, and that was fine, but when I was with Carter yesterday, on my first date in almost two years, I'd felt better than fine. I'd felt good. I hadn't wanted the date to end.

I hugged my knees tighter and stared into my wineglass. "I don't know about diving in, but sticking a toe in to test the waters is a viable option."

"Stick it in then." Rachel's shout was met with a split second of silence before we both guffawed at the innuendo. "You know what I mean."

"I do know." I drained my glass and popped to my feet, my confidence soaring. "And I think you're right."

❖

For the next two days, I grabbed that scrap of Halloween streamer from my bag and stared at it about once every hour. I even dreamed of looking at the phone number, scrawled in block numerals. I handled the flimsy paper so much the pencil marks started to rub away, sending waves of panic through me that I'd delay so long that I'd lose the number.

On Thursday afternoon, I finally decided it was time to make contact. I set the streamer carefully on my ink blotter and typed the number into my phone. I checked it a dozen times, making sure I'd transcribed it correctly, but I still couldn't bring myself to put the paper away. What if something happened and the number got erased from my phone? It was a completely nonsensical argument, but when did common sense ever overcome crush nerves?

I took a lungful of air and blew it slowly out. "Okay. You can do this. A simple text message. She likes you. She'll go for a second date."

My confidence grew with each word of the pep talk, and I finally started typing, reading the words out loud as I typed them. "Hey Carter."

I stopped dead. Should I keep the name joke going? It had made her laugh. Maybe it would again? I hit the delete button a few times and started again.

"Hey Donna." I paused. Had I guessed that one already? I couldn't remember, but that didn't matter. It was still part of the joke. "I had a nice time."

I stopped again. Nice wasn't the right word. It had been great. Amazing. Life changing. Okay, maybe that was a little too far. But nice wasn't right. I deleted the last two words to insert a better adjective when I noticed that I hadn't fully deleted the first greeting I'd typed. I must've hit "N" instead of the delete. It now read *HnHey Donna*

I growled and tried to tap on the first word, but the stupid cursor couldn't find the right spot. Instead, it highlighted the word and copied it. I accidentally pasted the messed up word rather than deleting it. After a few muttered threats, I admitted defeat. I'd need to type a longer message so the cursor would have room to roam or this would never work. I'd go back later and fix it.

"Okay. Keep going." I bit my lip and thought for a moment. "Great time. Maybe we could do it again sometime?"

I held the phone away and scowled at that sentence. It was so stupid. Like something out of an outdated advice book for dating. Carter had put me at ease by being honest about her interest. The least I could do was offer her the same honesty. I deleted the last part and thought some more.

"I'd love…no, too strong. Like? Hmmm. No. Maybe love was right. I'd love to do it again. Are you free tonight? Oh God, no, that's way too soon. Next week? No, too far away. I don't want to sound disinterested."

I was concentrating so hard that when my desk phone rang I jumped and dropped the phone. Unfortunately, my jerky movements made my thumb jam into the screen. I heard the tell-tale woosh of a text message being sent.

"Oh crap." I gasped. Unfortunately, I'd also snatched up the receiver of my desk phone. I jammed it to my ear and practically screamed, "Finance, Nicki Russell speaking."

Either he hadn't heard my outburst, or the accountant on the other end of the line was too professional to mention it. While he explained that he was handling the finances of one of my delinquent accounts, I snatched up my cell phone and read the text message I'd accidentally sent.

HnHey Donna! I HnHey had a ngreat time Maybe I'd love again HnHey

I was too shocked to be mortified, and I actually handled the call with the accountant pretty well. I hurried him off the phone, but I didn't get the impression he was interested in saying much. More likely his client had told him to make me leave him alone. In any event, I hung up quickly and stared at the screen. I tapped every button and icon available to me before Googling how to retract a text message. I knew it was a long shot, but what other option did I have?

Turns out once you embarrass yourself over text, it lives forever.

I dropped my forehead to the desk and groaned. Couldn't I have one interaction with Carter without embarrassing myself? As I contemplated changing my phone number and trying again, my phone chirped with a new message. I didn't bother raising my head, just dragged the screen into my lap so I could see her response without revealing my face to the world.

Carter texted, *Wrong number and also I don't know what this means*

Great. No doubt she assumed some drunken stranger had typed the message. At least she didn't know it was me. Maybe I could salvage this by throwing my phone into the nearest ocean and starting over? A new phone number seemed like a great idea. Then again, I'd probably screw it up worse the second time around. Or worse, chicken out and never speak to her again. I didn't want that. My conversation with Rachel had sealed it for me. I needed to stick my toe in the water.

I sat up straight and typed out a response. Well, a series of them.

Sorry
This is Nicki
Nicki Russell
We had coffee Monday morning

I cringed at the rapid-fire messages. Just me, being pathetic and weird again. I had resolved to try the message again when she typed back.

I remember

I could almost hear her laughing through the phone, but it was that indulgent laughter she used with me when I felt like I was being an idiot and she didn't seem to mind. My phone chimed again.

It was a great date.

That set my heart thumping in my chest again. She thought it was a great date, too. Maybe she'd be up for another one? I typed carefully this time. *Sorry about the jumbled message. I dropped my phone and autocorrect changed things.*

Carter wrote back right away. *Autocorrect can really mess up communication, can't it? I'm happy to hear from you anyway, even if it is HnHey ngreat*

I cringed again. *Sorry*

I love that I can tell you're blushing even through text message

An unintelligible chirp of pleasure escaped my mouth when I read that. My cheeks were indeed flame-red—I could tell from the heat radiating off them—but she liked that? Did she like it because I was someone she could laugh at or because she thought I was cute when I blushed? I had a feeling it was the latter and that made her different from basically everyone else in my life. Even Rachel had a good laugh at me whenever she could. But everything about Carter's personality told me she genuinely thought it was cute. Suddenly I was at ease again, calmed by her kindness.

Is my awkwardness that obvious? I asked.

Your awkwardness is that endearing

I jumped in my chair, lifting my fist in triumph. I knew she was as sweet as I'd hoped. How could someone like her truly exist?

Can I buy you coffee again soon? Or a drink? Dinner? She asked.

"Oh my God is this really happening?" I looked around, hoping no one heard me talking to myself. Or noticed that I was definitely not doing work. I was alone, so I could bask in this glorious moment.

I whispered to myself, "Just a toe. You don't have to dive in. Just test the water with a toe."

I wrote: *Coffee sounds great*

Awesome. The response took a little too long. My heart sank. She'd offered so many options and I'd taken the tamest one. Surely she was hoping things would move faster than this. Maybe that's why I read her response as deflated rather than elated.

"Be honest with her," I told myself. "She deserves it."

I'm sorry. I'm not great at this dating thing. Slow is better for me right now

I sat back in my chair, waiting for the polite but clear dismissal. A woman as gorgeous as Carter could have anyone. Women who were adventurous and bold. Women who didn't have to take everything at a snail's pace to feel comfortable. At least I was finding out now, not weeks down the road during a massive argument about how she had needs and I wasn't fulfilling them.

Carter's text cut through my panic spiral. *Relax, Nicki. I like slow. In fact, I need slow right now, too*

"She does?" *You do?*

Yeah

Why?

That's a perfect question to answer over another coffee. Tomorrow after work? Carter asked.

I laughed and spun my chair. The office walls whipped around as quick as my pulse. When the chair stopped, my head was as light as my heart. Obviously, she was just saying that for me. To make me feel better about needing things to go slow. But I could accept that for now. Maybe by the time she got tired of playing that game, I wouldn't need it anymore.

I wrote her back. *Sure! But that late I might need to stick to tea*

That sounds great. Tea is a talking beverage

And coffee isn't? I asked.

I'll talk over any beverage if you're across the table. Six o'clock?

I couldn't have been happier if all my dreams had come true in that moment. Who says sweet things like that after only one date? Apparently, someone who liked me enough to put up with my fears. *It's a date*

CHAPTER FOURTEEN

Luckily, traffic out of Charlottesville was a snarled mess. I'd still make it to Sallie Bell's in time for our date, but the traffic gave me a chance to channel my frustrations. If I let myself think about where I was going and who I was meeting, I'd lose my nerve and probably drive right through downtown and go home. Instead of worrying about surviving a date with a sexy farmer, I was able to worry about surviving bumper to bumper traffic over a very foggy Afton Mountain.

Since I didn't have time to focus on my fear, I arrived in Sallie Bell's tiny parking lot with only two minutes to spare and jumped out of the car before I could second-guess anything. I thought I'd have to distract myself further while I waited for Carter, but when I rounded the corner, there she was.

Carter hadn't noticed me, so I took a moment to study her with a leisure I hadn't done before. Like every time I saw her, the first thing I focused on was her wide jaw and thin, expressive mouth. Waiting alone, her expression was a disinterested neutral that could be seen as angry. I was sure many people who met her were intimidated by that stern expression, but not me. It gave her an air of capability. Like she could do anything and conquer anyone. I'd always found confidence in others a turn-on since I didn't really have any for myself.

I'd noticed the stacks of muscles before, but today her sleeves were rolled up to her elbows. Her right arm from the top of her wrist to her elbow and possibly beyond was covered in swirling tattoos in black and gray. From this distance I couldn't make out anything recognizable, but the sleeve of tattoos enhanced the sweep of muscle on her forearm. I'd never been a tattoo girl before, but I had the feeling Carter could change my mind.

Carter's eyes scanned the street and then landed on me. Her smile burst out like the sun rising over the mountains, erasing the neutrality of her expression but not the confidence. I forced my knees to bend and my feet to move across the concrete, but just barely.

"Hi," I said when I arrived at her side. I held out my hand to shake hers and then realized how ridiculous that was. Fortunately, I played it off as politeness when I saw her hands were full. "Can I take one of those for you?"

She handed me a massive paper cup with Sallie's logo stamped on the side. "You should. This one's for you. I hope you like chamomile lemon."

"My favorite." I wondered if she purposefully picked a stress relieving herbal tea because she knew how nervous I was or if she chose it because chamomile was the most popular herbal tea variety. Either way, it felt like fate that she chose my favorite herbal tea.

"I thought we might take a stroll with our tea." She jerked her chin toward the empty sidewalk behind her.

The anxious knot in my stomach loosened a degree. Without the pressure of having to look at her the whole time, I might not make as big a fool of myself on this date. It worked when we were setting up the Halloween festival, after all. I could be myself when I had something to do with my body.

"I like the idea of a strolling date." After a beat I added, "Diane?"

She shook her head and laughed, disturbing the butterflies that always filled my stomach when she was around. We fell into step beside each other, me picking at the sleeve on my cup, her shoving her free hand deep into her jeans pocket.

I watched Bucks Mill settle in for the evening as we walked in surprisingly comfortable silence. Todd Bailey flipped the sign on his hardware store door and switched off the lights. Becky Sanderson hustled into the pharmacy, one of her teenagers in tow. Lights flickered on or off in homes and businesses while the sun made its way toward the horizon. The peace of the scene and the warmth of Carter's presence made me feel like a character in an old movie. One with a dashing hero like Cary Grant or Spencer Tracy. If only I could pluck up the courage to be Katherine Hepburn, I might be worthy of hanging off Carter's arm.

When we got to the next corner, we had to wait for the light to change, and I took the opportunity to peek over at Carter. Her focus was on the scene around us, and I was suddenly desperate to know more about her.

"So you were going to tell me why you need to take it slow?" I said.

Carter met my eye and made a noise like the purr of a contented animal wakening from their sun-drenched nap. "I'll tell you my sordid past if you tell me yours."

I took a deep breath and steeled myself for the coming embarrassment. "I suppose that's fair. I haven't dated in a while. A long while. In fact, I haven't really dated much at all."

"That's nothing to be embarrassed about," Carter said in a low, smooth voice.

"When you're twenty years old, maybe, but it is a little embarrassing when you're forty and you've only had two serious girlfriends."

As we crossed the street, Carter said, "I hate to be contrary, but I disagree. There isn't a set amount of experience you have to have at any point in your life."

I wasn't sure I agreed with her on that point, but it was nice to think she felt that way.

"Besides, it's working out well for me that you aren't attached," she said.

There it was again. Her acting like this relationship was something she wanted. Something that she might even pretend she lucked out on. As though she wasn't scraping the bottom of the barrel with me. Normally I would ignore the comment, knowing

Carter was dead wrong, but the warm night and the gentle glow of streetlamps made me want to believe her. Rather than dismissing the comment, I tucked it away, hoping to believe it one day.

"Now it's your turn," I said to take the focus off me.

For the first time since I'd met her, Carter looked uncomfortable. Like she might have anything to be embarrassed about.

She ran a hand through her hair and then juggled her cup between her hands. "I guess I need to go slow for the opposite reason. I had a relatively recent breakup and it was a big life change."

Oh, that was it. That was the missing piece. She was still heartbroken over someone else and I was a rebound. The revelation wasn't a shock so much as a disappointment. Still, better to know now than fall hard and be disappointed later.

"Hence the living with my parents thing," she said.

"Completely understandable."

"I'm still adjusting. That's why slow is better for me."

I swallowed my disappointment. "Of course. That works out for both of us then."

We had to stop and move aside as Old Mr. Bamford burst out of his insurance office and commandeered the sidewalk to engage the many locks on the door. Carter watched his self-important fussiness and shook her head when he bustled away without so much as an apology for disrupting our walk.

"Don't worry about him," I said. "The Bamfords think they run this town and they aren't entirely wrong."

"That's Meaghan Bamford's husband?"

Carter's question came with a sparkle of mischief that had me giggling. "Her father-in-law. Although James has his father's warmth."

Carter leaned in conspiratorially. "For Meaghan's sake I hope he doesn't have his father's eyebrows."

"I wish he did. It would serve her right."

Carter asked, "Do you think she ever intended to help with the festival?"

"I doubt it. Honestly, I was surprised she volunteered. It must've been Tinley's doing."

Carter stopped next to a lamppost and smiled down at me. "From what I hear, it was out of character for you to volunteer, too. What made you do it?"

I couldn't help staring into her eyes. They were so bright and such a vivid brown. Like a glass of apple brandy reflecting the flickering light of a wood fire. Part of me wondered if I'd have been brave enough to sign up if I'd known I'd spend so much time around Carter. I hoped so. I didn't want a universe to exist where I missed out on this time alone with her.

"My niece begged me to and I can't say no to her."

"You're a good aunt."

"I hope so. She deserves all the love in the world," I said.

Becky Sanderson came bursting out of the pharmacy, hurrying her son along so loudly it caught our attention. After yanking her car door open, she spotted us across the street. She gave me an exasperated eye roll and mouthed "teenagers." We shared a wave before she dropped into her car.

"You know everyone in this town don't you?" Carter asked.

I leaned against the lamppost to make sure we didn't block the sidewalk and shrugged. "Most everyone. There was an influx of new folks a couple of years back. Small towns became all the rage when work from home was a realistic option. But I know a lot of folks."

Carter scanned the buildings. Most of them were residential in this part of town. The oldest and grandest of historic Bucks Mill. "I like that. It's comforting to know you have a safety net."

"You're a small-town kind of person?"

"Of course. I come from a farming family."

"But a California farming family. Slightly more impressive than Bucks Mill, Virginia," I said.

She leaned in like she was sharing a secret. "California isn't all movie stars and Silicon Valley, you know. A farming town's a farming town, no matter where it is."

"Ah, but Bucks Mill isn't exactly a farming town. We used to have lots of horses, but the bigger barns with more money and better pedigree wiped us off the map."

"Then what kind of town is Bucks Mill?"

"Just a Main Street town. You know—all charm and no substance. Except for those of us who love it," I said.

"Sounds like the kind of town I want to get to know."

The sun set behind the row of mountains behind us and the twilight made me bold. I slipped my hand around Carter's arm. "Let me be your tour guide."

For a heartbeat, I thought she might pull away. She looked down at my hand on her arm and hesitated. I nearly pulled back myself, but she smiled at me and nodded and I didn't let her change her mind.

"We're in Gingerbread Town right now," I said.

I pointed across the street at my favorite old Victorian house. The clapboard siding had faded from its original dusty rose, but the decorative woodwork at every corner still shone bright white in the fading light. The house next to it had similar shapes and angles, but the paint job was newer and pale blue.

"Gingerbread Town? We left Bucks Mill?"

I laughed at Carter's look of confusion. "No, we're still in town. Actually, it isn't really called Gingerbread Town. Not officially. Rachel and I called it that growing up because all the houses look like fancy gingerbread houses."

Carter looked around, scanning the houses and all their frills. "It does look like icing, doesn't it?"

"This is the oldest part of Bucks Mill. The original Main Street houses. You'll get to see them at Christmas. They do open houses to show off their fancy decorations." I didn't ask the questions hovering on my lips. Will you still be here at Christmas? Or will you be over your heartbreak and moving back into your regular life on the West Coast?

"I bet this place looks just like *It's a Wonderful Life* around Christmas," Carter said.

I led us back toward the shops and our cars. "Not exactly. We don't have a river to jump into."

Carter threw her head back and laughed, bumping against me as her footsteps faltered. "Then we won't have any angels to contend with this winter?"

"No angels here."

"I'm not sure about that."

I turned to catch her eye and found her standing still on the sidewalk, the smile replaced with a serious, thoughtful expression that dragged me to a halt. She took a step toward me and suddenly the air was too thick to breathe.

Carter gently swept the bangs from my forehead. "Is your head feeling okay?"

"Yes." My voice came out like a croak. I cleared my throat with difficulty. "No lingering effects. And the bruise is finally fading."

Carter stepped closer, inspecting my forehead in the dim light from the streetlight a few feet away. Her gaze slipped from my forehead to meet mine. Her fingers trailed away from my hair, but instead of removing them from my face, she let them slide down my cheek to trace the line of my jaw. Her eyes had settled on my lips and my heart skipped several beats.

I waited for her to tilt my chin up. To lean in, closer and closer until our lips touched. I wondered what her lips would taste like. They looked smooth, but her whole aesthetic screamed slightly chapped and wind-blown. All I wanted in that moment was to find out. To lose myself in kissing her here on the empty streets of my hometown.

As quickly as the moment had started, it ended. Carter's hand froze on my jaw and then she was stepping back. She shoved her hand in her pocket and stared at the toes of her boots. She shook her head and looked into the distance. "I'm sorry. I promise, I do know what slow means."

"It's okay," I said, shocking myself at my ability to speak. Carter didn't look okay, though. She was clearly upset with herself and I worried it would sour the date. "Really, Delilah, everything is perfectly fine."

The joke about her name did the trick and Carter laughed, holding out her arm to me. "Come on, let's finish this tour."

CHAPTER FIFTEEN

I got home just in time to see Lily walk out of the tool shed dragging my axe behind her. I don't think I've ever exited a vehicle so fast in my life. Based on the look on her face when I made it to her side, I was pretty sure I was screaming as I sprinted across the yard.

Lily hugged the axe handle to her chest. "Calm down, Aunt Nicki. I left the cover on so it doesn't get dirty."

I snatched the axe from her and dropped to my knees, checking her all over for signs of blood. "I'm not worried about it getting dirty. I'm worried about you cutting yourself. What are you doing with the axe anyway?"

"I was going to chop firewood for you since you're so bad at it." Lily crossed her arms over her chest and glared at me. "It was supposed to be a surprise."

I forced myself to count to five so I could talk to Lily with a calm voice. It wasn't easy, but I managed to subdue the screeching banshee that had sprinted across the yard.

"You should never, ever play with an axe alone, Lily."

"I wasn't going to play with it. I was going to use it like you do. I've been watching."

"You should never, under any circumstances, use an axe alone." I channeled my mother and paused for emphasis. "You aren't big enough to use this axe yet. Do you understand?"

"Well, you don't have a smaller one."

"Lily." I barked her name, I'll admit, but it made her stop talking and listen. "Do you understand?"

She pouted, but, for once, it had no effect on me. "Yes, Aunt Nicki."

I gave her a long look, trying to detect how sincere that promise was. I decided I'd need to keep an eye on her. Rules rarely stuck with Lily, especially when she determined she was right and the adults were wrong. "I promise to teach you to chop wood when you're older, okay?"

Lily shrugged grumpily, but I knew she wasn't too mad because she followed me as I took the axe back to the shed and firmly latched the door. Maybe it would be wise to get a padlock.

"Why are you coming home so late anyway?" Lily asked.

"I had a date," I said. The words felt good to say. I only wished I'd added a few embellishments to the statement. Like maybe second or heavenly, but she didn't really need to know any of that.

"With the pumpkin patch lady?"

"Yep."

"Is she going to move in with you when they don't need her at the pumpkin patch anymore?"

All the happy, glowy feelings evaporated. "That's a little fast for me. We're just getting to know each other."

Lily was quiet for too long, so I turned to see her staring at the scuffed toes of her Converse.

"Lily, honey? What's wrong?" I didn't hear her mumbled answer, so I knelt down.

"My dad moved his friend into his house today," she said quietly.

My heart clenched painfully. That jerk didn't really move her in so fast, did he? What was I thinking? Of course Stephen would move his girlfriend in. It probably didn't occur to him to talk to Rachel or the kids about it first. To prepare them. He'd never much cared what his actions did to his family, why would he start now?

I sat crossed-legged on the dirt and pulled Lily into my lap. She curled against me the moment she settled. Part of me was waiting for her to stick her thumb in her mouth like she had when she was little. She'd long outgrown the habit, but she felt just as small and vulnerable now as she had when she was a toddler.

"Things move at different speeds for different people," I said, cursing Stephen in my mind even as I defended him to his daughter. "What's okay for me and Carter isn't the same as what's okay for your dad and his friend."

I choked on the last word, remembering how he'd always defended his actions to Rachel.

"Bethany is only a friend. I'm allowed to be friends with my coworkers."

"I just had drinks with friends."

"Men and women can be friends without anything else going on."

Only something had been going on with his "friend" Bethany. Something that had resulted in an unplanned pregnancy and a family breaking to pieces. If only Stephen knew how small the pieces his daughter had broken into really were.

Lily stayed quiet, her cheek pressed to my chest and her little arms wrapped around her knees. I gave her time to think about what I said, and then asked, "Is it okay for you that your dad's friend moved in?"

"It's not okay for Mommy. She's been crying a lot today."

Oh God, Rachel. Was Lily there when she found out? Had Lily been forced to share the news with her mother? They'd taken to speaking through the kids more often than not these days. My heart broke for Lily and Rachel in equal measure. I tried to imagine how hurt Rachel had been to hear the news. How confused Lily must have been to see her mother sobbing.

"I'll go check on your mom in a little while." I was as gentle as possible when I asked again, "I still want to know if you're okay with it."

Lily sat still for a moment, then squirmed in my arms. "I don't know. I liked it better when Daddy lived with Mommy. I miss Daddy when I'm here with Mommy, but I miss Mommy when I stay with Daddy."

"It's hard not to be with the people you love. But you can make sure they know how much you love them and miss them when you don't get to see them."

Lily shrugged and squirmed again.

"Maybe you should write letters to your mommy when you stay with your daddy and write letters to your daddy when you stay here with Mommy?"

She shrugged again and popped up out of my lap. "I'm gonna go play with Blake."

"Why don't you take Blake over to my house? You can work on our puzzle with him."

Lily shouted her agreement as she ran off toward the house. I took my time standing up and following her. I had a feeling I didn't want to rush into my next conversation. I watched them until they closed the back door of my cottage before I went off in search of my sister. She was exactly where I thought she'd be—lying on the carpeted floor of her bedroom, her feet propped up on the bed and the ceiling fan blades lazily spinning overhead.

I slipped out of my shoes so I could join her, wiggling my sock-encased toes in the air. We used to do this as children when this was our parents' bedroom. We'd pick one blade on the ceiling fan and try to follow its path for as long as we could before we lost track of it. It became our favorite game.

She'd told me she was pregnant while we played it. I'd told her I was a lesbian. We'd come up here during our mother's wake while the town ate the casseroles they'd brought for us. All the tough moments of our lives were spent following those blades.

"He left his dirty underwear on the bathroom floor," Rachel said. "At some point I stopped picking them up for him. So there would be a pile of dingy boxers in the corner of the bathroom."

I lost track of my fan blade and had to start over. I pressed my palms against my stomach and chose a blade.

"At one point there were twenty pairs in that pile. I counted. He had to buy new ones," she said.

I lost the blade again and didn't bother to pick a new one. Out of the corner of my eye, I watched a tear fall out of Rachel's eye and leave a shimmering path toward her ear.

Emotion gummed up her voice. "He actually bought new underwear rather than pick up the dirty ones and put them in the laundry basket ten feet away." She wiped at the tear, but it had already soaked into her skin. "He was an absolute slob and he never cleaned a single thing in his life, but I miss him."

Rachel started crying then. She covered her face with both hands and they muffled her sobs, but the tears still leaked out. I laid my hand on her shoulder, holding it while she shook with tears. Her feet twitched in rhythm with the rest of her body, blurring the view of the fan blades.

"I don't love him and I don't want him back, but I miss him," she said. I squeezed her shoulder and felt the moment her sadness snapped into anger. She growled, yanking her hands away from her eyes and balling them into fists. "I left him. I kicked him out and I would never ask him to come back."

As she released a furious scream, I congratulated myself on sending the kids away. Rachel needed to scream. She needed to cry and rage and she needed her children not to see it or hear it.

"Why the hell do I miss that conceited, sloppy, cheating asshole?"

"Because you loved him. Because he was a big part of your life and you're allowed to grieve for that part of your life even though you're the one who chose to end it," I said.

Rachel sniffed and daintily wiped her nose. She focused on the fan blades and I watched the small, circular motions of her chin as she chased her high score. "It was a rhetorical question, Nick," she said.

That's when I knew she was going to be okay. The hint of annoyance couldn't quite be covered by the tears clogging her voice. She sounded like herself. A waterlogged version of herself, but herself.

I smiled. "I know. You hate it when I answer rhetorical questions."

"Then why do you do it?"

"I'm your little sister. It's my job to annoy you."

"You're very good at it."

I glanced over at her then and saw she'd let her cheek drop to the carpet. She was looking at me, a fond smile fighting through her sadness.

"You're really good at being a sister," she said quietly.

"I know."

Rachel wasn't done crying. Not by a long shot. She abandoned the game, rolling over to curl up against my side. She put her head on my shoulder and dissolved into tears again. Some of them were quiet. Some of them were wails. Some were angry, teeth-gritting floods. I took all of them and rubbed her arm until she fell asleep hugging me.

❖

I couldn't say when I stopped making my own bagels in favor of going to Sallie Bell's every morning. After the first time I ran into Carter there, I just got it into my head that I could see her if I got out of the house more. The morning after our second date, I went back to Sallie Bell's and Carter arrived a few minutes after me. We chatted as we collected our coffees and pastries and went our separate ways like we'd planned it.

Then the same thing happened every day for a week.

I didn't recognize the change until Ralph followed me into the kitchen one morning rather than staying in his spot on the bed. He plopped down in front of the coffee maker and swished his tail so hard it slapped against the cabinet. I couldn't help feeling like I was being chastised by a disappointed parent.

"I'm allowed to try something new, sir," I told him.

He didn't respond with words, but his glare was surlier than usual.

When I arrived at Sallie Bell's ten minutes later, Carter was waiting outside the front door. As usual, her face lit up when she saw me.

"Good morning, Nicki," she said.

"Good morning, Dawn," I said.

We laughed together at the familiar joke and I found myself moving closer to her. Her sleeves were rolled up again today, showing off the lower half of her sleeve tattoo. I reached out and touched one of the swirls—it looked like it was part of a flower, but the petals wrapped around her arm, out of sight. Her skin was warm and smooth. I could see tiny blond hairs on her skin, but I couldn't feel them. I wondered if the tattoos went all the way up to her shoulder.

I slid my hand up her arm. When I reached her elbow, I retraced the path down her skin and noticed those little hairs were standing up taller now. Was her skin tingling the way mine was? I should have asked for permission to touch her, in case the contact wasn't welcome, but I just couldn't stop myself from reaching out for her every chance I got and her every movement encouraged me.

I almost asked her about the tattoos, but another customer appeared on the sidewalk and we were blocking the entrance. Carter apologized for both of us as she stepped aside, but I couldn't even see who it was we'd blocked. I'm sure one of my acquaintances or old school friends was giving me a dirty look, but all I could focus on was Carter and the feel of her skin against mine.

"Should we get breakfast?" Carter asked.

"After you, Dolores." As Carter held the door for me, I had a moment of doubt. "Is that joke getting annoying? If it upsets you that I'm always trying to guess your name, I can stop. Sometimes I take things too far."

Carter smiled and stepped closer. I don't know when she'd learned her proximity had a way of silencing me, but she used the trick to great effect. "It doesn't upset me and it's not annoying. I love that we have a joke to share."

My brain stuck on the way her lips formed the word love and all I could manage was an unintelligible sound in reply.

"But that doesn't mean I'll give in and confess my biggest secret," she said.

"No? What if I ask really nicely?"

Carter leaned in and whispered, "Not even if you beg."

"Pumpkin spice latte and cheddar bagel with plain cream cheese." Sallie Bell's tone was a little too knowing as she handed over my order. "And here's the order to sign, Carter."

"Thank you, Sallie."

"Oh no." Sallie waggled her eyebrows in my direction. "Thank you."

Once she was gone, Carter cleared her throat and took a step back. "She doesn't even ask your order anymore."

"She knows I have simple tastes."

Carter collected the box of pastries from Sallie's nephew. "Do you? Good to know."

I said in a rush, "Not in women. I mean. I'm not saying you're simple. Not that you were implying. I, ugh, why does this always happen to me?"

Through her laughter, Carter asked, "Why does what always happen to you?"

"Why do I always embarrass myself in front of you?"

"You don't," she said. I held the door for her then followed her toward the parking lot. "You haven't fallen or spilled your coffee in…no, wait, you spilled your latte yesterday."

"Please don't remind me."

"I think your clumsiness is charming."

"I spilled the latte on you."

"Yeah, but once you fell right into my arms, so the occasional coffee burn is worth it."

We arrived at the farm truck and I turned away while she loaded the pastry box onto the passenger seat. I didn't really believe she thought my awkwardness was charming. She was being kind because that's the kind of person she was, but sooner or later she would get tired of it.

"Stop doing that," she said.

"Stop doing what?"

"Stop thinking I don't like you." She rubbed her thumb across my chin just below the edge of my mouth. "You get these frown lines and your expression is like someone with their head under a guillotine blade. I'm telling the truth when I tell you I like you. You can trust me."

The wild thing was, I did trust her. It was me I had grave concerns about.

A voice that sounded a lot like Rachel popped into my head and told me to dive in. I'd heard it off and on for a week, but today I decided to listen to it.

I swallowed hard and dove in. "I was wondering. If maybe we were ready to take the next step?"

Carter's throat bobbed and she ran a hand through her hair. "Which step is that?"

"A dinner date." There. It was out and there was no turning back. "Instead of coffee."

I held my breath and waited. I knew what it looked like when someone was excited but trying to play it cool. It was how I looked any time I saw Carter. This time she was the one wearing the happy, wary expression.

"I'm ready if you are, but there's no rush," she said, her voice a little too high.

All the air rushed out of me in a happy burst. "I know there isn't, but I'm ready. Are you free tonight?"

For three or four seconds, I thought she was going to say yes. She opened her mouth to respond, but then her face fell. "No, actually, I'm not. I'm sorry."

"Oh. Okay."

"I want to, but I can't. In fact, I don't know when I can do dinner. You see, the farm is staying open until eight o'clock every night from now until Halloween."

I smiled, trying not to look too deflated. "Right. Last minute pumpkin emergencies."

"I just don't want to make you wait until the farm closes. Then I'd have to wash up and change. We're both early risers. I couldn't ask you to wait that late for dinner."

"I understand. Makes sense. Your family needs you," I said.

"I really am sorry. It's just, you know, we're a pumpkin patch."

And once Halloween was over, her parents wouldn't need her anymore. She'd leave and I'd never get the chance to see where this might've gone. Even more reason to dive in.

"What about something unconventional?" I asked.

"What did you have in mind?"

"What if I brought a picnic dinner out to the farm?" I formulated the plan as I said it, but it actually sounded nice. "I could work on the festival barn and set up a picnic behind it. When the farm closes you could join me for dinner and it wouldn't be too late."

"It would still be pretty late. Sometimes we get stragglers."

"That'll give me more time to work on the decorations." I started to get nervous about the idea. What if her parents wanted to join since we'd be on their property? I wasn't sure I was ready for that. "Would your parents be okay with us finding somewhere private under the stars?" I snapped my mouth shut, realizing that could sound like a proposition for more than I was ready for.

Carter rubbed her neck and a dusting of pink showed on her cheeks. "I think they'd be okay with that." She smiled at me and all the hesitation was gone from her expression. "A picnic sounds perfect."

I couldn't contain the happiness bubbling up inside me. I dove in and she was interested. "Great. It's a date."

"I feel bad you'll have to do all the legwork. I can provide a bottle of wine or a pitcher of iced tea," Carter said.

"Tea would be better. Since I'll be driving home on dark, winding roads after." Not to mention I might forget I want to take things slow after a glass of wine or two.

Carter's smile nearly knocked me over. "I've never been so excited to make a pitcher of iced tea in my life."

Chapter Sixteen

When I arrived at Carter Farms after work, there was a man in overalls standing in the road, waving for me to stop. He was intimidating with his wide, heavyset frame and weathered skin. No one had ever stopped me before, and my stomach squeezed in fear. Had something happened? Had Carter sent someone to turn me away? He walked over to my window, and I was all set to explain who I was when he leaned down and looked at me with Carter's soft brown eyes.

"I understand you're here to see my daughter."

In all my years of dating women, I'd never gotten the lecture about how to treat someone's daughter, but it appeared as though there was a first time for everything.

"Um, yes, sir. I am."

"Well, you can't be showing up looking as scared as all that," he said. "She's as nervous as I've ever seen her and you can't both be like that or it'll be a boring date. One of you ladies needs to take the lead and she's too polite to do that."

My jaw practically hit the steering wheel, but he was too intent on his speech to notice me gaping in surprise.

He rubbed his chin very much like Carter sometimes did. "Suppose it's my fault. Raised her to be polite to a fault. But there's no changing that now." His eyes settled back on me and he tapped his palm on the door in a final sort of way. "Nope. It'll be down to you, I'm afraid." I managed a nervous laugh, but he was too intent on his instructions to pay attention. "Once you're done with the barn, set up over behind the old farmhouse. It's got a nice patch of lawn and the haunted house actors have all packed up for the night. You'll have that whole corner of the farm to yourselves."

"Yes, sir. Thank you, sir."

"Need me to help carry anything?"

"No, sir. I brought a collapsible wagon to carry everything from the parking lot," I said.

"Stroke of genius. Guess you're the smart one and the brave one in the relationship. Go on now and have a good time. Park by the entrance, I made sure the spot was clear."

I tried to thank him again, but he was already gone from the window. For a man his age, he moved with surprising speed. Maybe it was a lifetime of active farm work. As I pulled forward, his words echoed in my mind. Was I really brave? I didn't really think so, but maybe I should be. Her mother had said Carter was leaving, so I didn't have much time.

I loaded up my wagon as families filtered in and out of the farm. Children and adults alike looked happy as they carried their orange treasures to their cars. I stopped, padded blanket in hand, and watched a young couple with three small children march out in a line, each carrying a pumpkin and grinning from ear to ear. The whole place was alive with laughter and the anticipation of a silly, chocolate-coated holiday to come.

I couldn't help compare the atmosphere to my own workplace, where smiles were always forced and boredom was the prevailing emotion. How different must Carter's workday be to mine? To be surrounded by joy and know you have some small part in making happy memories.

I spent an hour hanging decorations and arranging games in the barn, but there wasn't much left to do. Carter and I had the place pretty much ready for the festival. It didn't take me long to put on the finishing touches. The lack of work was probably a good thing. I couldn't focus on anything. All I could think about was the date to come. When the noise from outside started to die down, I checked my watch. The farm was closing and it was finally time to set up our picnic. I slipped out of the small door at the back of the barn and dragged my wagon laden with food across the uneven ground.

Carter's father was right. When I arrived at the back of the haunted house, I found a lush yard of vibrant grass and a single gnarled sugar maple with leaves the color of sour cherries. I could only imagine that the lack of foot traffic kept the side of the house looking so idyllic. I decided to set up under the tree's canopy close enough to the house so the porch light would keep away the worst of the darkness.

I was setting up jar candles on the corners of the blanket when Carter came around the house, a corked jug in one hand and some oversized plastic wine goblets in the other.

"Just because we can't have wine doesn't mean we can't be fancy." She yanked out the cork with a flourish.

I complimented myself on the blanket and candle placement as she poured us each a small glass of tea. It wasn't bright enough in our little corner for Carter to see how nervous and awkward I was.

Carter handed me a goblet. "What should we toast to?"

"Dinner under the stars?"

"Wonderful. To dinner under the stars."

She raised her glass and I clunked mine against it. They made a sound like plastic ring toys dropping into place. We laughed at the absurdity of the sound, but the tea was absolutely perfect. Bright like it had been brewed in the sun and sweet enough to make your teeth ache.

"Not bad," Carter said.

"It's perfect Southern sweet tea."

Carter settled down onto the blanket. "I had to ask my mom how to make it. She grew up near here and drank tea growing up even though us kids don't."

"Is that why the family moved to Bucks Mill? Because your mom is from around here?"

"Not here exactly. Her family grew peanuts a little south of Charlottesville. A place called Petersburg? There's no farming there now so they settled here. She and my dad, who's from California, made a deal that they'd spend their first thirty years together in California, then the next thirty in Virginia."

"And what if their marriage hadn't made it more than thirty years and she never got her turn?"

Carter gave a half-smile and I could see the love she had for her family as clearly as if she'd spoken it. "I asked them that myself once. They said it never occurred to them that might happen. And the reason it didn't was because they never entertained the idea."

"That's sweet."

She looked up at me and her eyes flickered in the dim light. "Some people just have the spark, you know?"

The darkness made me bold. "I haven't in the past, but hopefully some day." I thought Carter would like the implications of that, but apparently I'd been too bold. She looked off into the night and I swear I saw a hint of discomfort in the line of her jaw.

After a moment, she shook herself and turned her attention to the food I'd laid out. "This is quite the spread."

"Are you ready to eat?"

"Absolutely. Farm work makes me hungry."

"Then let's tuck in."

I hadn't known exactly what Carter would like, but I figured the traditional local cuisine was the way to go. I loaded up her plate with biscuits, fried chicken I'd kept warm in an insulated bag, and a few different pasta and potato salads. I'd sourced most of it from my favorite local places, I'd preordered the biscuits and European tarts from Paradox Pastry. The way Carter's eyes rolled back when she bit into the biscuit was worth the effort. We made quick work of dinner and moved straight to dessert.

"You might have to roll me back home." Carter licked tart crumbs from her fingers. I'll admit to watching the process with relish.

"Think how hard it'll be for me to drive home. I might have to take a nap first," I said.

After I tucked the dishes back into the picnic basket, I flopped down with another goblet of tea and watched the stars twinkle overhead.

"You seem more relaxed tonight," Carter said in a low voice.

I found myself leaning toward her voice. "I do better away from crowds. I'm a bit of a home body. Too many people make me nervous."

"I had a feeling. That's why I chose a walking date last week."

"You did that on purpose?"

"I thought you might be happier away from prying eyes and distractions."

"I was." I looked over at her and she was definitely closer than I remembered. Our bodies were nearly touching. "I am."

Her eyes were so sincere, so kind, that I couldn't keep staring into them. I worried I'd get lost. That I'd forget everything and make a fool of myself. I dropped my gaze to the blanket and a lock of hair came loose from behind my ear. I reached up to tuck it away, but Carter beat me to it. Our fingers brushed as she lifted the hair off my cheek. She slid it behind my ear and let her fingers linger. Her fingertips were cold and her palm quivered slightly as she cupped my cheek. My body screamed to lean into that touch. To press my cheek into her hand or maybe bring her fingertips to my lips. To kiss each finger and then press my mouth into her palm. I craved her touch like it was oxygen. The only thing that could keep me alive.

But it was too fast and too soon and there were so many things that could go wrong if I let that happen. What if I'd forgotten how to kiss a woman over the years? What if our mouths didn't sync, proving our incompatibility? It was too scary. It might be the beginning of the end. It was too deep to dive in.

As uncertainty coursed through my veins, the chill of the night finally penetrated my skin. I couldn't say if it was the cold or the fear, but a shiver tore through my body. In a flash, Carter's hand was gone from my cheek and she was on her knees, peeling her jacket off and dropping it over my shoulders.

"I'm so sorry. I've kept you out late in the cold," she said.

"Oh, it's okay."

It was far more than okay. If Carter's touch had me nervous, the warmth and scent of her jacket had me reeling. It was the jacket I'd seen her in a dozen times, well-worn from use so that the flannel lining was soft as butter and the collar carried the mingled scents of her skin and fresh hay. I pulled it tight around myself and burrowed in. Not because I was cold, but because it felt like being hugged by Carter without the weight of expectation a real hug would bring.

"I hate to end this date," Carter said. She'd scooted even closer to me, running her hands up and down my arms to warm me. It certainly worked, but the warmth was spreading from deep in my chest rather than the arms she rubbed. "But we have early mornings here and I don't want to keep you on the roads too late."

I sighed. "You're right. The deer are out in force this time of year and I don't want to meet one."

Carter leapt to her feet. "I didn't think of that. It isn't safe for you to drive with the deer out."

I climbed to my feet with far less grace. "It's fine. I've driven in deer country my whole life. I know how to be safe."

"Are you sure? You said you were sleepy."

"I'm full, it's different." I slid her jacket off my shoulders and held it out to her. "I promise to drive safe."

"At least let me help you pack up."

"Deal."

I shouldn't have accepted the help because it meant the task was completed too quickly. Within moments we were trundling the wagon along the packed dirt of the parking lot, my car looming ahead like a stop sign at the end of a perfect night.

"Text me when you make it home safe?" Carter asked.

"It might just be an unintelligible bundle of letters. You know my texting skills."

She laughed and shoved her fists into her pockets, scuffing the ground with her toe. "I'll take it as long as I know you're safe."

"It really will be okay. I didn't mean to scare you. I know how to handle a country road at night."

Carter gave me a lopsided grin. "I know you can handle anything."

"Except haunted houses."

Carter leaned in close and gave me a wink. "Oh, you would've been fine if you'd just leapt into my arms immediately like your sister told you to."

I'd been mesmerized by her closeness and the twinkle in her eye. Then her words sunk in and my jaw dropped. "How did you know?"

"Lucky guess."

"I'm sorry. I shouldn't have been so childish and silly."

Carter leaned closer, propping herself up with one hand on the side of my car. I enjoyed the press of cold metal against my back and the solidity of her not quite touching me.

"It's okay. I actually have a confession of my own," she said.

"Really? What?"

She caught my eyes and held them, her breath washing across my cheek, bringing the sweet scent of her tea. "I don't usually pick up the pastries. The normal guy was sick and I complained about going the whole way there. I just took over the job after so I could see you every day."

I laughed and tried not to think how close her body was to mine or how much closer I wanted it to be. "I never go there for breakfast. I only started going so I could see you."

Carter's free hand slid onto my hip. I could feel the heat of her skin like a patch of fire in my core. "I'm glad we have the same ulterior motives."

"Me too."

"I have another confession," Carter whispered.

"I already guessed your first name and you lied about it to throw me off?"

Her chuckle was kindling on the fire her touch had ignited. "Good idea. I'll keep that in mind if you ever guess it. But that wasn't it."

"What is it?"

As soon as I asked the question my mouth went dry and my eyes fixed on the thin line of her lips.

"I want to go slow, but I also really want to kiss you right now."

I heard my breath hitch, muffled through the roar of the fire inside me.

"I'll back off if that's too fast, but I want you to know that I'm ready for our first kiss if you are," Carter said.

I bit my bottom lip to swallow the groan. Part of me wanted to slam our bodies together and devour her. Part of me wanted to run off into the darkness and hide. But the weight of her hand on my hip was too much for my fear to overcome.

"I think I'm ready for our first kiss, too."

Carter looked shocked at the answer, but the hunger in her eyes was unmistakable. "Really?"

I reached out to cup her cheek. My hand was trembling like a leaf clinging to a branch in a high wind, but her skin was soft and her jaw was hard. Her lips parted a fraction, the pale skin glowing in the moonlight. I nodded and leaned in, knowing it was up to me to close the final gap.

Her lips were soft but dry and still carried the sweetness of tea. We met gently and fit together perfectly. Carter didn't push to deepen the kiss and neither did I. It was sweet and chaste and made me feel safe. I'd never had a first kiss where my partner let me take the lead. Let me go just as far as I wanted and followed along happily. She held me as we kissed and I could have stayed locked together with her all night long.

When I pulled away, all the safety and happiness dissolved into fear. Was that too chaste? Would Carter be underwhelmed? If she'd been looking for hot and heavy, that's not what I'd given her. I opened my eyes, worried I'd see disappointment. Instead, Carter looked like a boxer who hadn't yet realized she'd been knocked out. Her eyes were unfocused and her lips now carried a bleary, almost dazed grin.

I had to gently remove her hand from my hip so I could slide out from her grip and open my driver's door. The click of the lock seemed to snap her out of it, and she stepped away from the car to let me leave.

Still, there was an unfocused joy in her words as she said, "Good night, Nicki."

CHAPTER SEVENTEEN

T hat was it? An amazing first kiss and you just drove away?"
My heart fluttered a little at the memory, which made
it hard to play it cool when I nodded to Rachel and went back to
chopping carrots for our salad.

Rachel reached across the counter and snagged a carrot chip,
narrowly avoiding the tip of my knife. "I don't think I've ever dated
anyone who was genuinely comfortable with taking things slow."

"She wants to take it slow, too. That makes it easier," I said.
I finished with the carrots and we both snagged a slice from the
cutting board.

"Do you know why?"

I dropped the carrots into the bowl and grabbed a sliver of
green pepper to snack on. "Just that she had a recent breakup."

"How recent? Do you know what happened?"

"No, I don't want to pry," I said. Rachel grabbed a cherry
tomato out of the salad bowl and I looked around the empty kitchen.
"Where are the kids?"

"With Stephen."

"Then why aren't we drinking wine?"

"Knife safety. No alcohol until the chopping is done," Rachel
said.

"I finished."

"Thank God."

Rachel hopped off the stool and yanked open the fridge. I took
the salad bowl over to the couch while she uncorked a bottle of

Chardonnay. We ate the undressed salad like popcorn out of the bowl while we sipped wine.

"Okay, give me all the juicy gossip parts," Rachel said.

"About Carter's breakup? I don't know them."

"But there's something more to this." Rachel waved a broccoli floret at me.

I looked around the room. "Are you sure the kids won't be home soon?"

"They're spending the night over there. Spill."

It was time I got this off my chest. "I don't really know what to do because I was the one who brought up going slow because I wasn't sure I was ready."

Rachel shoved some romaine into her mouth and waved her hand for me to continue.

"I'm sure," I said.

"Of what?"

"That I'm ready."

"To sleep with her?" Rachel sat forward like a happy puppy.

"No! Well, yeah. Maybe. Not yet," I said. Rachel rolled her eyes. "Look, the whole drive home last night all I could think about was kissing her."

"Mmm-hmm."

"And then I went to bed and I dreamed of more than kissing her."

"Sweetie, the kids aren't home. You can give me the details," Rachel said.

"It was an intense dream." I knew my face was blazing red, and I hoped Rachel didn't make me spell it out.

Rachel dropped back against the couch and sighed. "God, I want to have a wet dream about someone."

"That's not what I said. I said intense."

"Nicki, you are a nearly forty-year-old woman. You are allowed to get off in a dream. You're allowed to get off when you're awake. And you're definitely allowed to get off with her."

"I know. Please stop saying that word."

She smiled over at me. "Which one? Get or off?"

"Both. Together. You're my sister."

Rachel grabbed the empty salad bowl off the couch and scooted closer to me. She grabbed my hand and held it to her chest. "I'm your sister and I love you and I want you to be happy. And sex will make you really, really happy."

"I can be happy without sex."

"I know you can, but you want to have sex with Carter, right?"

"Yes. I do. I can admit that. Maybe not tomorrow, but…"

"But what?" she asked.

I threw my hands into the air. "I'm the one who pumped the brakes and now I don't know how to—you know—hit the gas."

Rachel burst out laughing. "Carter's dad was right. She's too polite, so it has to be you."

"But how?" I growled in frustration. Mostly frustration with myself for being wishy-washy, but there was a lingering frustration from last night's dream.

"You could try asking her for another kiss."

"How?"

"Nicki, sweetie. Do you really need help with how to phrase that request?"

"No, I mean how logistically? We had dinner at eight o'clock. She's working super long hours from now until Halloween. When can we see each other?"

"Go to the farm," she said.

"I'm not going to kiss her in front of her parents and all their customers."

Rachel's eyebrow went up and her smile was distinctly predatory. "I seem to remember a lot of barns at that farm. One of them, in fact, would be a perfectly natural place for the two of you to be alone."

I opened my mouth to argue, then closed it slowly while my eyebrow lifted so high my bangs fell into my eye.

❖

If I'd thought Carter's lips were sweet, they were nothing compared to her tongue. I indulged in the luxury of exploring every inch of her mouth as thoroughly as possible. With each press of lips and tongue, my worries about not remembering how to kiss a woman dissolved. Carter and I learned and taught in equal measure as I held her by her jacket lapels, dragging her body against mine.

I swiped the tip of my tongue across the ridge of her teeth and she groaned into my mouth. I pulled her harder against me, using her weight to slam me into the rough-hewn boards lining the barn wall. I could hear the rustle of tissue paper from the streamers above us. I clawed my fingers through her close-cropped hair, keeping her face pressed hard to mine. The fire that had ignited inside me during our picnic date was a raging inferno and I let it consume me. It made me ache to consume her.

The need for air forced me to break the kiss, but I didn't let Carter go. If her body wasn't touching mine in that moment, nothing would have held me anchored to the earth.

"Jesus." She panted, pressing a hand against the barn wall to prop herself up. I was starting to crave the feeling of her towering over me, pinning me against a hard object. "Holy…wow."

"Sorry. Was that too much?"

"God no."

Her eyes swam like that woozy boxer again, but I could see a healthy dose of lust mixed with the surprise. I was shocked how much that lust affected me. I dropped my hands from her jacket to her waist, still holding her close, but touching her now. We were tucked inside the darkest corner of the Halloween festival barn and I could barely see her. But touching her was a far more exciting way to feel her presence.

She laughed breathlessly. "If I'd known what you'd meant when you said you wanted to kiss me again, I'd have made sure I was sitting down. You make my knees weak."

An image flashed in my mind. Carter sitting on a wooden chair, me straddling her hips and kissing her as thoroughly as I just had. The thought of it made my hips roll forward in search of hers. She groaned at the contact.

"Sorry. Was that too much? Am I moving too fast for you?"

She chuckled and lowered her voice. "No. Absolutely not. I'm fine with the kissing." Her words trailed off as her lips found the side of my neck. A shiver that had nothing to do with cold cascaded through me and Carter pressed harder against me. Her lips brushed against mine. "I'm fine with lots and lots of kissing," she whispered.

"Show me."

This time Carter initiated the kiss. She crashed into me, a gentle hand cupped around the back of my head to keep it from hitting the wall. The rest of her was anything but gentle. Her body pressed against mine and I pulled her in harder still. Her tongue plunged past my lips and crashed into mine. Her lips were magic, pressing hard enough to show her passion but not so hard to bruise. Her whole aspect was a controlled roughness that had my head spinning.

I slipped my hands under her jacket, running my nails up her back across the thick fabric of her flannel shirt. She groaned and pressed harder against me. For a heartbeat our hips met and the friction I'd been desperate for made my head spin. She pulled away slightly and my whole body screamed for more. I pulled at her shirt frantically and the tail came loose from her jeans.

"Crap." Now I was the one panting when I broke the kiss. I looked down at her untucked shirt and the slice of flesh untucking it had revealed. "I didn't mean to do that."

She smiled as she shoved her shirt tails back in. "It's okay. Actually, it's more than okay."

"It's just that we agreed on slow. You said you wanted slow and then I came at you like this and this is not slow. Sorry."

She ran her thumb along my jaw. "I know we're going slow. But I don't have any doubts about wanting to be with you."

"I feel the same way."

Carter's eyebrows went up then a smile crept onto her lips. I couldn't keep my eyes off those lips. They were less pale than before and a little puffy from the kissing. I wondered if they would feel different now. If they'd be even softer and what patches of skin I'd like her to try them on.

I was reaching for her shirt again, excited where my hands might go if it was loose again, when the bolt on the barn door rattled open. Carter whipped around in front of me, shielding my body from sight, but I could hear Carter's dad talking to someone by the door. Clearly, he'd been distracted on his way in, giving us a chance to escape through the back. We slipped out the door we'd come in, trying to hurry without running and drawing attention.

"Do you think he saw us?" I whispered once she had the door shut and bolted it.

Carter checked her clothes and ran a hand through her hair to straighten it. "Nah. That was my brother he was talking to. They were probably arguing about the corn displays. They've been arguing about pricing on those for weeks."

Her words washed over me while I watched her hands trace the lines of her body. I knew she was just checking to make sure she wasn't disheveled from our barn adventure, but the movements were intoxicating. I wanted to make the same journey with my hands, caressing all her curves and sharp edges. Better yet, to have her run her hands over me like that. It took me far too long to remember to check my own clothes and hair. It was a good thing I had, because my ponytail was a frizzy mess, falling out of its tie.

Carter took my hand in hers as we emerged into the boisterous crowd. The route we took back to the parking lot was far more meandering than was warranted, even with so many people around. Clearly neither of us wanted to get to my car.

When we exited the farm gates, Carter turned to me. "Halloween is only a week away. You think everything is ready for the festival?"

"I think so. I'll bring the candy and prizes over that morning, and I've made sure the moms understand they have to help run everything. I'm sure they'll actually show up so everyone will see them working."

"My family will be here to run events, too."

"They don't have to do that. Don't they have to run the farm?" I asked.

"We have a couple of seasonal employees who'll man the registers. They can handle it."

The mention of seasonal employees reminded me that Carter was one of them. I hadn't had the courage to ask her about her future plans yet, but she had mentioned the desire to go back to her old land management job during our first date. Her days in Bucks Mill were numbered.

"The festival ends pretty early. What are your plans after?" Carter asked.

"I was going to bring that up, actually. What are your feelings about trick-or-treating?"

"I'm generally pro trick-or-treating. Are there people who are against it?"

"I meant how would you feel about trick-or-treating with me?"

Carter turned to me with a crooked smile. "Aren't you a little old for trick-or-treating?"

The smile drew my eyes back to her lips and memories of the barn. The thoughts made it hard to string words together. "Rachel has a late work thing."

"A late work thing on Halloween?"

"Yeah. She works at the library, and they're doing a trunk-or-treat. Anyway, she won't make it home until after what Lily has dubbed prime trick-or-treating time."

"Sounds like a crisis."

"Apparently," I said. Carter's smile was so sweet I wanted to pull her into another kiss, but there were too many people milling around. "And when I suggested she go to the trunk-or-treat, I was informed those events are for suckers and toddlers."

"Wow, this is serious business for her."

"Sure is." I took a deep breath and forged ahead. "I promised to take her and Blake trick-or-treating myself, but I could use some backup."

"You sure could. That little guy likes to bolt."

"I thought maybe you'd be available since the farm is closing after the festival."

"Are you asking me on a date?" Carter asked.

"I am. Are you interested? I know it's not the most exciting date, but it could be fun."

"It sounds wonderful." She gave my hand a squeeze and then rubbed her chin thoughtfully. "What exactly is required of a trick-or-treating chaperone?"

"Shoes you can chase a toddler in and a costume without a mask."

Her half-grin made my knees weak again. "Is that because you want my lips accessible at any moment?"

My face and neck heated up almost to the point of discomfort. "As nice as that sounds, it's because Blake is afraid of masks."

"And we don't need another reason for him to run away."

"Exactly."

"No mask it is, but I have to warn you, my costume will probably be pretty boring."

No one was looking our way, so I pushed up on tiptoes to kiss her cheek. "The more boring the better."

Chapter Eighteen

Y ou're absolutely sure it won't be a bother?" I asked.

Fred leaned against my office doorframe, a mug of tea in hand and an indulgent smile on his face. There were moments like this, when he looked at me like a precocious child rather than an employee, when I wanted to punch him very hard on the nose.

"Nicki, when was the last time you took a day off?"

"But this is a holiday."

"Halloween isn't exactly a business holiday. It's one day, we'll survive," he said.

"But what if that accountant calls back? What's his name? Shoot, I had a Post-it Note here somewhere."

"I know you'll check your voice mail every hour on the hour. The accountant won't know the difference." He took a sip from his mug and made a face. His tea must've gone cold while I was obsessing.

"I could work from home in the morning. The festival doesn't start until three."

"Sure. Save your vacation time for a real vacation and do a work from home day."

"But you know I don't really have enough work to take home for eight hours. What if I finish early?" I asked.

Fred shushed me and took a step into my office. "Don't say that out loud. You know none of us work eight hours at home. I don't care about that as long as you get your work done, just don't tell me."

"But then I would—"

"Don't tell me and I don't have to tell anyone else." He tried to give me a conspiratorial wink, but he'd never been able to wink. It was more like a pained blink.

Honestly, I probably wouldn't get much work done anyway. Between my nerves over pulling off the festival and the way seeing Carter made me breathless, I would be absolutely useless on Friday. I should just take a vacation day.

"I've told you to stay home for work sometimes. We're all more efficient from home."

"I don't want you to feel like I'm taking advantage of you," I said.

He shook his head and his smile wasn't condescending anymore. It was bordering on thoughtful. "You ought to spend more time thinking about what makes you happy and stop focusing on other people's expectations."

Tears immediately sprung to my eyes. It was like he'd seen right through me. All these years he'd spent so much time trying to connect with me in weird ways, but maybe he really did know me after all?

"I've embarrassed you. I'm very sorry." He stumbled a little as he backed out of my office.

"No, it isn't you." Frustratingly, the tears fell down my cheeks and I had to grab a tissue to dab them away. "I've been thinking a lot recently about setting aside my fears and doing what makes me happy. Diving in, you know?"

"I'm glad to hear it. You deserve to do things that make you happy."

"I think I'm ready to do that." I felt myself stand taller when I said it. Perhaps speaking it into the universe had been the key all along. Maybe I could be brave with Carter Friday night.

"Great. So you'll work from home more?"

"What? Oh no, I couldn't do that." I chewed on my lip, thinking about how I could relax into taking the next step with Carter. What even was the next step? Was it sex? How many steps were there in relationships?

"Are we having the same conversation?"

"Definitely not," I said, my face heating up at the thought of having sex with Carter.

"Is that okay?"

The thoughts of sex with Carter didn't elicit the fear they had even a few days ago. They made me feel warm and safe and happy.

"It's more than okay." I smiled widely.

Fred didn't say anything else. He just looked vaguely confused as he walked off toward the break room. While I was shoving my laptop into my bag, my cell phone vibrated on the desk. A notification with Carter's name on it popped up, so I dropped into my chair to settle in.

I haven't had a spare moment since we talked. My costume will be even more boring than I thought

I hurried to text back, *Then it'll be perfect*

Carter didn't respond immediately, but her message was worth the wait. *I've been thinking a lot about the last time we saw each other.*

Warmth bloomed in my chest and I closed my eyes, letting the memories of Carter's lips and tongue and body wash over me. I texted back, *Me too. I can't wait to see you Friday.*

I wish it was tonight

Me too, I texted and really, really meant it.

❖

I was ten minutes from home when my cell phone rang. I'd been lost in more thoughts about Carter and ways we could continue moving our relationship forward, so I didn't even look at the caller before I answered.

"Nicki, we have an emergency." Rachel's voice barked through the car speakers.

"What's wrong?" I frantically searched for somewhere to pull over. "Is one of the kids hurt?"

"Lily will be soon because I might strangle her."

"What?"

"Your niece is being a spoiled terror," Rachel said.

I heard said niece angrily shouting in the background and told myself to calm down. "So this isn't a real emergency. It's a Lily Emergency."

"Exactly," Rachel said. I could hear her grinding her teeth through the phone. "She took some of our pumpkins to her father's house and apparently now our display doesn't have the appropriate number."

"Why can't you handle this Lily Emergency?"

"Because Blake found my chocolate stash and he's practically bouncing off the walls. I can't handle both of them and she is insistent that our display is ruined until we get more."

"Oh God, not that again. It's two days before Halloween, no one will see it."

"Believe me, I have told her. There's no escape from this. She needs to get last minute, emergency pumpkins."

I couldn't help but laugh. "Rachel, there has never, in the history of the world, been a pumpkin emergency."

Apparently, I announced this too loudly because an inhuman squawk sounded on the line. The muffled sound of Rachel trying to cover the phone meant I only heard the fury in Lily's voice, not her words. That was probably for the best. I loved my niece, but Rachel was right. She was a spoiled terror when it came to Halloween. She'd given me an hour-long lecture during dinner last night about costumes.

Rachel came back on the line, but her voice was quiet and hissy, like she was trying to hide the conversation from her daughter. "She's doing you a favor, Nicki. There's only one pumpkin patch in town and you want to stick your hands down the operator's pants."

"Rachel!"

"Stop bleating about it. Be a good girl and take your niece to get the fricking pumpkins."

I drifted onto the shoulder thinking about putting my hands down Carter's pants. Maybe in that dark corner of the barn? I shook myself out of it and dragged the car back onto the road. It would make me feel way too weird at the festival if I had memories of seducing Carter in the corner where my niece was playing ring toss.

"Okay."

Rachel sighed. "Fine. Don't take her because of Carter, take her because we'll never have a moment's—Wait. What did you say?"

"I said okay, but I won't be able to put my hands down Carter's pants unless you come, too. Are you coming?"

Rachel was quiet for a long time. "You aren't sputtering or protesting or anything," she said in an oddly calm voice.

"No. I'm not." I laughed at my own bravado. "Isn't that weird?"

I heard hurried footsteps and could picture her rushing down the hall to hide in the dining room. "So you aren't nervous about being intimate with Carter anymore?"

"Oh no, I'm super nervous about it. But I still want it." I took a moment to bask in how excited I was about the idea. "Like I really, really want it."

"Calm down there, tiger, your niece has superhuman hearing."

"Well then, she should hear me honk cause I'm in the driveway."

"Already?"

I threw my car into park and honked the horn. "Stop slowing me down. Send your kid out here so I can go see my girlfriend."

I swallowed hard at the word and the line went eerily quiet. Had I just said that? Was Carter my girlfriend? Was that one of the steps I was nervous about taking? As Lily burst through the front door and careened across the yard, I stared at my headlights illuminating the overgrown grass.

"Did you just say—"

"Stop. Don't say it. Pretend you didn't hear anything," I said.

"Pretend I didn't hear what?" Lily asked as she climbed into the car.

"Nothing. Never mind. Nothing happening here," I said in the same shrill voice as I hung up on Rachel. It didn't matter because she sprinted out of the house, Blake in her arms, and clambered into the back seat. I didn't have to warn her to keep quiet, she knew better than to use the G-word around the kids, but she did keep a hawk's eye on me in the rearview mirror while I drove us all to Carter Farms.

We snagged a parking spot near the entrance and Rachel hustled the family off so quickly I didn't see them go. I was slower getting out of the car since I was scanning the crowd for a familiar jawline and Carhartt jacket. I was still wearing my business suit and heels, the tight, knee-length skirt not ideal for the farm's uneven ground.

I spotted Carter kneeling to chat with a little boy not much older than Blake. She was wearing that indulgent smile she saved for sweet kids and me. Her forearms were propped on one knee and she held out the most perfectly round pumpkin I'd ever seen. Suddenly the warm evening was too hot for my blazer and I unbuttoned it to give air flow to my silk blouse.

I was just noticing how low cut my blouse was when Carter stood and looked toward the parking lot. Her eyes locked on mine and the pumpkin dropped from her hands. It missed the little boy's head by inches but smashed onto her toe. She swore loudly and hopped on one foot, cradling her abused toe. I tried to stifle my laughter while Carter apologized to the little boy's family and made her way toward me. When she got close, I noticed a slight limp and that set me off again.

I reached out to take her hand. "I'm really sorry to laugh. It's just that's usually my move."

She scowled at the wet pulp staining her boot. "I liked it better when it was you. My mom's going to kill me for that."

"Then I'm glad I get to see you one last time." A young couple carrying a wailing infant walked past us, nearly bumping into Carter. "Walk with me?"

"Gladly."

We set off toward the end of the parking lot where there were fewer people and less noise. Carter set a slow pace, and I was grateful for it. The heels weren't particularly high and the ground was far more even from the constant vehicle traffic, but we'd already had our tumble for the day. I didn't want to add to the list.

"You look amazing," Carter said. Then she bumped her shoulder against mine. "I'm glad you lied about me not seeing you until Friday."

"Oh, no. I wasn't lying. It's just that we had a pumpkin emergency and I was on my way home from work and Rachel talked me into it. I would never…"

I trailed off when I heard her laughing over my words. Somehow, even with a bruised toe and broken pumpkin, Carter already had the upper hand again. How did she manage to do that? We reached the end of the parking lot and ducked between the farm truck Carter always drove into town and a cargo van with their logo on it.

"I was only teasing. I like it when you get all nervous and flustered," she said.

I rolled my eyes. "Why on earth do you like that?"

She leaned her shoulder against the van. "It's sexy. It reminds me of when we first met."

"I'm still like that." I looked into her eyes and let myself get lost in them. "For the same reason."

Carter took my hand and pulled me closer. There wasn't a soul around and the sun was setting behind her. "What reason is that?"

My mind screamed at me to be brave. Dive in. Ask for what makes you happy. "All I can think about when I see you is kissing you. It's become an obsession."

Carter pulled me to her and I went willingly, slipping my arms around her waist and looking up at those incredible lips. If she'd asked, I would have begged her to kiss me. I would have gotten down on my knees and done anything she asked just for one taste of her mouth.

She dipped her head down toward mine, stopping a breath from my lips. "I better stop this obsession before it gets out of hand then."

"Please," I whispered.

Her mouth was just as delicious as I remembered, but our kiss was more frantic this time. I was probably the desperate one, but I honestly didn't care. I was kissing Carter and she was kissing me back. Not only was she kissing me, she was touching me.

Her hands slid up my sides, catching occasionally on the thin silk. They slid up under my blazer, her thumbs grazing the sides of my breasts for a heartbeat before wrapping around my back and holding me close. They slid down, settling on my lower back when I would have wished she'd go lower. She drove me wild, but she never crossed the line and my lust-drenched mind still appreciated the care.

We were in public, so I should have been more chaste, but the van offered the illusion of privacy and my body screamed for me to take advantage. Carter released my lips, trailing a line of kisses across my cheek and down my jaw. When her first kiss landed on my neck, I lost all self-control.

I don't know when I'd settled my hands on her waist, but suddenly I was yanking her shirt out from her pants so I could slide my hands across the bare skin on her stomach. I had expected hard, defined muscles like the six packs I saw in superhero movies. Carter's stomach was certainly toned, but there was nothing hard about it. She moaned and pressed against me as I raked short nails across soft skin and firm muscles.

She groaned into my neck. "It's not fair. You show up, dressed in this killer suit, when I have to work." She nipped at my neck and I gasped when her teeth scraped against my skin.

I grabbed her waistband and dug my fingertips in. "What about how unfair it is for you to always dress like the hot lesbian model in a Carhartt catalog?"

She chuckled and kissed back up my neck. "That's not a thing."

"It should be. More lesbians would buy Carhartt if it was."

She pulled away to look at me. I was simultaneously devastated and relieved when she stopped kissing me. I certainly didn't have the strength to stop, but we were treading in dangerous waters.

"You're serious, aren't you?" she said.

"What? That I find flannel hot? I'm a country girl, of course I do."

"I'll keep that in mind."

She stroked her thumb across my chin and gave me one last, closed-mouth kiss on the lips before stepping away to tuck her shirt back in. I tried to rearrange my clothes, but I doubted there was any hope for it.

"I better get back to work before I get in trouble."

"I thought you couldn't get in trouble since you work for your parents."

"It's you that'll get me into trouble, not them." She walked to the end of the van and peeked around like a teenager sneaking back into the house after an elicit date. "See you Friday."

I should have followed her out of our little nook, but I took a moment to lean back against the van and smile up at the first stars poking through the darkening sky. Each time I saw her, the thought of her leaving at the end of the season hurt a little bit more.

CHAPTER NINETEEN

I didn't work a single minute on Halloween. I tried. A little.
I sat at my computer and thought about logging into the VPN. Then I thought about the feel of Carter's skin under my fingertips and her tongue in my mouth and I couldn't sit still. I texted Fred to say I was taking vacation after all and then cleaned every inch of my cottage. Somewhere between dusting the baseboards and bleaching the drain traps for the kitchen sink, I recognized that I needed to get out of the house.

So that's how I found myself chopping firewood again. The chore was becoming tedious, but at least I was getting better. It still took me ages to chop a log into burnable pieces and I tired quickly, but I hardly ever missed the wood when I swung my axe. That was a marked improvement and I allowed myself some pride that I was mastering the task.

The timing couldn't be better. It was starting to get chilly and tonight would be the perfect night for a real fire. One that wasn't just for show but really warmed my cottage with both its crackling noise and its heat. We were supposed to get a real frost overnight. One that would coat everything outside in that beautiful, crystalline shimmer. I looked over at the porch and the arrangement of pumpkins. My mother had a saying about frost on the pumpkins, but I couldn't remember it. Maybe it was a poem?

"Hey, Lily," I called between axe swings. "Do you remember Granny Russell saying something about frost on the pumpkins?"

Lily had taken to watching me chop firewood. I kept a close eye on her since I still wasn't sure she could be trusted not to drag the axe out on her own. Something about the chore seemed to interest her, though, so I hoped to keep her in line by letting her watch. Plus her school had a half day for the holiday and the festival, and I didn't want her to get too bored. The only thing more dangerous than Lily with an axe would be bored Lily with an axe.

She scrunched up her face. "I don't remember. What was it about?"

"I don't remember either. I was hoping you would."

"Did Granny Russell like pumpkins, too?"

I laughed a little breathlessly after my last swing. "Not as much as you, sweetie."

Lily kicked her feet for a while as I tried to conjure my mother's voice in my head. It was a hard task. It felt like she'd been gone forever, but that was just because my life had changed so much when we lost her. I hadn't really felt like a grown-up until I didn't have the option of calling my mom for advice.

"I don't remember Granny Russell much. I think I remember her funeral? There were a lot of people at the house," Lily said.

"Yes, there were. You were just four and all your cousins wanted to play with you, but you didn't want to mess up your nice dress."

"I don't like dresses," Lily said, her face scrunching again.

I laughed as the axe split perfectly through a log and sent the two halves flying. "You did back then. It was a purple dress with ruffles underneath so it stood out like a tutu. You wouldn't take that off for months."

After a moment, she said, "I looked like a princess."

I took a break to lean on the axe and pant a little more than I'd like to admit. "You sure did. That's cause you are a princess, whether you're wearing a fluffy purple dress or not."

Lily beamed and hopped off her log seat. "If you're tired, I can take a turn chopping."

"No, you most certainly cannot. We've had this discussion. You are not old enough to use the axe."

Her pout had an air of defiance to it and I was suddenly rethinking the strategy of letting her watch me chop.

"Am too," she said, stamping her little foot into the dirt.

"Are not and that's final." I could see the temper tantrum building, so I deflected. "But you are old enough to help me carry this wood inside. I have to get ready for the festival, so I could use your help."

That worked for exactly two armloads of firewood. I balanced a couple of pieces in Lily's arms and loaded myself down, but I could tell before we even got inside that she wouldn't stick around too long. Sure enough, she dumped her second pile on the hearth and announced she needed to go check on her brother, leaving me to finish the job.

This time around, I was able to fill the inside rack and even stack a few pieces in the shed out back. It wouldn't last long, of course, but it would be enough for tonight. I took the time to arrange newspaper, kindling, and a few choice logs in the grate for that evening. Trick-or-treating would be a chilly event, and I was looking forward to coming home after and curling up on the couch with a roaring fire and a good book.

I dropped the log I'd been placing. Carter was going trick-or-treating with us. She'd be helping me walk the kids home. The kids who lived right next door to me. What if I invited her inside? Maybe I could curl up on the couch with something far more enticing than a romance novel.

Before I could get carried away, I settled the log into place and went to take a much-needed shower. If I showed up smelling like bleach and sawdust there was no chance she'd join me in front of the fire.

❖

My costume came together more easily than I'd thought. The hardest part was curling my hair, a process neither my hair nor I was used to. It took some trial and error, but it ended up giving my hair more body and shine than the usual ponytail offered. I'd made the costume itself several years ago in a fit of independence and a desire for accuracy. It was a perfect replica from my favorite movie, *A League of Their Own*. That night it had been a hit, but I wasn't so sure recycling my favorite costume was actually a great idea.

When I'd told Rachel that morning about my plan, she'd argued that it was a mistake. "You're spending the whole afternoon with Carter. You should've picked something sexy. The stores are full of those costumes. Sexy pirate or sexy nurse or sexy cat."

"First, cats are cute, not sexy. Second, we're spending the first couple of hours at the school Halloween festival. It would be weird to dress sexy. Plus, it's too cold for a teddy and tights."

As I adjusted the Rockford Peaches logo on my chest, I second-guessed my decision. The skirt was still pretty short, even if the tall socks helped with the cold. But was it a good idea to wear the costume from a thirty-year-old movie?

Hammering of tiny fists on my front door told me that, mistake or not, it was too late for me to change my mind. Lily and Blake sprinted through the door and I waved good-bye to their babysitter. Rachel had brought the kids costumes over this morning and Lily insisted she could dress herself. Blake took a little persuading to do his Spiderman outfit. It wasn't a costume, per se, but onesie pajamas with a loose hood. He insisted on red face paint to complete the look, but wouldn't sit still long enough for me to complete the job. It ended up as uneven smears of red paint down his cheeks and across his forehead and a dot on his nose. He looked more like Rudolph than Spiderman, but he seemed happy enough.

Lily had graduated from cheap, store-bought costume sets to what she referred to as a "curated look" this year. She'd dragged Rachel to a dozen thrift stores to find just the right dress and coat. She'd torn both to shreds and somehow ended up with a pretty convincing gown and cape to go with a witch's hat Rachel had made. Actually, Rachel had made the hat three times. The first two attempts were admittedly hideous, but Lily had squealed with delight at the final product.

My phone rang just as I finished a last-minute inspection of the kids.

"Did you go get a sexy maid outfit?" Rachel asked.

"No, I did not."

"Why? You had plenty of time. You didn't even go to work today."

I rummaged through my utility closet with the phone wedged into my shoulder. "I did work today. I had chores around the house. And I wouldn't have gotten one anyway. I'm not that kind of woman."

"What? A sexy one?"

"Gee, thanks, sis."

"Come on, Nicki. You're sexy, you just don't let yourself show it."

"I don't have to hang my tits out for Carter to think I'm sexy." Did I?

"No, but it would help," she said.

"Good-bye, Rachel."

"I'll see you at six thirty. Thanks for this. I owe you one."

I tossed the phone on the couch and dove headfirst into the closet, pushing dusty wreaths and Fourth of July bunting aside as I searched for that stupid plastic pumpkin. All the while telling myself Carter wasn't looking for a sexy maid. I repeated it to myself a dozen times, but the doubts kept creeping in.

"Aunt Nicki, we have to go." Lily drew the O out for at least thirty seconds.

I shoved the closet door shut. "Fine, but I can't find my extra candy pumpkin."

Lily scrunched her face up. "You're not allowed to ask for candy. You're a grown-up."

"It's for Blake."

"You didn't prepare for this?"

I opened the door again and the plastic pumpkin fell off the top closet shelf directly onto the top of my head. I really needed to be careful for the rest of the autumn or I'd get permanent brain damage. "I was busy."

"So was I." She unfolded a piece of notebook paper on the coffee table, spreading it out like an ancient treasure map. "I've planned out our route. Fortunately, the pumpkin patch is the perfect spot to start our trick-or-treating."

Sure enough, the page was covered in a rudimentary if surprisingly accurate map of Bucks Mill. Our two houses in the bottom left corner and Carter Farms, indicated with a massive pumpkin sticker, was at the top right corner. She'd used a red marker to draw arrows leading us from one corner to the other.

"Obviously we'll collect Carter at the farm after the festival. She knows to be ready as soon as it's over, right? We can't wait too long for her to get ready," she said.

"She'll be ready. We're all wearing our costumes to the festival," I said. In my head, I added, and hopefully she won't beg off when she sees I'm a thoroughly non-sexy baseball player from the forties.

"We may as well hit Forest Lakes first since it's walking distance from the farm." Lily's exasperated expression showed clearly that she thought the first leg was a waste of time. "From there, we'll go to the stores. Mr. Bailey at the hardware store usually gets the good stuff."

"Reese's," Blake yelled. He clapped and bounced up and down.

Lily then gave us a rundown of the rest of our evening. After downtown, we'd head to Gingerbread Town, then down the hill through the country club before circling back to Archcroft Court, the neighborhood where Tinley Bamford lived. It didn't escape me that Lily had plotted our route to hit all the posh neighborhoods in town. She certainly knew how to prioritize her time. I had a feeling her pumpkin would be full to bursting by the time we made it back home.

The moment Lily finished laying out her plan, my phone chirped with an incoming message from Carter. It was a selfie of her making a silly face in front of the festival barn followed by a simple "can't wait to see you" message. It was nothing overly romantic or personal, just a casual message anyone might send to the person they were dating. The casual nature of it put me at ease.

Carter didn't try too hard. She wasn't afraid to tell me she missed me or that she was thinking of me. She didn't push for more or complain. Nothing she did implied I should feel lucky for being with her. When I laid it all out like that, it didn't sound like something extraordinary, but it was still the first time I'd experienced anything like that from a partner. Carter was good to me and that was a wonderful feeling.

I expected that the happiness would morph into anxiety by the time Lily, Blake, and I arrived at the Halloween festival, but it didn't. In fact, as the three of us walked through the parking lot, I was radiating as much if not more of the barely controlled excitement I felt from them. We'd had to arrive a half hour before the festival started to get everything ready for the crowds, and there were only a handful of cars in the lot. I hoped to see Carter with every step I took, but I made it all the way into the farm without seeing her.

Meaghan squealed my name as soon as I entered the barn. "Nicki! Didn't we do a fabulous job setting up the festival?"

I turned to see Meaghan, wearing the gracious hostess smile she usually reserved for her annual Christmas mixer. Inside my head, I made a cutting remark about how I didn't remember seeing her climb into the rafters to hang papier-mâché ghosts. I couldn't say it out loud though. Not with her mini gang of Carolyn and Becky flanking her and Karen within earshot. Karen was beaming from ear to ear as she looked around at all the decorations and games. I couldn't burst her happy bubble. Not after ghosting her.

Instead, I applied my own fake smile and said, "We make a great team. Maybe we should do this again next year."

It felt good to see their three smiles falter simultaneously. Tinley came to collect Lily and Blake at the same moment Karen caught my eye. I had a distinct memory of avoiding her at back-to-school night. Had that really only been three weeks ago? It didn't seem so painful to see her now. More like an old acquaintance I had vaguely fond memories of.

"You did all of this work, didn't you?" Karen asked, leaning close so we wouldn't be overheard.

"Not all of it."

Carter's brother walked into the barn at that moment, two massive boxes of candy balanced precariously in his arms. I'd seen

TAGAN SHEPARD

the color of his hair and his build and thought it might be Carter, and my disappointment must've been evident. Karen watched my reaction with an all too knowing expression.

"I'm glad you had some help," Karen said.

"I, um…"

"It's okay, Nicki. Carter seems great and I can tell you really like her. I'm happy for you both."

She sounded genuine and I couldn't detect any lingering resentment in her smile. I worried again that I might've been unfair to Karen, but Meaghan's crew invaded our circle and Karen wandered off.

"Nicki, are you still okay working the sucker pull game?" Meaghan asked, consulting the schedule I'd made.

"Of course."

"Excellent. Becky, you'll be at the Plinko game."

Before Becky could accept her assignment, I spoke up. "Carter's supposed to be working Plinko. It's her favorite."

"We need a member of the family at the gate in case someone has questions about the farm." The excuse seemed thin and I had the direst suspicions, which were confirmed when she shot a wide grin over her shoulder. "Plus, Carolyn really needs the help, don't you?"

The sparkle in Carolyn's eye sent a pang of jealousy through me. There was a crude drawl to her tone when she said, "You know I do."

"It's settled then. Let's make this the best Halloween festival ever," Meaghan said.

Becky gave me a shrug and an eye roll but didn't say a word as we all dispersed to our assigned tasks, Carolyn with far more pep in her step than the rest of us.

• 168 •

CHAPTER TWENTY

Unfortunately, I didn't get the chance to follow Carolyn and save Carter from the wandering eyes of my fellow festival volunteer. Meaghan waylaid me en route to organize the extra parents who'd agreed to work the various booths and games. I'd made a spreadsheet of assignments and printed three hard copies to distribute, but Meaghan insisted I was the only one who could direct everyone. By the time all the volunteers were situated, the first of the kids were arriving.

I was happy I'd assigned myself to the sucker pull game. It required the least interaction with kids and parents alike, so it was the natural choice. All I had to do was make sure each kid only pulled one sucker out of the hay bale and hand out little plastic toys to the ones whose sticks had black marks on the end. I figured I could handle that task since the festival was only two hours long. There was little chance I'd run out of fake spiders or pumpkin-shaped sunglasses. To my surprise, it was kind of fun. Especially since the kiddos were far more excited for the cheesy toys than I thought they'd be.

The other benefit to that assignment was that I had the best possible view of the Plinko game. Had Carter been stationed there, I would've been able to drool over her all evening. Instead, I was able to watch Becky work the most popular booth at the festival. There was a line at Plinko from the moment we opened the doors, and I was excited to tell Carter she'd made a good choice of activities when the whole thing was over.

The festival had been scheduled to end at five o'clock so that the kids could get in some trick-or-treating before it got too dark. Most of the neighborhoods had organized carpools, but others decided to walk into town from the farm like Lily had planned for us. She joined me behind the sucker pull hay bale fifteen minutes early.

"Aunt Nicki, when do we get to leave?" She was fidgeting beside me, watching with evident concern as a group of fifth graders headed noisily for the barn door.

"The festival isn't over yet. Don't you want to get in another round of games before we leave?"

"No, I want to go trick-or-treating before all the good stuff is gone."

"There's plenty of candy to go around," I said.

Lily scoffed at my optimism. "I hope Carter's already in her costume. We're not waiting for her, you know."

"Yes, we are waiting for her, but she won't be late. I'm sure she's already in costume."

I considered enlisting Lily to go see what Carter's costume was, but it felt too desperate a move even for me. Instead, I let her stand beside me while the festival wound to a close. Lily counted down each minute by tapping her foot on the packed earth and hay. I was getting nervous again at the prospect of trick-or-treating with Carter. We hadn't had time to even greet each other, so I still didn't know if she'd have preferred a sexy maid costume to my nerdy baseball gear. Unfortunately, the festival crowd had thinned to almost nothing so there wasn't much to distract me from my nerves.

As the last miniature ghosts and goblins scuttled out of the barn, Karen joined me. "You really did an amazing job."

Meaghan popped up beside her. "We did, didn't we? This was much better than last year."

I was a little worried Karen would be offended, since she'd organized last year's event, but she nodded her agreement. "Make sure to thank Carter on behalf of the school, would you, Nicki?"

Once Karen was out of earshot, Meaghan leaned close. "I'm sure you can find an appropriate way to thank her."

I couldn't manage more than a furious blush in response. It heated my cheeks almost to the point of pain, but Meaghan didn't seem to notice. She gave me a wink and left to gather her children and head to the parking lot.

"Can we go now, Aunt Nicki?" Lily whined my name and pulled on both my hand and Blake's.

I collected our trick-or-treating supplies and my purse from behind the hay bale. "Yes, we can go. I'm sure Carter is outside waiting for us."

Carter's brother-in-law pulled the barn door closed behind us as I scanned the crowd. I wasn't shocked to see Meaghan, Becky, and Carolyn circling Carter at the entrance to the farm. She was a head taller than all of them, so I could just barely see her, but there was no mistaking that smile or the twinkle in those eyes, even in the waning light. It was a relief to see she found the attention amusing rather than enticing.

Lily spent the short walk to the gate expanding upon her trick-or-treating strategy, including the families famous for excellent candy selections. I let her ramble and twisted my skirt between my fingers.

This had been a huge mistake. Carter would take one look at me, in my boxy costume and run the other direction. If she hadn't already planned her post-holiday escape, she'd figure it out tonight.

"Are you even listening to me, Aunt Nicki?"

"What?"

"I was telling you that Tinley gave me the details on her neighbors and their candy trends. Mrs. Cauthorn is the only house in Archcroft Court we're avoiding."

"Why?"

"Everyone avoids her house. She's mean."

"That's not very nice. I remember her daughter. We went to school together and she was very sweet," I said.

"Then something happened in the last fifty years because she's mean now."

"Excuse me, it has not been fifty years since I went to school."

Lily held on as Blake tried to bolt across the grass. "Whatever. We're not going to her house."

Before I could ask which house was Mrs. Cauthorn's, the mothers left and every thought flitted out of my mind. Carter was standing alone, fidgeting and looking adorably nervous.

Apart from the uncertainty, she looked pretty much like she did every other day. Her costume consisted of her normal worn jeans and a red flannel shirt. The sleeves were rolled up to her elbows, showing off her toned forearms and sleeve of tattoos. The new additions were a red knit cap and a child-sized plastic axe.

Her cheeks flushed as she smoothed her shirt. "Told you my costume was boring."

"You look amazing," I said.

"Who are you supposed to be?" Lily asked, her eyebrows knitting together.

Carter pointed to a name sticker on her chest and I read it aloud, "Hello, my name is Paula Bunyan."

"Dad needed help collecting the last of the pumpkins from the field and one of the haunted house actors tore her costume right before opening. It's the best I could manage. Sorry."

I burst out laughing and held onto her arm. "It's adorable. Where's Babe, your blue ox?"

"He had a date." Carter smiled sheepishly. "Actually, I wanted to use some hair dye on the family's yellow lab, but Mom freaked out. She loves that doofus."

"Were you referring to the dog or yourself?" Lily asked with a sneer.

"Lily! That's not very nice."

But Carter was laughing and Lily smiled along with her, clearly proud of her teasing. Blake jumped up and down by way of greeting and Carter knelt to chat with him about his costume.

"Cool!" Blake shrieked, yanking at Carter's axe.

"It's about your size." Carter handed over the fake weapon.

He waved it around and bounced, squealing with glee to have a new toy. Seconds later, he dropped the axe in favor of rattling his pumpkin with both hands.

"You look really great." Carter gave me a once-over that sent my blood humming. "I love that movie."

It gave me a little boost that she thought of the movie first, not the new show. "Thanks. Geena Davis was my gay awakening. Actually, a mix between Geena Davis, Rosie O'Donnell, and Madonna."

"They really pulled out all the stops to hurry our generation out of the closet, huh?"

"It's time to go." Lily scowled at us, making her displeasure with our conversation clear.

Embarrassment flooded me, but, once again, Carter laughed at Lily's rudeness. "She's a character, isn't she?"

Lily started walking, dragging Blake behind her. I took the opportunity to move closer to Carter. "I'm sorry about her. She gets really into Halloween."

"That's cause Halloween is the best," Carter said.

The kids came bustling down the driveway of the house closest to the farm, their first candy bars rattling around in their plastic pumpkins.

Lily propped one fist on her hip. "Everyone know the plan?"

Carter grabbed Blake's hand and smiled at Lily. "Knock on doors, ask for candy?"

Lily clearly wasn't as impressed with Carter's good looks and winning smile as I was. She turned to me and said, "You're in charge of her. Let's go."

Lily let me take her hand once we arrived in town since the streets were busier than usual, but I knew that wouldn't last. We made it through the shops downtown and had already collected a fair amount of candy when Lily decided she should hold Blake's hand and lead. She allowed us to pause long enough to empty Blake's pumpkin into the pillowcase I was carrying. His pumpkin was smaller than hers and becoming precariously full.

The moment we arrived in Gingerbread Town, we found the streets crowded with costumed kids. Most of them were making a beeline for the Winchester House, but Lily was too methodical to take the houses out of order.

"Trick-or-treat," Lily and Blake called in unison at the first house.

"Well, aren't you just the best looking witch out tonight." Amber Bennington held out the candy bowl to Lily. We'd gone to school together and she was one of the few acquaintances from back then who hadn't batted an eyelash when I came out. She turned her attention to me and then raised an eyebrow when she glanced at Carter. "Hey, Nicki, how've you been?"

"Great." I sounded a little too peppy and a little too breathy. "How about you, Amber?"

"Can't complain. Have a great night." She gave me what I'm sure she thought was a sly wink before closing the door, but I couldn't tell if Carter saw.

Carter was being a good chaperone, keeping a close eye on Blake and humoring Lily's bossiness. Still, it looked like she was having fun, even though it wasn't much of a date.

Next, we found out why everyone was so eager to get to the Winchester House. They were handing out full sized chocolate bars and ladling out cups of punch from a cauldron wreathed in smoke.

"Nothing to spike it with, I'm afraid," Frank Winchester said as he handed me a cup. "And it's costing me a fortune in dry ice to keep the smoke going, but the kids love it."

Carter toasted him with her punch. "I love it, too. You're the most popular house on the block."

He puffed up at that and slid a Snickers bar into her hand when she handed over her empty cup.

As we walked away, I whispered to her, "Nice work. You know how to get that extra candy, don't you?"

"I'm naturally charming." She slipped an arm around my waist.

"I couldn't agree more."

Nearly every homeowner in Gingerbread Town greeted me by name and most of them recognized Carter from the pumpkin patch. A few held her back to compliment her family on turning the farm around and gush over how well the pumpkins were holding up. Eventually, Lily got tired of waiting for her, so the kids paired up together, leaving me to walk with Carter in the lull between the country club and the brightly lit sign announcing Archcroft Court.

"I really appreciate you inviting me. I haven't been trick-or-treating in years," Carter said.

"That's the great part about having young kids in the family. You have an excuse to dress up and act like a kid all over again."

She playfully slapped her forehead. "All these years and I haven't taken advantage. What an idiot I've been."

"Do you have a lot of nieces and nephews?"

"Just two nephews, but they still live in California. My other sister and her husband are dog people and my brothers both love themselves too much for kids yet." She leaned in and whispered, "They're both too pretty to settle down if you ask them. Only one of them is right." Her breath tickled my neck, sending a shiver through my whole body. She stepped closer, wrapping an arm around my shoulders. "I'd offer you my coat, but I didn't bring one."

A voice in my head that sounded a lot like Rachel suggested asking for her shirt, but I ignored it. "No problem. I'm fine."

Lily and Blake stopped in front of a house with a white picket fence and an intimidating wall of hedges. Lily consulted her notes, then pulled Blake away from the gate.

"What's wrong with this house?" I asked, checking to make sure the porch light was on.

"Oh my God, Aunt Nicki, do you even listen to me?"

"I try not to."

She squinted angrily at me, then marched over. "That's Mrs. Cauthorn's house. I told you we're skipping that one," she whispered.

Carter leaned in, making us look like a football team huddling up to discuss a play. "Who's Mrs. Cauthorn?"

I'd been taught that, if you didn't have anything nice to say, you shouldn't say anything at all, but apparently Rachel hadn't made that message clear to Lily yet. "A really mean old lady who only gives out boxes of raisins to trick-or-treaters."

"Cool. I love raisins. Let's go get some," Carter said.

Lily gasped in horror and tried to stop Carter from entering the gate, but she was too late. Carter had already rung the bell. I approached a little less enthusiastically, Blake holding on tight to my knuckles. Despite her daughter being a sweetheart, Mrs. Cauthorn had not been the nicest woman in town when her husband was alive. She seemed to have made it her mission to turn the whole town against her since his death. She was the sort of woman who would get kids to spend hours cleaning her yard, then pay them a single quarter and lecture them about how they should be grateful for the exercise. Not that she'd ever done that to me. Or Rachel and all our friends.

The doorbell echoed through the house for a long time, sparking my hope that Mrs. Cauthorn had chosen to ignore the holiday. The sound of multiple locks clicking and a chain rattling from inside killed my happy dream.

"Trick-or-treat," we said. Lily and I said it apprehensively, but Carter's cheerful shout drowned us all out.

Mrs. Cauthorn's voice crackled with age as she stared daggers at me. "Aren't you a bit old for trick-or-treating? I don't remember seeing you in the neighborhood before. Came down from Charlottesville to double up on candy, didn't you?"

Carter was undaunted. "We heard you have raisins, and these two love raisins."

Blake scrunched his face up in a clear sign of distaste while Lily's smile was plastered so tight it was incredible she could breathe. Still, Carter smiled that winning smile and must have melted something inside mean old Mrs. Cauthorn. She reached for a tiny bowl overflowing with raisin boxes.

"You only get one, mind you." She held out the bowl with trembling arms. Carter grabbed a box for Blake and Mrs. Cauthorn pointed a bony finger at her. "And you won't get one next year if I see you again. You're too old for trick-or-treating."

Carter stifled a giggle. "I assure you, ma'am, you won't see me next year."

Mrs. Cauthorn's only reply was to slam the door in our faces. Lily seemed to gain a level of respect for Carter after that. The two of them put their heads together and teased each other, but I was too busy obsessing over her words to join in the fun.

She had been so clear that she wouldn't be back next year. Was that because she'd avoid the house, despite her professed love of raisins, or because she had no intention of being in Bucks Mill this time next year? Of course, the family business was seasonal and she wouldn't be needed anymore. Not until strawberry season at least and surely she had something better to do with her time than hang out in Bucks Mill, Virginia, over the winter.

"That went even better than I thought." Carter dropped back to walk with me.

I hadn't noticed how far I'd fallen back from the group and had a moment of panic realizing I hadn't been paying attention to where Blake and Lily were. Fortunately, they had found a gaggle of Lily's school friends and the kids had formed a small roving band, heading from one house to the next in the neighborhood's cul-de-sac.

"I wouldn't get used to it. You won't get those raisins again if we do this next year," I said as much to myself as to her.

"You're giving up on trick-or-treating already? Those two will be in prime candy collecting age for years to come."

"I, um, didn't want to presume that you would be joining us again."

Carter took a step closer and slid her fingertips into my palm. "I think it would be very nice for us to do this again next year."

I didn't let myself look up into her eyes. It was just that she would be back next year for pumpkin season. That's what she meant. She didn't mean she'd stay. Just that once a year, for a month or so, we would share the same space. I would be a perfect distraction while she worked long hours selling pumpkins.

She slid her fingers between mine, keeping a light grip on my hand. "Now I know all the best places to go. That knowledge is too valuable to waste."

All I could do was push a burst of air from my lungs in a sound that vaguely resembled a laugh. Anything more would have been too taxing when she was standing this close, holding my hand like she meant it. She continued to hold my hand as we made our way out of the neighborhood and up the winding road back home. I didn't feel the chill of the air or hear the excited squeals of my niblings. I focused entirely on the feel of Carter's slightly calloused palm against mine and the occasional eye contact we shared. They were fleeting glances, but enough to make me wish the kids weren't around so I could kiss her in the fading sunset.

We were nearing the house when I remembered Carter was just here because she was on the rebound. At least I could be content with the fact that I helped her move on after her ex. When she picked up the pieces and headed out of town, she'd credit me with helping pull her out of that rut. I could live with that. I could look back fondly on this month with her while she was out in the world, restarting her life. I could accept just being a distraction for her.

"Fat chance," I mumbled.

"What was that?"

"Huh?"

"You said something." Carter squeezed my hand and said, "What'd you say?"

"Oh, I was just…" Wishing I had the nerve to ask you to stay. "Realizing how early it is. I forgot that trick-or-treating happens before the sun goes down."

"Yeah. Why do I remember running around in masks in the dark?"

"Probably because our parents weren't as attentive as this generation."

"Or the world is a scarier place," she said.

"That's true."

"Glad I have you here to protect me."

"You're the one with the axe," I said.

"I have a secret," Carter said. She tapped the toy axe against her forehead, creating a hollow thunking sound. "It's fake."

"Then we're in trouble alone here in the dark."

The porch light flipped on at the main house and Rachel stepped out, waving to us. Lily just waved, but Blake screamed "Mommy" and broke into a sprint.

I held up the pillowcase, now bulging with most of Blake's candy, and started to shout his name, but Rachel called from the porch, "Don't you dare. I can't handle him with that much sugar on board."

I shouted back, "What am I supposed to do with all this?"

"It's your payment for taking the kids trick-or-treating."

Rachel then hustled the kids into the house and pulled the door shut behind them. Everything went quiet and I found myself standing in front of my own cottage, Carter's hand still linked with mine.

I swallowed hard and steeled my courage. If this was the last time I was going to see Carter, I might as well be bold. I nodded toward my cottage. "Maybe you should come inside where it's safe."

Her eyes widened just a hair and I swear I saw excitement sparkle in them. "I wouldn't want to intrude. If you have plans."

My earlier, impure thoughts of sharing the couch with Carter flashed through my mind. "Nothing concrete. In fact, I'd offer you dinner, but all I have is a pillowcase full of candy and half a bottle of apple pie moonshine."

"Sounds perfect."

CHAPTER TWENTY-ONE

The fire crackled and the burning logs resettled awkwardly, but I didn't get up to add more wood. I was laughing too hard, tears streaming down my cheeks and mingling with the sticky sweetness in the corner of my mouth.

"Who knew moonshine went so well with Kit-Kats." Carter tipped her glass back. It was a juice glass because I didn't have a proper cocktail set, but she didn't seem to mind. "Where did you get this stuff?"

I tossed an empty Milky Way wrapper onto the rug. We'd amassed quite the collection of candy wrappers. "My sister dumped it on me a couple of weeks ago. She's more of a wine drinker."

"And you're a liquor girl?"

I shrugged and rummaged through the candy stash. "I'm not picky."

"Oh really? Then can I trade you this box of Nerds for your Reese's pumpkin?"

I took a long sip of moonshine. It was more cinnamon than apple, but this was my second glass, so I didn't mind as much. I squinted at Carter over the top of my glass. "Two boxes of Nerds. Everyone knows Reese's pumpkins are the best."

"Does everyone know that? Are you sure?"

I held up the debated candy, pointing to the orange and purple wrapper. "Reese's are already top shelf candy, but the seasonal shapes are by far the best. They have the ideal chocolate to peanut butter ratio."

"Really? I like the mini cups."

"Blasphemy. They have the worst chocolate to peanut butter ratio."

"Explain." Carter stretched to retrieve the moonshine bottle from the raised brick hearth.

I took a moment to admire the length of her body and the inch of bare skin at her stomach the stretch revealed. She was more fit than anyone I'd ever dated, faint lines of muscle bracketing her abs. Carter sat back straight and I was able to connect the distracted thoughts in my head.

"The ideal ratio is one part chocolate, three parts peanut butter. That's what the shapes have. The minis are the opposite," I said.

"What about the regular old cups?"

She reached out to add another couple inches of liquor to my glass, and the muscles on her tattooed forearm rippled as she titled the bottle. I forced myself to speak, though I couldn't quite force myself to look away. "They're like one to two. Not the worst, but not worth the calories."

"But Nerds are?" Carter rattled the box.

"I like fruity candy."

"Me too. That's why I'll only give you one box."

I wasn't really smooth enough to keep up the teasing so I handed it over. Totally worth it. She slapped the box into my hand and snatched the pumpkin away with a shout of triumph. Then she peeled the wrapper open and dropped the pumpkin on her tongue. Her eyes rolled back and she groaned. When a smile pulled her lips tight, the slightest smear of chocolate appeared on her lip. While she chewed, I fantasized about climbing onto her lap, straddling her waist, and licking the chocolate off.

"Good trade," she said through a mouthful of chocolate and peanut butter. I looked away. "What? Is there chocolate on my face?"

"As a matter of fact, there is."

I don't know if it was the moonshine or the roaring fire or the fear of Carter leaving, but something gave me a burst of confidence. I leaned forward and wiped the chocolate off her lip with my thumb. She froze when I touched her, but I didn't let myself hope that she was as affected by the touch as I was.

"Got it," I whispered.

"Thank you."

I should have kissed her then. It's not like I hadn't been brave and kissed her before. But those times had been in public, when nothing more than a kiss—even an intense, toe-curling make out session—could happen. Now we were alone in my house, a thick rug beneath us and a roaring fire behind us. As much as I wanted her to be here, I didn't want to start something I wasn't sure I could finish.

"I should put more wood on the fire." Carter leaned away, her cheeks as pink as the box of Nerds I clutched.

Carter took her time rearranging the glowing coals to better catch the new wood. She stacked the logs expertly, maintaining air flow between them. I took the opportunity to rip open the box of candy and dump every last crunchy strawberry-flavored kernel into my mouth. Crunching through them gave me an outlet for my nerves. She settled down and selected another piece of candy.

"I've never asked what brought you to Bucks Mill," I said. I left off the question about how long she'd be staying. It felt far too dangerous to ask.

Carter swirled her moonshine, following the wave of clear liquid with her eyes before answering. "I spent the last three years homesteading in the Pacific Northwest." She paused and glanced up at me. "With my ex-girlfriend."

"Oh?"

"We had a yurt with a view of the Pacific Ocean and an acre of fully organic, self-pollinating garden."

Great. She liked women who lived off the land and I couldn't even manage to chop firewood. "Sounds wonderful."

"Yeah." Carter was still staring at the ocean inside her juice glass. "It pretty much was."

I swallowed a gulp of liquor. "So what happened?"

"I woke up one morning with a three-foot long snake curled up like a cat on the foot of our bed."

"Oh my God!"

Carter finally met my eye and I was shocked to see something like embarrassment in her gaze. "I hate snakes."

"That sounds scary."

Carter tore open a fun-sized Snickers and shoved it into her mouth. She sighed through a mouthful of candy. "Turns out I hate homesteading."

A laugh burst out of me before I could stop it and Carter's cheeks went flame red.

"Don't get me wrong, I love the outdoors and chopping wood and stuff." She pointed a desperate hand at the blazing fire behind me and groaned. "Only I want to carry the wood inside a real house with electricity and central heat and flushable toilets."

"Oh."

Carter went back to staring at her glass. "She took it pretty well. Truth is we weren't super compatible."

I knew that look and that tone. I'd used it often myself. What she clearly wasn't saying was that she'd thought they were compatible until she found out they weren't. I knew exactly what that was like. Not just the grad student. Pretty much any woman I'd gotten serious with had known we wouldn't work out when I hadn't.

My heart melted at her vulnerability, but all I could manage to say was, "I'm sorry."

I'm not sure she heard me, because she leaned in and pointed toward the window with her moonshine for all the world like her ex was on the other side of the glass. "You know she kept the damn snake? Named him Carl or some shit."

The last of her speech came out like a sulky child and it was so endearing I wanted to pull her into a hug. I didn't because I was busy processing what she'd said.

"So you aren't, um, heartbroken?"

"Nah. She was sweet, but we wanted different things. She loved that homesteading stuff." Carter's eyes reflected the flickering flames. "You know what I love?"

I couldn't speak, so I just shook my head. Carter reached over and grabbed the bottle of moonshine. Then she scooted closer to me on the rug, empty candy wrappers crinkling beneath her hip.

Her shirt smelled like woodsmoke from tending the fire. Her breath smelled like cinnamon and peanuts. The blazing warmth of her hip next to my bare knee chilled the heat from the fire at my back.

She rested her forearm on her knee and stared deep into my eyes. "Modern conveniences. The outdoors are amazing, but you know what the modern world has?"

I leaned in. She was so close I could nearly taste her skin on the air. I smiled. "Pumpkin spice lattes," I said.

Carter's smooth chuckle shattered the stillness of the air. Her eyes held mine so close I could fall into them. Then they left mine and glanced down. At my lips? Or maybe at my neck? I caught my bottom lip between my teeth to keep from begging her to kiss me. The air between us hummed with electricity. My shoulder rubbed against hers before I realized I'd been leaning in.

Carter set her glass on the rug deliberately. Slowly. I thought she was reaching for my hand. It was resting in my lap and I could tell it was trembling.

But she didn't take my hand. She reached across my lap, her long, calloused fingers disappearing from view. Then she was smiling and holding something up for me to see. "Raisins."

The tension snapped like steam popping inside a burning log. I laughed and snatched the box out of her hand, swiping a teasing slap toward her shoulder.

"Are you trying to steal from me?" I held out the pilfered raisins.

"I have every intention of paying up." Carter dipped her head, catching my lips with hers. The kiss was gentle, but so unexpected that I jumped at first contact. Carter released me the moment I moved. She scooted away from me, nearly spilling her drink in the speed of her retreat. "I'm sorry," she said. Her cheeks were brighter red than ever. "I shouldn't have. I misread the—"

I didn't let her finish an apology. A reckless courage burst out of me and I launched myself at her. It wasn't graceful. I definitely spilled her drink. I didn't care. My lips were on hers again. My hands cupped her cheeks, keeping her close. I was desperate for her mouth and I wouldn't let her apologize for wanting me. For once in my life, I would be brave and take what I wanted without worrying about tomorrow.

I was still me, though. Awkward, bumbling me. As I clung to Carter, pressing my tongue past her lips and into the heavenly sweetness of her mouth, my momentum carried me too far. Carter's hands slipped around my waist as we tumbled backward, our bodies sprawled across the rug and all the discarded candy wrappers that constituted our dinner.

"Oof." Our kiss broke as her head banged against the rug. It was a thick rug, shaggy with faux fur and thick padding beneath, but not thick enough to cushion the blow when the back of her head connected with the floor.

"Oh God," I said. I pawed at her head helplessly. "Carter, I'm so sorry."

I tried to scramble off her, but she was too quick for me. With the arm wrapped around my waist, she pulled me onto the rug, switching our positions. Any thought of further apology died in my throat as she settled on top of me.

"No apologies necessary." She leaned down, pressing the full length of her body against me and catching my lips again. I melted beneath her, the weight of her body holding me steady as my heart fluttered in my chest. Wrapping my arms around her back, I held her close. Carter's lips caressed mine gently, reverently, but with an unmistakable need that mirrored my own. "Is this okay?" she whispered.

I wrapped my legs around her waist, praising myself for the loose cut of my costume skirt. "So much more than okay."

Carter's lips trailed down my neck, teasing the delicate skin beneath my jaw. Waves of mingled anticipation and delight washed over me. "We don't have to do anything you're not ready for."

"I'm ready for everything with you." And I was. Without my notice, all my fears and doubts had fled, leaving certainty and fiery need in their wake. Part of me knew there was every chance this would be my only night with Carter. All of me didn't care. Whether we had just tonight or a lifetime, I needed it to start here. Tonight. Now.

Carter shifted slightly above me, her thigh pressing between my legs. I welcomed her eagerly, the friction sending another wave of desire through me. I tore the shirt from her waistband, opening a path to the skin of her back. I raked my nails lightly from her lower back to her shoulder blades and Carter arched into me. I couldn't help grinding against her leg, desperate for more pressure where I needed her most.

When Carter's teeth grazed my neck, I lost all semblance of control. Before I knew what I was doing, I tore her flannel and the soft white undershirt up and off her. She held herself above me, arms braced on either side of my shoulders while I examined every inch of newly exposed flesh. Her tattoos ended in a sharp line after rounding her shoulder cap, but another peaked out of the waistband of her jeans. I followed the line of it with my eyes. When clothing hampered my view, I gracelessly tore open button and zipper to peel back her jeans.

I lost interest in the tattoo when her jeans were open. Carter's breath came in ragged gasps and her arms shook. I wondered if she was as desperate as I was. If her core ached to be touched like mine. I captured her eyes with mine and slowly, carefully slid my fingers beneath the tight fabric of her boxer briefs.

Her eyes rolled up when I cupped her. Sweet, burning heat coated my fingers and the ache in me roared as I touched her. I should have gone slower. I should have touched her breasts or at least waited until we were both naked. I couldn't. She groaned when I slid a finger easily inside her. When I added a second, she dropped to one elbow, unable to hold herself up on shaking arms.

I kept my rhythm slow at first, giving her the chance to ask for something else. Everything about the way she moved, rolling her hips in time with my thrusts, and the noises she made told me this was what she wanted.

A lock of hair fell across her face as our pace quickened and I reached up to push it away. She pressed a kiss into my palm and then gasped as I pressed against her front wall, finding the place that made her moan with each pass. I cupped her face and watched her as she fell apart, screaming incoherently as her body quivered above me. Watching that woman—every sweet, strong, kind, thoughtful inch of her—in ecstasy from my touch was pure bliss. The tendon in her neck that stood out when she threw her head back. The color that burst up her neck. The thin sheen of sweat that popped out at her hair line. Every inch of her was perfect and perfectly designed to make me want her.

The ache inside me would not be ignored another moment. I tightened the grip of my leg on her hip, grinding hard against her thigh. She was still sluggish, her eyes unfocused from her orgasm, but she responded to my need. Her hips moved in time with mine, though I admit there was little semblance of rhythm. It was more a flailing desperation, and I couldn't quite find the right pressure. I whimpered and squirmed, trying to grasp on to the pleasure that seemed to always be just out of reach.

"Nicki," she whispered, her lips grazing my ear. "Come for me? Please?"

Raw need gave her voice an edge that cut through the woodsmoke scented air. She pressed down into me, I pushed up into her, and my body exploded with ecstasy. I knew I was screaming, but I could barely hear the sound over the pounding of my heart. All the pent-up desperation of far too many lonely nights burst as I clutched Carter to me and sobbed through wave after never-ending wave of ecstasy. I clawed at her skin, but she held me gently, the weight of her on top of me a constant in the roiling mess I'd become.

Sweat soaked my skin and candy wrappers stuck to me in strange places, but I held Carter tight while my heart slowed to a normal rhythm and the embers of a dying fire warmed us both.

Chapter Twenty-two

I woke up cold, under the thin cabled blanket from the couch, the spent ashes of the long-dead fire illuminated by weak morning sunlight through the windows. The rug was plush, but not soft enough to cradle my body for the full night. My right shoulder ached and I rolled onto my back to relieve the pressure, candy wrappers crinkling beneath me as I moved.

That's when I realized I was alone. The cold should have tipped me off, but my brain was still groggy from a long night with Carter. I was naked under the blanket, though I couldn't remember when I'd finally wriggled out of my Halloween costume to give her full access to my body. I did remember peeling Carter's clothes off. The sight of her body, slowly revealed to me with each tug of fabric, was not one I'd soon forget.

Looking around, I noted that Carter's clothes were missing along with the woman herself. My skirt and blouse were neatly draped across the arm of the couch, a bra strap peeking out beneath.

"How considerate of her," I mumbled.

A long, plaintive meow echoed in the empty room in response. The sound made me jump, a movement my sore shoulder was not thrilled with. I scanned the room and saw Ralph lying on the center couch cushion, his front paws tucked beneath his chest and his eyes boring into me like a disapproving parent.

"You meow?" I asked him.

He didn't answer. Both of us knew perfectly well that he had not uttered a sound in years.

"You leave the bed?"

He pulled one paw out and started licking it lazily. Sure, he arrived at his bowl in time for breakfast and dinner every day, but I rarely saw him out of the bedroom any other time. Maybe I was late for his breakfast? I tried to check my watch, but I'd flung it aside at some point last night. There was a massive clock over the mantle, but I was at the wrong angle to see it. Also, I was too sad and embarrassed to truly care what time it was.

Last night had been incredible. By far the best sexual experience of my life. I'd known that Carter probably wouldn't stay in Bucks Mill forever. I just assumed she would stay at least through the morning. I guess I'd thought our night together warranted a good-bye? Clearly not. Maybe that sort of mind-blowing sex was par for the course for her. Nothing worth sticking around for. If she'd wanted anything more between us, she would have at least left me a note, right?

I was thinking about getting up to search for a note when I heard noise from outside. I rubbed my eyes and listened hard, trying to tease apart the sounds. There was the whoosh and thwack of an axe hitting wood. Then the ringing notes that were unmistakably Lily's giggle.

"Oh God, no," I shouted, jumping to my feet.

I didn't waste time putting on my clothes. Lily had disobeyed me and was playing with the axe. If she chopped an arm off while I searched for my underwear, I'd never forgive myself. Wrapping the blanket around me, I sprinted for the mud room door. I launched through it and leapt to the ground rather than navigating the stairs. I ignored the cold mud on my bare feet. I expected to be met with arterial spray and Lily shrieking in pain.

I found most of what I'd been expecting when I arrived in the side yard. Lily was shrieking and she was holding an axe. It wasn't my axe, though. It was Carter's plastic toy axe barely the length of her arm. Carter pried the real axe out the chopping block and set half a log on top.

Carter stepped back. "Okay, you chop first. Show me where to hit it," she said.

Lily stepped up to the log and set her feet, wiggling her hips and holding the plastic axe out in front of her.

"Don't forget, put your opposite foot forward," Carter said.

Lily scrambled to change her stance, then looked to Carter for approval. Once she received a proud nod, she lifted her little axe and swung with all her might. The plastic made a hollow thump against the wood, a third of the way across the half circle.

"Excellent placement. That's exactly where I'll chop. Step back now, okay?"

Lily giggled as she ran around behind Carter, far enough behind that she was well out of the way of the axe. Carter put her left foot forward, hauled the axe up above her head, and swung down in a powerful, graceful arc. A wedge of wood—exactly a third of the piece—flew effortlessly off and landed a foot from my bare toes.

"Aunt Nicki!" Lily squealed and ran over to me, a massive smile lighting her features. "Carter let me chop firewood with her."

"She's still in training," Carter said, color dusting her cheeks.

To my utter horror, I burst into tears. I don't know what was making me cry. Fear that Lily had hurt herself? Embarrassment from waking up alone? Relief that Carter hadn't just ghosted after our night together? Whatever the cause, I couldn't seem to stop crying.

I noted absently Carter telling Lily something and her running off back home, but I was too busy stifling my tears with the corner of the blanket. A moment later, I felt Carter's hands on my shoulders. I wanted to fall into her arms, but fear kept me rooted to the spot.

"I'm sorry," I said wetly.

"Are you okay?" Carter's hand rubbed up and down my arm, which only made me cry harder.

Swallowing my tears best I could, I went with the easier explanation. "I thought Lily was out here chopping wood. She's been trying to play with the axe."

Carter laughed and tugged at the edge of my blanket wrap. "You aren't exactly dressed for a rescue."

"I didn't have a chance to get dressed."

Carter tucked a loose piece of hair behind my ear. "It was cold when I woke up and you didn't have any more firewood. I thought I'd come out and chop some while you slept."

I fell into her chest and let myself cry again. Carter wrapped her arms around me, holding me close in one of her powerful, gentle hugs. This time I knew exactly why I was crying.

"I thought you'd left."

Carter's arms tightened around me. "I'm so sorry, Nicki. I didn't think of that. I hoped you would sleep through me getting more wood, but I didn't find any more chopped out here."

Her arms around me had an immediate and amazing effect. Not to mention the fact that she hadn't run away screaming when I started blubbering.

"I'm not very good at the wood chopping thing," I said, snuggling into her.

"Then it's a good thing you have me around." Carter pressed a kiss on the top of my head. "I've got all these outdoorsy skills and I don't get to use them at my parents' place. They have gas logs."

I sniffled, trying to clear my nose, and looked up at her. I knew I looked pathetic and maybe even desperate, but I was well past caring if Carter thought I was helpless. If there's one thing she must have learned from the previous night, it was that I was, in fact, quite desperate. Especially when it came to her. I had spent most of the previous night begging her for more and she had been not only willing, but enthusiastic. Maybe it was time for me to believe her when she said she wanted me and wanted to be with me. That's what a brave version of me would do.

I swallowed hard to clear my throat. "You're, um, welcome to come around and flex your outdoorsy muscles any time you want."

"Oh yeah?" she asked, grinning down at me.

"Yeah. In fact." I tried to smile while I reminded myself to be brave. "I can offer regular access to wood chopping and gutter cleaning and even grass mowing in the summer. If—you know—you're around then."

"Summer is strawberry season, but I'm pretty sure I can talk my parents into a day or two off to…what did you call it? Flex my outdoorsy muscles."

"So you're coming back for strawberry season?"

"Where else would I be?" Carter pulled away so she could look into my eyes. "Have you thought I was leaving all this time?"

"You never really said one way or another."

"So you expected the worst?"

I couldn't look at her anymore, so I snuggled back into her shoulder. "It's sort of what I do."

"Well, you don't have to think the worst of me."

"It's not you I think the worst of," I said.

"You don't have to think the worst of yourself either."

"Maybe you could—you know—help me with that lesson."

"I think we could work something out," she said.

"But what about that bug you want to murder? Don't you need to go off and track them down?"

Carter's laugh rumbled through her chest and into mine. "Gypsy moths are invasive on the East Coast."

The hope that had been fluttering in my chest was now coursing through me. "They are?"

"Weren't you listening on our first date?"

"I was distracted by your eyes and your arms. Plus I'm pretty sure you didn't mention that part. Also, your mom said you weren't going to be on the payroll for much longer."

"My brother's opening a Christmas tree farm on the plot next to my parents' place. I start helping him clear out brush next week. I'm not going anywhere any time soon," she said.

"You aren't?"

"You don't have to sound so surprised. I told you I like Bucks Mill."

My heart was thudding so fast that it made my head spin. If Carter hadn't been holding me up, I'd probably have fallen over. The smile that lit Carter's eyes was so genuine and so sweet. It made me hope the same way I had last night. The way I always felt when her arms were around me. Like I'd found my missing piece.

"I'm still not pushing though. I know you need slow. I'm not asking to move in or anything. I'm just asking to be a part of your life," she said.

"I don't think I'm as interested in going slow as I used to be."

Her smile had a hint of mischief in it. "Oh yeah? What changed your mind?"

I lifted my fingertips to her face and traced the line of her jaw I loved so much. The easy answer was that she changed my mind, but that wasn't exactly true. "I've spent so much of my life being afraid of not being enough. Maybe I've finally learned I was the only one who thought that."

Carter's smile grew to positively glowing. "I'm glad you finally caught on. I've known that for ages."

Her teasing laughter made my heart flutter. I could get used to having her around more often, helping me be brave. That thought was thrilling enough to drown out the knowledge that Rachel would be insufferable after this. She always did love being right.

"Well then. If you want to make this chore thing a more formal arrangement…" I trailed off.

Carter laughed and ran her thumb along my chin. "This was your plan all along, wasn't it? To seduce me with the promise of butch chores."

I shrugged and the blanket fell off my shoulder, exposing my collar bone and a significant portion of my chest. Carter's eyes lit up, fixed on the bare skin. "Did it work?" I asked.

Carter lowered her lips to mine, cupping my cheek and pulling my body hard against hers. Her tongue explored my mouth hungrily and I kissed her back with every ounce of passion I possessed. When she pulled away, I was left gasping for air.

"I've never heard a more tempting offer," Carter said.

CHAPTER TWENTY-THREE

When I pulled into the parking lot of Carter Farms on Sunday, everything felt very strange. For one thing, every time I'd been there in the past, the farm had been buzzing with life. Even when I came just before closing time, there were cars filling up the gravel parking lot and families scurrying around with armfuls of pumpkins and festive decorations. This time I was greeted by an empty parking lot and a cheery little wooden Closed sign strung across the entrance gate. I felt like I was still at a party the morning after, when the hosts hadn't quite slept off their hangovers and the stillness was tinged with exhaustion.

The other reason it felt weird was because I wasn't nearly as nervous to see Carter as usual. I'd spent the night with her and somehow both the worst and best thing had happened. Anything seemed possible now that I knew Carter wasn't leaving town quite yet. Knowing I wasn't just a distraction for her and knowing she was actually excited for the possibility of a continued relationship did wonders for my confidence.

Honestly, I should have just asked Carter what her plans were. I'd like to think it would've saved me many hours of uncertainty, but I knew myself well enough to know that wasn't quite true. My nerves and my lack of confidence would still have gotten in the way, but at least Carter would have been warned before my meltdown. It was Carter's gentleness when I freaked out that made me finally start believing in us.

When I arrived at the festival barn, I found the doors wide open and heard the sounds of movement from inside. I didn't bother praying the moms would skip this final day of volunteering. I might have neglected to mention the scheduled clean-up to them. I didn't want them to actually show up for once and ruin my last chance to corner Carter in the corner of the hay loft. Sadly, I arrived just in time to see Carter climb down the last few rungs of the hay loft ladder, carrying a massive coil of orange and black streamers over one shoulder like rope.

When her boots hit the ground, she turned and spotted me, a crooked smile growing on her perfect lips as she looked me over. Apparently, she saw something she liked in my outfit of a droopy cable knit sweater, old blue jeans, and hiking boots. I'll admit I selected the outfit to appeal to her preference for casual and practical outfits. Only a week ago, the smile she gave me when she finished her once-over would've had me dropping the two pumpkin spice lattes I held, but I managed to keep it together. The memory of her hands trailing over my bare skin was a heck of an ego booster.

"I missed you." Carter tossed the streamers onto the floor.

"It's been less than a day."

Eighteen hours and thirty-three minutes to be exact, but who was counting. After starting a new fire in the hearth the previous morning, Carter had taken her time reassuring me that she was staying in Bucks Mill. It had been nearly dinner time before she headed back home.

Carter trailed a thumb along my jaw and leaned in close enough to make my mind go blank. "Far too long without you."

I didn't wait for her to close the distance between us. I hadn't been able to stop thinking about the taste of her kiss, even in my sleep. The brush of her lips against mine was far more satisfying than it had been in my dreams the previous night. The taste of her breath as she opened her lips to let me inside was far more intoxicating. As she explored my mouth, I felt the flutter of her eyelashes against my cheek and I swore I could feel the pounding of her heart. Maybe it was my own heart I was feeling, but the lines between us were already starting to blur.

Carter broke the kiss. "Is one of those for me?" she asked.

I didn't want to open my eyes and break the spell, so I kept them closed. "You can have anything of mine you want."

I felt Carter's chuckle more than heard it as she slipped one of the paper cups out of my hand. "I'll keep that in mind for later."

We fell into work with ease after so many weekends spent setting up the festival. It was almost a little sad, dismantling the games and decorations we'd built while also building our relationship. I was particularly disappointed to watch her take apart the Plinko board, but at least I could tell her it was the biggest hit with the kids. We decided to pack it away carefully to bring it back next year.

After an hour of me slowly rolling up streamers and getting caught several times staring at Carter's butt, she called for a break. We sat on the hay bale I'd used for the sucker pull game and sipped our lukewarm lattes with several breaks for some teenager-like making out. I was practically in her lap and she was playing with the end of my ponytail when disaster struck.

Carter cleared her throat. "Hey, can we talk about yesterday morning?"

I'd never had a good conversation that started with the phrase "can we talk," so I was, of course, having a massive internal panic attack. Hadn't we already gone through the breakup scare? We had makeup sex and everything, so I'd thought we were past it.

I did my best to sound casual. "What about yesterday morning?"

"I just wanted to check in and make sure you were okay." There was an ominous pause at which I made noncommittal noises and Carter continued, "We had a big relationship step and I want to make sure you're okay with it."

Relief nearly had me toppling off the hay bale. "I'm very much okay with it."

"I'm happy to hear it." Looking up, I was surprised to see her cheeks flush pink. "I wanted to check in, though, because...well, yesterday morning, when you thought I had left."

"Sorry about that."

If a hole could've opened up in the barn floor, I would have gladly tossed myself in. I was hoping she'd forget all about the crying and the weirdness.

"Your reaction seemed a little over the top, so I wanted to make sure everything was okay."

God, why hadn't a hole opened up for me to fall into? I was pretty sure I'd never been more embarrassed in my life. I seriously considered running home and hiding under my bed like usual, but I knew I couldn't do that this time. I was already too far gone with Carter to run away now. It looked like I might have to go with honesty instead.

"I was really nervous you would leave after the season ended," I said. She nodded at my words, but I knew they weren't enough. I took a deep breath. "But it was more than that."

"What was it?"

"I've never really been good at relationships," I said.

That was the understatement of the year. Most people had issues with relationships because they didn't want commitment. I had issues for the exact opposite reason. I wanted forever. A wife and maybe kids, but mostly the growing old with someone. I wanted what my parents had. What it looked like Carter's parents had. My missing piece. My soulmate.

I wasn't far gone enough to admit all that to Carter this early on. Instead, I said, "I've never really been on the same page with my partners. I wanted commitment and they wanted distraction. Someone for right now. Sometimes I went with it because I was in love. Sometimes I hoped they'd change their minds. Those times I knew I was bending for them, but the last time I was just completely caught unaware. Since then I've been afraid to start something because I was always worried about how much it would hurt when it ended."

Carter's hand stilled on my hair and she tilted her head to catch my eye. "What made you take a chance on me?"

She was so gorgeous in that moment. The gentleness in her gaze and the lightness of her tone while she was sitting there, staring at all my baggage. I wasn't sure I'd ever met someone so thoughtful and sweet. And here she was asking me why I'd fallen for her?

I sat back and smiled up at her, earning one of those dazzling smiles in return. "You know you're really hot, right?"

The joke was worth it to see her face light up and laughter bubble out of her chest. "Nice." She grabbed a fistful of hay from the bale beneath her. She laughed even louder when she tossed it at me. A couple of pieces landed in my hair and stuck, but I was too busy grabbing my own projectiles to notice.

I was sure we made a ridiculous scene, a pair of adult women giggling and dodging handfuls of hay. Soon we both had hay stuck in our hair and clothes and our shared seat was dwindling beneath us. As a last-ditch effort, I flung myself into her arms, taking advantage of her catching me to drop a massive pile of hay on top of her head.

"No fair," she said.

I wrapped my arms around her neck and pulled her lips close. A small shower of hay fell between us, so I had to rub dust off her lips before I brushed mine against hers. I watched her eyes flutter closed as she held me and I'd never felt so safe in all my life. Her kiss set my pulse racing but was so gentle and sweet it made my chest ache.

I pulled away and waited until her eyes fluttered back open to whisper, "No one's ever worked so hard to make me feel comfortable before. I don't know why you did that for me."

The way she looked at me then made the world spin around me. Her eyes shone like precious gems in the light filtering through the chilly air. I couldn't pull myself out of them. I didn't want to.

"I've never met anyone like you. I couldn't help myself," she said.

Our next kiss was less sweet and more heat. She always said the right words. She always made me feel like I was the only woman in a room. I would do anything to make her see what that meant to me. I dragged her closer and explored her mouth with mine. A sound like desperation bubbled from her throat and she dragged me closer still. Without breaking contact with her lips, I swung one leg over her lap so our bodies could press together in all the delicious ways we'd found Halloween night. Her fingertips pressed hard into my shoulder blades, begging and claiming. As I pressed harder into her, the hay bale, abused during our silly hay fight, crumbled beneath us.

With a squeak, I tumbled forward, knocking her backward to the barn floor. The impact knocked the breath out of her, but she held on tight so I didn't topple over her onto my face. Before I could check to see if she was okay, laughter erupted from her.

"Oh, Carter. Are you okay? You didn't bump your head did you?" I was too busy pressing my hands over her shoulders and head, looking for injuries, to stop her when she rolled over, pinning me beneath her against the hay-covered ground.

"You know, this is becoming a habit. You don't have to knock me over to seduce me."

"I didn't mean to. I'm so sorry."

Carter was wearing one of her crooked smiles as she looked me up and down, settling more comfortably between my legs. "I can't really say I mind at the moment."

She leaned down to kiss me again, taking her time pressing her body against me before covering my lips with hers. Everything was going in a much more interesting direction than I'd anticipated when I heard someone clear their throat from the direction of the barn door.

Carter jumped up to her feet so fast I barely registered the movement. "Seriously bad timing."

"Seems like I arrived just in time for the show," a deep voice said.

"Stay right there," Carter said. "I'm gonna drop a tractor on you."

I'd finally managed to settle my clothes into a somewhat decent position and looked over at the door. The man standing there looked like he'd stepped out of a Brawny paper towels ad. He sported the same flannel and dark blue jeans that Carter was so fond of and he even had her same nose, but the lower half of his face was covered in the bushiest beard I'd ever seen. It was neatly trimmed, just like his perfect swoop of hair, including Superman curl, but it was still more hair than any human should have on their face.

"I'm confused about the logistics of that," he said. "You're going to pick up a tractor and drop it on my head? Seems like too much even for you."

"You're right. I should've done it when you were still in the cradle. It would've saved me thirty years of grief," Carter said.

He clutched his chest dramatically. "You wound me, sis."

Carter leaned down to take my hands and help me to my feet. "Stick around and I really will wound you."

Her brother laughed and it sounded so much like Carter's laugh I couldn't help but like him just a little. Based on how warm my cheeks were, I'm sure I was blushing just as hard as Carter, so I tried to hide my face while I brushed dirt and hay off my clothes.

"Nicki, this is my annoying little brother Nate. Nate, this is—"

"Your girlfriend. I figured that one out all on my own." Nate held out a hand roughly the size of a garden shed. When he smiled his eyes sparkled almost the same shade as Carter's. "Nice to meet you, Nicki. I've heard a lot about you. This idiot never shuts up about you."

Carter blushed even harder and some of my embarrassment washed away with his charm and her adorable discomfort. "Shut up, Nate."

"Her description didn't do you justice," he said as he released my hand. "I can see why she's kept you all to herself."

"Time to leave, Nate," Carter said, a protective growl to her voice that had my self-esteem jumping up a few points.

Nate stepped back to a respectful distance before he gave me a wink and laughed. "You can't keep Nicki away from us anymore, you know. We'll be seeing a lot more of each other now that I'm your boss."

"You will never be my boss, little brother. And stop embarrassing yourself by flirting with my girlfriend."

"Flirting? Never. I'm merely being a charming gentleman, as always."

"You're merely being a pest."

Watching their brother-sister sniping back and forth was so wonderfully endearing. It reminded me of Rachel and it gave me that tingle of warmth that a close family always inspired. It made me hope that Carter might have the same goals as me for family and a simple life.

Nate's booming baritone cut into my musing as he looked around at the barn. "You two haven't gotten much work done on cleaning this place up. What on earth have you been doing all this time?" He gave me a cheeky wink that had me blushing all over again.

Carter wrapped an arm around my hip. "Didn't I mention it was time for you to go, Nate?"

"Sure thing, sis," he said, looking at me. "Only Mom sent me to invite Nicki to dinner. Maybe y'all hadn't noticed how late it was?"

"Thank you for the invitation," I said. It seemed wise to keep it noncommittal since Carter was looking distinctly uncomfortable again.

Once Nate had left and pulled the door shut behind him, Carter turned to me. "Dinner is totally up to you. I told you before that my family's a lot. They're going to be even worse after Nate tells them about finding us kissing. If you don't feel like getting the third degree tonight, I can make an excuse for you."

I was definitely nervous about meeting the whole family, and seeing Carter fidget honestly made me even more nervous. Still, after all the time Carter and I had spent together recently, I couldn't imagine going home to an empty house anymore. I already knew her parents and her brother was just an extreme version of Carter herself. How much worse could the rest of them be? And the pull of that loud, loving family atmosphere was so strong.

I reached out my hand and Carter took it without hesitation. "If they really are so much to handle, I'm going to need you to hold my hand all night."

CHAPTER TWENTY-FOUR

When I walked into Sallie Bell's shop two weeks after Halloween, I was greeted with the mingled aromas of pastries baking and coffee brewing that had become so familiar. I couldn't help smiling at the memories Carter and I had made in this shop over the previous month. I'd never thought those walls would remind me of anything other than my grandmother, but it hadn't taken long to prove me wrong.

"Hello, Nicki, dear," Sallie said from behind the counter. "Back again?"

"You know I can never get enough of your coffee." I scanned the room and didn't spot Carter.

Sallie wasn't fooled, but she only acknowledged it with a wink. "Pumpkin spice season is winding down, you know. After Thanksgiving I'll be rolling out my eggnog and peppermint selections."

"I'll be sure to get my fill before it's over, but you know how much I love eggnog."

"I should've known," Carter said from behind me. Her breath on my neck made me shiver pleasantly from head to toe. "Is there any seasonal treat you don't like?"

"I can't think of any." I snuggled back into her as her arms wound around me.

While Sallie sliced our bagels, she asked Carter, "What are your plans now that pumpkin carving season is over and it's too early to plant strawberries?"

Carter and I stepped down the line to clear away from the register. She kept her arms around me so we shuffled together. I'd found in the last few weeks that Carter was very affectionate, even in public, and I found that I didn't mind in the slightest.

"I'm helping my little brother with his Christmas tree farm," Carter said. "He's equally helpless with business and growing trees, but I'm trying not to rub in how much he needs me."

That wasn't strictly true. Nate was hopeless, but Carter never missed an opportunity to tell him so. Since that first family dinner, I'd spent a lot of time at the farm and I'd gotten a good handle on Carter's family. Her mother was the brains of the business and her father had an almost innate connection to the land. He was a born farmer and he'd passed the same along to most of his children. Her older brother was being groomed to take over the strawberries and her sister and brother-in-law the pumpkins if her father ever decided to retire. Carter seemed to be the only one with a penchant for trees, so there was some talk of a peach orchard, but Carter derailed the conversation whenever it started. Nate's main asset seemed to be charisma, hence his need for Carter's help.

Sallie gave me a not-so-subtle wink. "Glad to hear you'll be staying put, Carter."

When Sallie bustled off to complete our orders, Carter turned toward our usual table. An impulse born of Sallie's approval had me pulling Carter back toward me. I laid as chaste a kiss as I could muster on her bottom lip, but when I opened my eyes I saw Becky had walked in. She gave me a thumbs up before turning to Sallie's nephew to put in her order. I was torn between embarrassment that someone had seen us kissing in public and pride in my hometown that everyone here was not only okay with me being gay, but rooted for me. I knew how rare that was for queer people in small towns.

We settled into our usual table and Sallie delivered our pumpkin spice lattes within seconds of us sitting down. Carter took her first appreciative sip. "How's it going, sweetheart?" she asked.

I loved how she always checked in on me, even though we saw each other every day. I entwined my fingers with hers. "Pretty great now that you're here. Although it is a little weird to have a breakfast date on a workday."

"Not getting used to working from home yet?"

I shrugged. "Fred keeps insisting I not start work until nine, but it feels like cheating to be awake for so long before I start working."

"That's the benefit of cutting out a long commute."

I squeezed her fingers with mine. "I am definitely enjoying these benefits."

Carter picked up our joined hands and pressed her lips against my knuckles. "Same here. Remind me to send Fred a bouquet of flowers."

As much as I wanted to pull her into a kiss in that moment, Becky kept shooting us glances and I decided to save it for when I could really show Carter how much I appreciated her. Instead, I asked, "How about you? What's in store for you today?"

Carter sighed and sat back in her chair. "Turns out things aren't nearly as rosy at the tree farm as Nate led me to believe. We won't have trees ready to sell for at least another year."

"But you're supposed to be opening for sales in a month. I've seen the ads all over town."

"Yeah. Mom's pissed at him about that."

Sallie's nephew dropped off our bagels. The moment Carter's bagel hit the table, she attacked it with gusto. I could see the strain lines around her eyes, so I let her eat rather than pushing her on the details of her farm woes. A few bites of Sallie's excellent baking and she found herself sufficiently bolstered to continue her story.

"Nate decided to use an organic farming method for the trees. I totally agree with the choice, but that means he can't fertilize the way he'd been planning and he can't intercede when pests attack the crop."

"Are pests an issue? Not those moths you want to murder, right?"

Carter laughed and some of the stress seemed to leave her. "No issues with gypsy moths or anything else yet, but the trees are growing slower. We think we've found a farmer who can supply a crop for us to sell this year. The profit margin will be razor thin, but we'll get customers and that's the main point for now."

"If you want me to crunch numbers, I'm happy to help. I can work off some of that relationship debt I'm wracking up with you chopping firewood."

"I told you I'm happy to do that."

I gave her hand a squeeze. "And I enjoy watching you do it, but I could still return the favor."

"I'll keep that in mind," Carter said. "So, what about your day?"

"Tracking down delinquent accounts and filling out spreadsheets. Nothing exciting, but I'll be able to have dinner on the table for us at six."

Butterflies erupted in my stomach again at the thought of our dinner date. It was strange since Carter had spent plenty of time at my house and even spent the night a few times since Halloween. We had settled into a comfortable relationship, but every now and then my nerves reminded me how gorgeous and perfect Carter was. Maybe the very fact of how domestic we were becoming accounted for the nerves. My little cottage was starting to feel too big and too empty when Carter wasn't around.

Carter's voice shook me out of my churning thoughts. "Uh-oh. That crease is back between your eyebrows. Do you want to cancel for tonight?"

"What? No. Of course not."

"Two dates in one day is a lot. It's okay if it's too much."

"I definitely don't want to cancel," I said.

"Then why the worry lines?"

If I knew the answer to that question I was sure I would be able to banish the butterflies. "I don't know. Forget it. I'm just tired."

"If you're sure," Carter said.

"I'm sure." I forced the butterflies down and managed a genuine smile. "I guess you'll just have to take me to bed early tonight."

Carter's wink made me melt. "If you insist."

❖

I felt out of sorts all day. I had fallen into a pretty good routine of working from home in the last few weeks and I enjoyed the extra time I got with the kids and Carter because of it, but the strange, unsettled feeling I had at breakfast just wouldn't go away. By the time I clocked out at five o'clock, I'd nearly driven myself over the edge. I spent a half hour just pacing the house, ostensibly cleaning but really just staring into the distance until I finally forced myself to start cooking.

Once dinner was in the oven, I wandered back into the living room to start a fire. The chill of autumn was well settled in Bucks Mill, and I kept a fire lit every night. After creating a nest of newspaper and kindling, I reached for a few logs from the stack Carter had kept full since Halloween. I couldn't help thinking about how I used to depend on my brother-in-law to keep my house warm and now I depended on Carter.

Maybe I was feeling unsettled because I was putting too much pressure on this new relationship. Was I just depending on Carter to take care of me? Why couldn't I take care of myself? It was something small, but the small things could multiply before I knew it. What if Carter started to resent my helplessness? What happened when it was all too much for her? Would she tell me about how she felt or would she just run out the back door?

The sound of knuckles rapping on my front door dragged me out of my panic spiral. A moment after announcing herself with the knock, Carter let herself in. It constantly charmed me the way she did that. Ever since she'd become a regular visitor to my home, she always knocked first, even if she was expected. She never just barged into my space. No one else in my life was that thoughtful. Even Rachel just let herself in as though nothing of mine was sacred.

Carter carried an armful of firewood, which she carefully balanced while stepping out of her boots on the mat. Before she'd completed the tricky maneuver, Ralph came sprinting out of the bedroom to twine around her ankles. She chuckled at his antics and scratched behind his ears. Even while she chatted with my cat, she looked up to give me a radiant smile.

The domesticity of the scene made my heart thud in my ears and the prickle of happy tears itched my eyes. I wrapped the sweetness of the scene around me like a favorite blanket. Before I knew what I was doing, my mind painted a slightly altered picture of the scene. Picturing us together like this three or five years down the road. Instead of Ralph running in to greet Carter, it was a little girl with my button nose or Carter's mischievous brown eyes.

The scene was still fresh in my mind while Carter carefully stacked the wood into the rack on the hearth. She walked over to me and wrapped an arm around my waist, pulling me close to the scent of firewood and her delicious skin.

After dropping a kiss on my cheek, she asked, "Hey, honey, what's for dinner?"

In that instant, the nerves and restlessness that had plagued me all day suddenly made sense. When I'd first met and started dating Carter, the butterflies in my stomach were half attraction, half fear. What I was feeling today was totally different. It was the excitement of realizing I was falling in love. Yes, it was early, and yes, it was probably foolhardy to picture my life with Carter years in the future. For the first time in my life, though, I could see getting everything I wanted with the person who wanted to be with me, too.

As the happiness of these revelations spread over me, I couldn't hold back a small, choked sob. The smile melted off Carter's face and she took a step back. "Sorry. It was a joke. Too much?"

I stepped back into Carter's arms and pulled her down into a kiss. She came willingly and I did all that I could to put the swell of my emotions into the kiss. Because she was incredible, she followed my lead, allowing me to drag out the brush of our lips and the dance of our tongues into a languid, sensual rhythm.

Pulling back from the kiss, I looked up into her hazy, unfocused stare. "I've waited a long time for someone to walk in my front door and ask me that."

A corner of her mouth twitched up, but she still had the dazed look of woman who didn't quite have her feet beneath her. "I'll have to remember to do it more often."

The answer was so utterly perfect. The slight tease of her words. The lack of hesitation. The confidence and vulnerability. I couldn't help myself.

Leaving her there, I went into the kitchen and turned off the oven. There was a question in her eyes, but none on her lips as I took her hand and led her back to my bedroom. The setting sun cut through the sheer curtains, giving the room a warm glow that mirrored the warmth in my chest, inspired by the feel of Carter's palm in mine.

Again, she let me take the lead, standing still as I took my time unbuttoning her shirt and pressing it back off her shoulders. I'd learned her body well enough by now to keep my eyes locked on hers while I undressed us both. With each discarded garment, the brown of her eyes deepened. With each newly revealed patch of skin, the fire in my belly burned a degree hotter.

Each time I saw Carter's body, I found a new feature to delight me. That first night it had been the strength of her chiseled shoulders. One afternoon last weekend I had spent hours admiring the subtle sweep of her collarbone. The weight of her breasts and her slim waist—perhaps the only part of her body that screamed traditional femininity.

Tonight, I was enchanted by the spot where her neck swept into her shoulders on a thick column of muscle. When she took a deep breath, it swelled. When I nipped at it, the skin quivered and jumped. Her breath hitched as I ran my tongue up the full length of it to capture her earlobe between my teeth.

Carter whimpered my name and her fingertips trembled against my hips. More than her humor or her wit or her kindness, I was absolutely captured by the way she let me drag her to the edge. She never took. She always gave. She would beg if I made her. There was never any question that she was mine and I loved to show her I was hers.

When we lay down, I pulled her body on top of mine so I could feel the length of her against me. More than her hands and her mouth, I wanted her skin. Every inch of it against every inch of mine. Our eyes were locked together and neither of us seemed interested in looking away. Even as her fingers slid easily inside me, I held her body and her eyes in place. I felt as much as heard her gasp as the full extent of my desire covered her hand. There had been times in the past when I was embarrassed at my body's response, but I wanted Carter to know how she affected me. I wanted her to revel in the wetness she inspired.

She moved slowly, recognizing my mood and adapting her lovemaking to my needs. As with everything between us, she focused on my needs first. As much as I wanted that slow, sensual night with her, I wasn't interested in waiting my turn. Shifting our bodies slightly, I was able to reach between us. Carter's groan when my fingers settled on her clit was almost as intoxicating as the press of her fingers inside me.

We settled into a deliciously slow pace, our skin pressing against each other and our gazes fixed. I couldn't remember if I'd ever made love with my eyes open like this. Needing to see and be seen while touching and being touched. The connection of our bodies was secondary to the connection we created through our eyes. It felt like she was looking into my soul and I wanted nothing more than to see into hers. To find the shadowy corners and the wounds that needed my healing touch. I wanted her to know all my fears because I'd already started to shake free of them, thanks to her. Not just my fears. My hopes, my dreams. All of me.

I was so lost in those beautiful brown eyes that my release crashed over me before I was ready. I heard the whimper in my shout, but Carter's roared repetition of my name soothed my disappointment at the speed of my climax. When she collapsed on top of me, sweaty hair sticking to my cheek, I reveled in the opportunity to wrap all my limbs around her and hold her close.

Later, while we ate chicken and rice casserole straight from the baking dish with the sheets twisted around our legs, I had a moment of pure insanity. I looked over at her, shoving a fork so overloaded with food into her mouth that it made her cheeks puff out like a chipmunk when she chewed. She was the sexiest, sweetest, most wonderful human I'd ever laid eyes on, and the words just tumbled out of my mouth without checking in with my brain first.

"I love you."

Her eyes bulged almost as wide as her cheeks and the room went so silent it hurt my ears.

"You don't have to say it back." I babbled and felt the heat on my cheeks, but I wasn't going to take it back. "I know it's too soon and it's ridiculous of me to say it. But the thing is, it's true and if I didn't say it right now, I'm pretty sure I'd explode."

I dimly noted her chewing frantically as I spoke, and when she swallowed, her throat bulged like a cartoon character. It felt like the words came from the far end of a tunnel when she said, "I've been waiting so long for you to say it first."

"What?"

"I didn't want to freak you out, so I was waiting for you to say it so I could repeat it without scaring you off. But I've felt it for so long and now I can finally say it." She took a breath and smiled. "I love you, too, Nicki."

Our forks clattered down onto the glass baking dish at the same moment and I wasn't quite sure who pulled whom into the kiss. It didn't really matter. All that mattered was we were kissing and it tasted like chicken and rice and forever.

CHAPTER TWENTY-FIVE

The next two weeks were surprisingly difficult for Carter and me. Despite easing into our relationship and the comfort of our time together, that comfort was hard to come by. Mainly because Carter's free time was hard to come by.

As we rolled through November, demands on her time at the Christmas tree farm seemed to multiply every day. It seemed that Carter's initial assessment of the crop was a bit too optimistic. During one of our rare dinner dates, she explained the integrated pest management program Nate had decided to use. I didn't understand most of it, but it boiled down to the difference between regular produce and the organically grown options. Just like the slightly smaller, less impressive tomatoes in the grocery market, Nate's trees were smaller and less impressive than they could be. Worse, it turned out they did have a pest problem on about a hundred acres of the farm, and their options for saving the trees were limited and laborious.

Carter, being the tree expert, was carrying the lion's share of the load in saving the crop, but she was also doing most of the work finding a supplier for this year's sales. She had been driving all over the state and once over to Tennessee to find a partner. It meant she tended to collapse into my bed hours after I was already asleep and sometimes leave before I was awake.

We'd started having "dinner dates" via long telephone calls while she drove back from whatever farm she'd been visiting that day. At first the dates were wonderfully romantic. We talked and teased without the option of interruptions for having sex. Soon enough, however, the frustration set in when I couldn't make out with Carter after she said something sweet or sexy. The calls became a hollow substitute for real dates and we were both desperate for any time together we could get. She'd finally worked out a contract with a farmer near Roanoke, but the drive was over two hours each way and there were a surprising number of details to work out before they could schedule delivery.

On Thursday night, Carter and I were an hour into our dinner phone call date. I was teasing her about her name again, guessing Diana, Dana, and Darla before I realized she'd stopped laughing at my attempts. When I said her name, she didn't answer. The second time I screamed her name, the icicle of fear in my gut making me panic. She grunted and I heard her tires on the rumble strip along with an impressive string of profanity as my shout woke her up. She was only a fifteen-minute drive from home, but I made her talk to me the whole way. I didn't sleep that night I was so rattled. What if I hadn't been on the phone with her? There were several spots during the drive that she didn't have cell reception. If she'd fallen asleep behind the wheel at any of those spots, I might have lost her. That thought sent me into a spiral that had me sobbing in Rachel's arms for longer than I wanted to admit.

Carter was embarrassed and apologetic about the whole thing, but nothing could shake the fear that had settled into me. She clearly felt guilty about the separations and the scare, so I decided not to make it worse by confronting her about her work hours. It seemed to me like she was doing all the heavy lifting for what was supposed to be Nate's farm, but she assured me it wouldn't always be like this. I would've rather she force Nate to do some of the driving, and she promised to bring it up with him. She even scheduled a romantic hike for us for Saturday and I couldn't turn down a picnic on top of a mountain with the woman I loved.

The fear I felt listening to her on that phone call, though, was nothing compared to what I felt when she arrived Saturday morning. She looked more haggard than I had ever seen her, her hiking boots scraping along the gravel drive. Her eyes were sunken and dull. She looked like she could sleep for a week and still be tired. But when I suggested we skip the hike and have a relaxed carpet picnic in my living room instead, she flatly refused.

"You were so excited when I told you the plan. Don't you want to go on the hike?"

"I am excited, baby, but we can do it another day," I said.

"No way. I promised you spectacular views at Spy Rock, and I'm not going to break my promise." Then she gave me one of those smiles that melted my heart and I couldn't say no.

I promised myself to make sure we took it slow and took our time over lunch. I wasn't averse to using my seductive powers to ensure Carter got a nice long break on top of the mountain. I knew all too well the restorative powers of a nice long make out session.

The hike started out just as wonderful as Carter had promised. I'd been wanting to try this trail for years and my obvious appreciation of autumn in the Blue Ridge Mountains was clearly infectious. There hadn't been much rain recently, so the trail was dry and in great shape. Carter was full of her usual energy as we started along the Appalachian Trail.

The rustle of leaves underfoot and the occasional far-off crash of animal or tree was the only sound to be heard. We were far from traffic or home up here and the peace of nature seeped into my bones. Not far along the trail, we came to a break in the trees that revealed rolling hills and breathtaking vistas of mountains and valleys disappearing into the horizon. Carter and I shed our packs and shared our first kiss in days with sunshine on our faces. I couldn't remember a more perfect Saturday morning.

I don't know how long the idyllic landscape distracted me, but by the time we turned off on the spur trail to Spy Rock, Carter was noticeably flagging. She stumbled a couple of times over easily avoided obstacles. I'd had enough. I marched in front of her and stopped with my fists on my hips. It was indicative of how out of it she was that she nearly walked right into me, only seeing me in front of her at the last moment.

"We need to go back," I said when she finally focused on me.

"Why? What's wrong?"

"You're dead on your feet and we aren't even halfway up the trail."

"I'm fine. Seriously."

"No, you're not. You're too tired for this. Let's go home and take a nap. We can do this hike another time."

For the first time since I'd known her, there was something like annoyance in the way Carter spoke to me. "We're already here and you really want to do this hike." She tried to walk around me, but I shifted to block her again.

"Please don't be stubborn."

"I'm not being stubborn, you are. I told you I'm fine," Carter said with a bite in her voice.

I was honestly so shocked at her tone that I didn't move in time and she got away on her second attempt to skirt around me. I didn't want the day to devolve into arguing, so I followed after her, content for now to argue with her in my head. I had no doubt that, when we got back down this mountain we would have our first real fight as a couple.

When the inevitable happened, I was too far away to stop. All I could do was watch in what felt like slow motion as the toe of Carter's hiking boot, dragging low to the trail all day, caught on a protruding rock. It was a testament to how tired she was that she barely reacted as she went down. She was nearly on the ground before she threw her arms out to catch herself. Since we were on a downhill stretch, her fall was farther than normal, and her toe was trapped beneath the rock that had tripped her. She fell in a heap and her yell of pain tore through my chest.

My world went from slow motion to hyper speed as I raced down the path to her side. She'd managed to free her foot, but she was clutching it with white knuckled fingers. It wasn't just her knuckles, though. Her face was so pale I thought she might pass out and she was obviously in a ton of pain.

I dropped down beside her, searching her for blood or protruding bones. "What hurts? Stay still."

"I'm fine," she said, though her voice was thin and strained.

When she tried to stand, I lost it. I slapped my open palm on one of the rocks on the path and screamed. That caught her attention and she sat still, staring at me like I was on the verge of losing my mind. To be honest, I already had.

"Damn it, Carter. If you say you're fine one more time I'm going to absolutely lose it." I snapped my next words, one at a time and over-enunciating. "You. Are. Not. Fine."

"I just tripped."

"And you're in pain. Tell me where it hurts."

She tried to smile, but it was a shadow of her usual playfulness. "Just my ego. You're usually the one who falls down in this relationship."

"Stop joking. This isn't funny."

"It's a little funny." She looked at my face and the smile wilted at the edges. "I'm sorry to scare you, but I'm not hurt."

She scrambled up and I just stayed on my knees, watching. I couldn't believe her. There was bravado and then there was stupidity and I honestly thought she knew the difference. Worse, she was shutting me out. Lying to me about what was going on. Pretending. All the confidence I'd had that this time things would be different, and yet here I was again, my girlfriend hiding things from me.

Carter took two steps and went down again. Hard. Fortunately, there weren't any rocks in the section where she tumbled this time, but there was runoff from a stream beside the path and she landed with her hands and knees in a patch of mud. She bit back a cry of pain, but I wasn't about to let her tell me she was fine again.

I hopped up and hurried over. She had rolled onto her butt, her hands on her ankle again. If I'd paid more attention, I'd have noted that she wasn't trying to stand again, but I was so furious I could barely see. "That's it," I shouted. "I'm not taking another step up this trail. You are going to listen to me. We are going to turn around now and head back to the car."

"I just need to rest."

"Damn it, Carter, I cannot carry you down this mountain."

She wouldn't look at me, but she sounded like Lily when I told her she couldn't play with the ax. "You're just overreacting. Calm down."

Clearly, no one had ever told Carter that you never tell a woman to calm down. Especially not a woman you are romantically involved with and definitely not when she's angry. I balled my fists together so hard I could feel my short fingernails cutting into my palms and I loomed over her.

"If you expect me to ignore the fact that you're injured, you've got another thing coming."

It was Carter's turn to snap at me and the twinkle I always loved so much in her eyes were more like sparks threatening to burst into fiery rage. "Damn it, Nicki, I'm not helpless or useless. You don't have to baby me."

"I never said you were helpless."

"You're sure acting like it." Her voice was ringing through the wilderness, amplified by the empty forest and the cold rock. "Like you think I can't handle a real job and a real relationship at the same time. Fine, I was a little tired after a long week, but all I wanted was a romantic hike with my girlfriend."

We were both shouting now and honestly it felt good to release some of the tension that had clutched at my body since Thursday night. "And all I want is my girlfriend to be alive and healthy!"

"This is about the other night in the car."

"No, this is about you trying to hike up a mountain with a twisted ankle. It's not safe and you know that."

"I can handle myself outdoors, Nicki. It's who I am. It's what I love."

"Part of being comfortable in the wilderness is recognizing when you aren't safe."

"You think I don't know that?" Carter shouted.

"I think you're being a stubborn idiot right now and you're scaring me!" The moment I admitted that I was scared, all the anger burst out of me and I felt that fear. I felt it wrap its arms around me like it used to. Like every time I thought about trying again after the grad student. Like every time I thought about how temporary love was. Like Stephen leaving Rachel. I'd thought I had conquered that fear, but it had only changed shape. Now it wasn't Rachel's blank stare when Stephen had pulled away with a trunk full of suitcases. It was the emptiness in Dad's eyes when the trailer pulled away carrying the last of the horses that had defined our family for generations.

I'd never really understood the expression "burst into tears." In my experience, tears always announced themselves before they arrived. Bursting was a word of surprise and that had never fit with the way I'd cried in the past. Now I understood the expression. One moment, I was angry and shouting, the next moment, a flood of tears was streaming out of my eyes. It was like I was feeling everything at once. The anger and fear, but also love and fear and frustration. They poured out of me all at once and I was helpless to stop them.

The moment I started crying, I saw the fight leave Carter, too. Her shoulders slumped and her eyes drooped. While I collected myself, she peeled the backpack off her back and held out a handkerchief to me. I wasn't quite ready to forgive her stubbornness, but I didn't want to have snot running down my chin while I dragged her down the mountain. I cleaned up my face while she searched through the pack.

"Can you find me a couple of sturdy sticks?" she asked quietly. "I think it's best if we splint my ankle. Just in case."

She still sounded sulky and withdrawn, but at least she was being reasonable. I found a fallen tree limb a little thicker than my thumb that I thought would work and managed to snap it in half with a little effort. We used the cloth napkins from our picnic to secure the two pieces on either side of her ankle. My anger flared again when she winced as the knots tightened, but it wasn't time for I-told-you-sos.

Another thick branch worked as a walking stick, but I thought we might have another fight when I grabbed both backpacks. Fortunately, Rachel had been giving me lessons on her "Mom's death stare" to use on Lily, and I must've been catching on because it worked on Carter. It was rough going through some patches, and

Carter eventually asked if she could lean on me when the walking stick wasn't enough to help her walk on the ankle.

We were both physically and emotionally exhausted by the time we got back to Carter's truck. Helping settle her into the passenger seat, I could see pain etched into every inch of her face. I wanted to hold her and let us both cry again, but I didn't have the energy. Carter was asleep before we made it back to the main road and I let another batch of tears silently fall during the drive.

CHAPTER TWENTY-SIX

Carter's peaceful nap didn't last long. The hum of my tires on the interstate had soothed my frayed nerves, but an hour into the drive, Carter woke up in obvious pain. Sweat was beading on her brow, and a grimace was more or less permanently affixed to her thin lips by the time I turned into the Emergency Room entrance to Martha Jefferson Hospital. Her pain couldn't have been better displayed in the fact that she didn't argue with me when she saw where we were going.

I convinced someone in scrubs to help me get Carter into a wheelchair, and they took her straight back into an exam room. When I would have followed, one of the folks at the intake desk stopped me. She was on the young side, with a kind smile and muddy brown hair pulled back into a neat ponytail. She guided me over to her desk and started asking me questions the moment I sat down.

"Can you tell me your friend's name?" she asked.

"She's my girlfriend."

She didn't skip a beat. "Okay. What's your girlfriend's name?"

"Carter."

"Last name?"

"That is her last name."

She gave me a fake smile. "What's her first name then?"

How was I supposed to explain that I didn't know my girlfriend's first name? She was polite enough about the name when I explained the nickname, but I could see her frustration grow when

I also didn't know her personal medical history, family medical history, insurance information, or even if she had any allergies.

"Is there a family member we could call?" Her patience was clearly running thin. "Who's her emergency contact?"

I had no intention of admitting I didn't know the answer to that question either, but it seemed a safe bet to hand over her mother's name and number. When she turned to her phone, I bolted. I think she called after me, but I was well past caring. Each question she'd asked me had pricked another tiny hole in the happy bubble Carter and I had built over the last few weeks.

What did I expect? We'd only known each other since the start of October. We'd talked about our families and our workdays, but we'd never really delved into anything important. To think I'd pictured us having kids together and I didn't even know if she was allergic to latex. I'd done it again. Fallen in love so fast I didn't take time to allow reality in. But reality had a way of bursting onto the scene whether I wanted it there or not.

I marched in a loop around the hospital parking lot while I texted Rachel to tell her what was going on. It took a long time for me to compose a text I thought wouldn't worry her, but I'd obviously failed. She wrote back a string of follow-up questions and I answered them as briefly as I could. I didn't want to admit to yet another person that I was at a complete loss.

I should've gone back in to check on Carter. I needed to know she was okay. Instead, I did a couple more laps around the parking lot, staring into the fog that had crept in around the base of Pantops Mountain. This time of year the morning fog hung around the valleys well into the afternoon and Martha Jefferson was high up on the slope.

As I stared and walked, I couldn't help comparing my relationship with Carter to the impenetrable fog. We'd talked about our relationship after Halloween. She'd been open and pushed me to be open, too. But then she kept holding back. I'd found it romantic at the time, but, in retrospect her reluctance to tell me she loved me until I said it first felt like a red flag. Like she was playing her cards close to the chest. Like she didn't trust me.

I stopped dead in my tracks, the faux stone exterior of the hospital swaying in my vision as I accepted certain truths I'd been avoiding. Carter didn't trust me. If she trusted me, she would have said she loved me when she felt it, like I had. If she trusted me, she would have put herself out there. Instead, she made me take all the leaps. She made me put my heart on the line while she hung back and waited.

That's not how love worked. That's not how relationships worked. They only worked if both partners opened up and allowed themselves to be vulnerable. It wasn't until that moment that I realized Carter hadn't done that with me. She hadn't taken any real risks since she asked me out the first time. She was sweet and caring and thoughtful, but she wasn't honest. Even about her own name. I'd thought we were on the same page, but here we were, almost a month later and I didn't really know anything more about Carter than I did the day I crashed my cart full of pumpkins.

As confused and hurt as I was by Carter's reluctance to open up to me, she was still hurt and I needed to get over it at least until we knew what was going on with her. I took a few deep breaths and turned back into the ER. The intake clerk was clearly still annoyed with me, but she showed me to Carter's room anyway. I slipped through the curtain just as her nurse was slipping out.

Seeing her there, propped up on a hospital bed, surrounded by all those machines and sterile smells, spiraled me right back into fear. She still looked pale and her clothes were dotted with speckles of flaky dried mud. Our makeshift splint had been removed along with her boot and sock and her pants were rolled up to her calf. The sight of her ankle was sickening. It was hugely swollen and was already turning the red-purple of raw meat. Just looking at it was bad enough, I couldn't imagine how much pain she was in.

"Hey, you," Carter said in a quiet, almost defeated voice.

"Hey."

She held out her hand and I hurried across the room to take it. When she looked up at me like that, regret and love mingled in her eyes, I felt like a jerk for how I'd shouted and how I'd cried. I brushed Carter's bangs back out of her eyes.

"They're taking me to get an X-ray soon," she said.

"Did they give you something for the pain?"

"Not yet, but they're working on it. It's okay. I'm fine."

Those words threatened to flare my annoyance again, but I held it back as best I could. She was clearly not fine. She was on a hospital bed in an ER, waiting for an X-ray on her ankle that had swollen to the size of a pumpkin. The only thing that saved her from my wrath at the moment was the fact that she was very clearly not fine.

Carter cleared her throat. "I'm sorry for getting angry and shouting at you."

I shook my head as a sliver of guilt needled me. "I'm sorry, too, baby."

"I just really wanted to do something special with you and then I ruined it by falling down like it was my first time on a rocky trail."

My fingertips stilled in combing through her hair. "Why do you keep doing that?"

"Doing what?"

"Why do you keep putting yourself down? People twist their ankles, especially if they're too tired to be hiking in the first place."

Okay, that last part wasn't strictly necessary so maybe I earned the scowl Carter gave me, but any pretense of apology was wiped away with the snap in her next words. "I know my limits, okay? I don't need a lecture."

The rebuke rang in my ears and I was about to shout back at her when the curtain was roughly pushed aside. Carter's nurse came back, a little paper cup in one hand and a motherly smile on her face.

"You're fourth in line for the X-ray, so I brought you a couple of happy pills while you wait." The nurse did an admirable job of ignoring the tension in the room as she watched Carter take her pain pills and ask if she needed a blanket or something else.

Carter was extra polite to her, probably so she wouldn't know we'd been fighting. I tried not to let that stoke my anger and pushed away the childish thought that she could've directed some of that politeness my way. The nurse gave me a smile almost as warm as the one she gave Carter before she slipped back out, promising to be back soon. Knowing how hospitals worked, soon could be anywhere from thirty minutes to three hours.

Once we were alone again, Carter made a point of avoiding my eye. I couldn't tell if she was pouting or feeling guilty, but I honestly didn't care. If we didn't talk about our feelings now, things would deteriorate and I couldn't let that happen. Not without a fight.

"What's your name?" I asked.

Maybe it was the softness of my tone that made Carter think our fight was over. Maybe she just wanted it to be. Whatever the reason, she turned to me with that half smile of hers. "The drugs haven't kicked in that quickly. I'm not going to reveal my secret, you have to guess."

"This isn't a joke," I said. The smile had faded from her lips. "I don't know you. Not as well as I should for the way I feel about you anyway. I told you everything that morning after Halloween. All my fears and desires. You won't even tell me your first name."

"That name isn't me. It won't tell you anything about me you don't already know."

"Then tell me something I do need to know." I still held her hand and I could feel I was gripping it too hard. Desperation ripped through me and I leaned close to her, begging her to understand how I felt. "Tell me what's going on with you. Tell me why you're running yourself so thin you fell asleep behind the wheel and why you're so stubborn you wanted to march up a mountain with a broken leg."

"It isn't broken."

I closed my eyes and took a deep breath, willing myself to stay calm. I wanted her to open up to me, I had to do the same. I had to explain. "When they wheeled you back here, the intake nurse asked me all these questions—medical history, insurance information. I couldn't even tell her your name. I'm in love with you, Carter, and you don't even trust me enough to tell me your name."

I opened my eyes and I saw exactly what I wanted to see. I saw Carter looking at me with that same sweetness she usually showed me. I saw the woman I had fallen in love with. I saw the determination in her eyes and I knew I was finally going to get the answers I needed. The answers we needed.

As Carter's lips parted, the curtain was torn back and a burst of noise washed through the room. Carter's mom pushed through first, quickly followed by her dad, Nate, her middle sister, and her brother-in-law. Her mom gave me a quick one-armed hug, but then took Carter's hand from mine and leaned between us to kiss her forehead.

I stepped back to let her get to her daughter but also because the noise of so many members of the Carter family all talking at once, teasing Carter, and asking her how she was, made my head ache. We'd been having a moment, Carter and I, and I'd felt like we were finally coming back together. Suddenly, I felt again like an outsider again. A shadow in Carter's life.

"You okay?"

I was so shocked to hear Rachel's voice so close to my ear that I jumped. I had backed away from the bed, sliding along the counter until I was brushing against the privacy curtain separating Carter from the rest of the ER. I hadn't noticed Rachel come in with the rest of them, but she looked just like I felt. Overwhelmed and out of place in this close family unit.

I watched the family interact for a while. Nate punching Carter's shoulder and ruffling the hair I had tucked neatly behind her ear. Her mother cradling her hand, petting it with her own in that peculiarly tender motherly way. Her father, bouncing on the balls of his feet with his hands in his pockets, clearing his throat in a transparent attempt to push back his emotions. Her sister perched on the edge of her bed, a gentle hand on her uninjured leg. Her brother-in-law offering her water or snacks and offering to get everyone coffee.

These people were Carter's family. They knew her the way I wanted to know her. They cherished her the way I did, but the difference was she let them. She didn't resent their concern or try to be someone she wasn't with them. She would drive all over the state for Nate, but she wouldn't relax on my couch with me. All I wanted was to be part of this group in her life, and I had never felt less a part of it.

"Nicki?" Rachel put her arm around my shoulder. "You okay?"

I wanted to turn and bury my face in her shoulder. To run back to my big sister like I did every time my heart was broken and my dreams were dashed. I had the same thing Carter had, just on a smaller scale. I should be grateful for that and patient with Carter, but right now it hurt too bad to be shut out and I needed to be out of this tiny room full of faraway love.

"I'm not really sure," I said. "Can you take me home?"

I couldn't quite read the look Rachel gave me. She was clearly surprised I wanted to go, but she knew me too well to argue with me. She kept her mouth shut and nodded, pulling her keys out of her jacket pocket.

"Sure, honey."

Carter finally looked at me then. Her look was much easier to read. She was always easy to read and regret had been plain on her features a lot in the last couple weeks. I pushed through the crowd to kiss her forehead and tell her that I was going to go and that we would talk later. She just nodded in response. Her dad pulled me into a hug and her mom thanked me, but the rest of the family, including Carter, let me walk away without another word.

Chapter Twenty-seven

Ralph had become more lively since Carter had become a regular visitor to his domain. Even when she wasn't there, he'd started walking around the house, looking for trouble to get into and being more affectionate. When I'd told Fred about Ralph's personality transplant, it only reinforced his belief that Ralph was the wreck-it type, but the truth was he just spent more time lazing around on the couch with me.

That's how I spent the remainder of my Saturday and most of Sunday. Lying on the couch, Ralph stretched out along my legs, snoring. Ralph was snoring, not me. I was sulking. Carter had texted me well after dark the night before to say she was finally home from the hospital, but her mother had her on lock-down for a few days of healing. Other than my response that I was happy she was okay and back home, we'd gone radio silent.

The silence gave me plenty of time to think, which was always bad. There were very few things I was great at, but overthinking was certainly one of them. I could spend entire hours worrying over one disturbing thought. Like why Carter was acting so strange. Why she was shutting me out. Why she still hadn't told me anything of substance about herself.

I knew there'd been a breakup recently—that's why she was in Bucks Mill with her family—but I knew nothing else about it. Was she still pining for her ex? Did I do something that reminded her of unhappy memories? How long had they dated? What did that woman mean to Carter and why hadn't she told me about the relationship even though I had walked her through my whole sordid, disappointing romantic past?

I couldn't answer any of the questions that rippled through me like waves crashing onto a beach, but boy could I spend hours obsessing over them all. The more I sulked and brooded, the more everything felt impossible to resolve. Thanksgiving was coming up this Thursday and I was supposed to join Carter's family at the farm for the holiday. I was starting to have nightmares about getting dumped while carrying a plate full of candied yams and cranberry sauce.

When the orange glow of sunset shone through the kitchen windows, I nearly cried out in relief. Sunday was ending which meant the work week would begin. I'd never looked forward to diving into spreadsheets so much in my life. Delinquent accounts and angry accountants sounded like a vacation when I'd been stuck in my head for so long.

I was just wondering if it was genius or pathetic to go to bed at six o'clock when Rachel walked through the front door, a pizza box in one hand and a bottle of red wine in the other. She dropped the pizza box on the coffee table with a thwack of cardboard on wood and gave me a challenging look.

"This is an intervention," she said.

I pointed at the bottle of wine. "People rarely bring alcohol to an intervention."

Rachel made a face like she smelled a dirty diaper. "Why would you go to a party that doesn't have wine?"

Despite my burgeoning depression, I laughed, which sent Ralph sprinting for the safety of his bedroom. "Interventions aren't exactly parties."

Rachel's eyebrow climbed to her hairline. "Are you sure? Because it seems to me like you're having a pity party."

Sticking my tongue out at my big sister seemed very childish, but I was feeling childish, so I did it. Rachel responded by cracking the twist top off the wine bottle and grabbing a pair of glasses. I couldn't come up with the energy to object to wine, so I let her go ahead and pour. I also couldn't come up with the energy to move my legs to give her room on the couch, so she perched on the opposite arm and stared at me. I wasn't going to give her the satisfaction of speaking first. Instead, I just sipped my wine and waited for her lecture.

"I really love my kids," Rachel said after a few minutes of silence.

"I certainly hope so."

"Shut up, I'm trying to be profound and mysterious."

"Can you refill my glass before you do?" I asked. "The mysteries of the universe require a full glass of Merlot."

"It's Pinot Noir."

"Whatever."

"You're a brat." She refilled our glasses and pushed my feet off the cushion so she could sit cross-legged on the far end of the couch facing me. "What was I saying?"

"You love your children."

"Right. I love my kids," she said. "They're the best thing that ever happened to me."

"I thought I was the best thing that ever happened to you."

"You're a close second. You want to know what the third best thing is?"

The banter was starting to lessen my bad mood, though I tried to pretend it wasn't. "What?"

"Stephen."

That caught me off guard. "The guy who cheated on you and shattered your heart into a thousand pieces?"

"A million pieces. I always say a million pieces. You never listen when I talk." She winked at me. "Yes. That guy. The guy who never picked up his underwear and broke my heart. You want to know why?"

"You're going to tell me."

"Because I loved him." She smiled that sad smile and a blush crept onto her cheeks. "I loved him so much it felt like flying and falling and all the scary, wonderful, exhilarating things."

I smiled along with her, remembering the way she talked about him when they'd first met. She'd been head over heels. She was like me. We both fell hard and fast. Of course those thoughts of Rachel falling in love with Stephen made me think of me falling in love with Carter. The feelings she described were exactly what I'd been feeling, though the scary falling feelings had been predominant the last couple of days.

"I don't regret my marriage for a second. I've got two perfect kids and a lot of really beautiful memories," Rachel said.

"Doesn't that make it even worse that it's over?" I asked.

Rachel rubbed her hand along my sweatpants-clad calf like Mom used to do. "Something doesn't have to last forever to be beautiful, kiddo. More importantly, never giving love a chance is an act of fear, and the only thing stronger than fear is love. It's clear you love Carter, and it's even more clear that she loves you back with everything she has."

She almost had me. Like she started out really strong, but the last part just brought back all the doubts I'd been chasing this weekend. "That's just it. She doesn't. Not with everything she has. Not really. I don't even know her."

Rachel had clearly thought she'd dropped her truth bomb and had already sat back to bask in the glow of her success. My response was not what she had expected, but, to her credit, she pivoted pretty well. "Tell me why you think that."

Boy did I tell her. This list of reasons was obviously pretty fresh, since I'd repeated them in my overactive mind at least once an hour for two days. I went through the whole thing with Rachel. I explained about the strange behavior and the way she had held back our whole relationship. She thought the waiting for me to say "I love you" first thing was cute, just like I had, but I burst that bubble when I laid out how it was just another thing she held back so she didn't have to risk her heart. She actually looked like she was listening to hear me rather than to respond when I told her about the questions from the intake clerk at the hospital.

After I'd run through everything, I set my empty wine glass down on the coffee table and summed it all up. "It's just starting to feel like she's keeping secrets from me. Like she's not all in."

Rachel shook her head at my conclusions. "I know it's like a whole lesbian thing that y'all share too much too soon, but you're expecting a little too much here, Nick."

"You don't get to invoke the lesbian thing. You aren't part of the club."

"I'm just saying that you two have only been dating a few weeks. You can't expect to know everything about her yet. Let go of your fear and trust her to get to that point," she said.

"You don't get it. I don't even know her name." This was my ace in the hole. The most obvious example of why I was right that Carter was holding back.

To my complete surprise, Rachel broke out her sternly disappointed face. "That isn't fair. Carter chose her name. The one that matters to her and the one that expresses who she is. You're putting weight on her birth name instead of honoring her chosen name. As a queer person, don't you see how unkind that is?"

I opened my mouth to argue, but I couldn't come up with anything to say. I couldn't believe that my straight-as-an-arrow sister was giving me lectures on queerness. I really couldn't believe that she was right. I should be honoring Carter's right to choose her own name. It was one of the most personal decisions anyone made, especially a queer person.

Still, I had practical reasons to be upset, and I made a last ditch attempt to defend this hill I'd chosen to die on. "Okay, I hadn't thought of that, but you have to see it from my point of view. Do you know how humiliated I was in that ER? Maybe it's too early to know Carter's medical history, but having to admit that I didn't know my girlfriend's first name? I've never been more humiliated in my life."

Rachel winked. "I find that hard to believe."

"I'm serious. It isn't just her name. You have to admit, she's holding back. The way she's acting—it isn't like her. At least the her I know. I can't help thinking that, if I really knew her, I would understand her actions, but I don't."

"Sweetie, you just have to trust that she'll tell you in time."

Time. That was the real thing that was scaring me. That Carter was just marking time.

"I'm just so afraid," I said.

"What are you afraid of?"

"That I'm a distraction. That I'll be over at Thanksgiving dinner and she'll stand up and announce that I was a lot of fun for a while, but there are more interesting people for her to date and I can find my own way home."

I didn't realize I was avoiding Rachel's eye until I felt her take my chin in her hand and pull my face up to look at her. "Carter is not the grad student. She would never do that to you."

I knew that. Deep down inside, I truly knew Carter wasn't that kind of person. I just wish I knew what kind of person she was.

"It's just so hard to believe someone like Carter would want a home and a family with me."

For a moment, I thought Rachel hadn't heard me. I'd spoken so quietly, I'd barely heard myself. But she had heard me, of course. Even if she hadn't, Rachel knew all my fears. She knew better than anyone why I had such a hard time trusting Carter, even though she'd given me every reason to believe she could be trusted.

"It isn't fair for you to punish Carter for your own baggage," Rachel said finally.

"I don't want to," I said on a rush of tears. "But I don't know how to quiet this fear. I don't know how to let it go."

"I know, kiddo."

"How did you do it? How can you still be so hopeful even after the way Stephen treated you?"

Rachel didn't hesitate. She didn't have to overthink it or work to put her thoughts together. Her confidence in her answer made me realize she was like me in other ways, too. She'd conquered the same doubts I wrestled with, which meant she'd spent a long time sulking and spiraling, just like me.

"I remember the way Mom smiled that sad smile at Dad's funeral." She straightened her shoulders. "I want to love someone that much again. I want to find my forever person like Mom did and I can't do that without hope. It feels good to love someone that much, doesn't it?"

My head filled with memories of Carter's smile. Of the way she winked at me and the sound of her laughter. It made my heart skip just to think of the sound. I thought of how good it felt when she wrapped me in her arms as we fell asleep. Not just the moments after sex, either. Even when she came over to my place in the middle of the night and crawled into bed while I was already asleep. Those quiet moments were so precious.

"Yeah," I said. "It feels really, really good."

Chapter Twenty-eight

First thing Monday morning, I texted Fred to ask to work from home. I felt bad about it since it was last minute and I'd worked from home on Friday, but he wasn't upset at all. In fact, he congratulated me for prioritizing my work-life balance and also attached an NPR article about how working from home was great for the environment because it cut down on unnecessary carbon emissions. Sending the article was so purely Fred, I couldn't help being touched. Since he was so sweet, I sprinkled some torn up printer paper around Ralph and sent pictures to him with a "Wreck-It Ralph strikes again" text.

I skipped breakfast and dove hard into work, determined to squeeze eight hours of productivity into a short workday. I even saved showering until my lunch break so that I could dive right in. I was determined to finish by three so I could make it over to Carter Farms before the family sat down for dinner. Carter and I needed to talk and I didn't want Nate or her parents interrupting. Especially during the beginning part where I would beg forgiveness for being a pushy jerk and bailing on her while she was in the hospital.

While I wasn't letting Carter off the hook on letting me in, Rachel had helped me see that I wasn't blameless in our fight. Carter had a right to open up to me in her own time. Honestly, I was looking forward to it. Carter was worth waiting for. Not that I would ever admit that to my sister. She was unbearable when she was smug, and I was already hearing constantly how she was right about the haunted house.

All kidding aside, I was grateful for Rachel's intervention. I'd expected to spend a long night brooding after she left, but it turned out I was done with that. Carter was the right woman at the right time in my life and our relationship was worth working on. She had proven that I could trust her, and I would. It was really as simple as that. If, of course, I hadn't made her so angry with my pushing and nagging that she decided to give up on me. But I decided that thought wasn't worth entertaining. All I had to do was get to the bottom of whatever was going on with her, and the best way to do that was prove she could trust me with her fears the way she had shown me she could be trusted with mine: with patience and support.

That determination helped me power through work faster than I ever had. Honestly, the timing had as much to do with it as my determination. Most of the college was closed for Thanksgiving week. Only Finance and Administration were open, so the email and messenger chat traffic was down considerably. At three o'clock on the dot, I slapped my laptop closed and rushed to my bedroom to change clothes.

I was just considering what get-well pastry to pick up from Sallie Bell's when my doorbell rang. Assuming it was the kids wanting to play, I rushed to send them away, grabbing my keys on the way so I could hop in the car as soon as they were back in their house.

I dropped the keys as soon as I opened the door. It wasn't Lily on my stoop. It was Carter. Carter with a massive boot on her foot, a pair of crutches tucked into her armpits, and a slightly battered bouquet of flowers clutched in her hands. Over her shoulder, I could see the farm truck pulling away, a flash of silver hair that I was pretty sure belonged to her mom behind the wheel. I couldn't be sure, though, because I was having a hard time keeping my eyes off Carter. I hadn't seen her in two days and the last time neither of us had been at our best. I hadn't realized until this moment how much I missed the sight of her. Maybe if I hadn't been such an idiot, I wouldn't have needed Rachel and her wine-soaked intervention at all. Looking at Carter now, I couldn't imagine why I'd been so upset. Looking at her now, I knew we could figure it out. We could figure anything out together.

After a long moment of staring at her, I picked up on a couple of oddities. She was as gorgeous and captivating as ever, but, for the first time since I'd known her, there was no confidence in the set of her shoulders. In fact, she looked so small and nervous standing there on my stoop you'd think I was the suave one in this relationship. The longer we stood there in silence, the more nervous she looked. Her hands twisted around the stems of the flowers so tight I could hear a few of them crunch under the pressure.

Apparently, Carter heard it, too, because she shoved the bouquet toward me. "Doris," she said.

Between the strange introduction and the sunflowers thrust underneath my nose, I had a hard time collecting my thoughts. "Did you hit your head, too? My name's Nicki."

Carter blushed from the collar of her long-sleeved Henley to the tops of her ears. It was so adorable I couldn't stop myself from reaching out and brushing my fingers through her hair. The short strands were just as silky as I remembered, and she stood a little straighter at the contact. I took the flowers before she destroyed them and held them close to my chest.

Carter cleared her throat. "It's my name. Doris Lucille Carter. Doris for my grandmother and Lucille for my great-grandmother."

Every time she said the name, a little flinch cut lines around her eyes. Her obvious embarrassment sent a wave of sickening guilt through my limbs. I had pushed and pushed until she thought this was her only choice. I had forced her to admit a truth she wasn't ready to share, and I hated myself for it.

I reached out to cup Carter's cheek and watched some of the anguish smooth out in her features. I pressed my lips gently against hers, trying to show her how sorry I was without forcing an intimacy she might not be ready for. When I pulled away and watched her eyes flutter open, I didn't see recrimination there. Even the pain I knew I'd caused had washed away.

"Thank you for telling me." I forced myself to emulate her strength and patience. "I think I'll keep calling you Carter if that's okay."

She rewarded me with one of her half smiles. "Thanks." The smile faded as she said, "I owe you an apology for this weekend. Do you think I could come in so we can talk?"

I offered to help her inside, but it was easier for her to move on her own with the crutches. She didn't argue when I brought an ottoman over to the couch for her to prop her foot up on. While I propped up her crutches by the fireplace, Ralph came over to scold her for her absence. They had quite the conversation about it, but she persuaded him to let me sit beside her and he waddled back to the bedroom, clearly smug about having made his point.

"I think I need to start by telling you the whole story about my ex. There's more than what I told you at Halloween," Carter said.

The last thing I wanted to talk about was some other woman Carter had loved, but she had accepted my baggage, it was time I learned about hers. "More than a perfect yurt life and a big snake?"

"Yeah, more than that. Is that okay?"

I took her hand in both mine and laid it in my lap. "Yes, I'd like to hear the story. Anything you're ready and willing to tell."

Carter nodded and rolled her shoulders like she was about to step into a boxing ring. Maybe she was. Wrestling with the past was rarely easy. "Her name's Kayla. We met while I was working for the Bureau of Land Management in Oregon. She was a homesteader with a plot of land on the fringe of a wilderness area we managed. We had a run-in over some foraging she was doing on government land."

The way Carter blushed had me grinding my teeth. While she avoided my eyes, I reminded myself that Carter was here now, with me. Not in Oregon with some mushroom hunting hippie with a sense of entitlement. Okay, I wasn't sure about that last part, but I was pretty sure there was nothing that could make me give Kayla the benefit of the doubt.

"Long story short, we spent some time together and that's when my job bumped up too uncomfortably against her lifestyle.

Homesteading isn't something you can really do in the after-work hours. There's a lot of hard work involved, and Kayla never really followed the rules if they interfered with what she wanted. She thought I was prioritizing work over her. Eventually, I quit my job, sold my condo, and moved onto the homestead full time."

When Carter met my eye, I had a pretty good idea why she freaked out when she thought I was questioning her ability to work for Nate and be my girlfriend. Obviously, the situation was different here with us, but given my own recent panic spiral, I couldn't exactly blame her for having a sore spot.

"I poured everything into our…her plot of land. She was a few years younger than me—just starting out—and there wasn't much there when I arrived. It's a lot of work, building a sustainable home and food sources. I was happy to do it, though. I thought we were building a life together. Building a family." Carter's jaw was clenched so tight it looked painful and she kept swallowing hard. I could tell she was holding back tears.

I wondered how many times—if ever—she'd told this story. I knew her family pretty well by now. They were sweet and fiercely loving, but they were practical people. Farmers. There wasn't a lot of room for emotions in their family. Had they asked her for the story when she arrived at their doorstep? If she only told them part of the story, would they press her for more? I doubted it. They weren't like Rachel, who would never let me fester the way Carter clearly had.

"You said you wanted a family and a forever home. I want that, too," Carter said. "After three years together, working together the way we did, I thought Kayla and I had that. When she picked a damn snake over me, I realized we had been building her life, not our life. She didn't love me. She wanted my skill set, but she didn't want me."

Carter's hand curled into a fist between my palms. I could feel the strain in her ligaments and the stretch of her skin. My heart broke for her. The blow of losing so much. The grad student had hurt me and humiliated me, but she had never promised me forever in word or deed. Kayla had done that to Carter. Had made promises and tossed them aside when her yurt was waterproof and her garden was thriving. I held Carter's fist in my hands and promised myself I would never use her like that. I would learn to chop wood and I would be a partner to her, not a project.

"When it was over I didn't have anything," she said, her voice noticeably thinner. "I didn't have anywhere to go or anything to do. We hadn't had any money in over a year. We were feeding ourselves so we didn't need it. I hiked ten miles to the closest general store and called my mom collect. She sent me enough money for a plane ticket and all the junk food I could eat while I waited to slink home with my tail between my legs." She spit the last words with so much venom I couldn't take a full breath. The way she blamed herself—the way she hated herself. It was all too much.

I scooted as close to her as I could on the couch and pulled her close. She let her head fall onto my shoulder without protest. The way she let herself flop against me like a rag doll was shocking, but her story wasn't quite through.

"All I could think about on that eight-hour flight home and the hour layover in LAX was how I wasn't enough. I wasn't lovable enough. I wasn't useful enough on the homestead. I wasn't smart enough to have a backup plan or experienced enough to get my old job back after three years off the grid."

"Baby, that's not true."

Carter either didn't hear my words or ignored them. "Now I'm not enough of a farmer to be useful to my parents. I'm not enough of an arborist to be useful to Nate. I'm not a good enough girlfriend to you. I just keep trying to be more and more, but it's never enough to chase away all those doubts."

I worried she might push me away and try to collect herself like a tough butch, but she did the exact opposite. She sobbed so hard her body shook like a leaf in a hurricane. She threw her arms around me and gripped me so tight I could feel each fingertip digging into my back. She buried her face in my chest and cried and shook and tried with all her might to hold me closer, even though she was holding me so tight my shirt caught every tear that fell from her eyes.

For a heartbeat, I was afraid. Afraid I'd do the wrong thing and make her run screaming from my house. Afraid that I wouldn't say the right thing or do the right thing and somehow make it worse. I always made it worse. I always spilled the cart of pumpkins and dumped my latte and split open my forehead at the haunted house. I never knew what to say. But Carter had accepted all of those silly mistakes and loved me all the more for them. And I loved Carter all the more for her tears and her insecurities and her broken heart. I'd wanted her to trust me and be vulnerable, and that's exactly what I got. It was everything I wanted. She was everything I wanted.

Because I loved her, I found I did know what to do. I held her just as strong as she held me. I pressed my cheek to the top of her head and kissed her as she wept. I rubbed my hands up and down her quivering back and I whispered into her hair how much I loved her. The harder I held her to me, the more she loosened her grip. Eventually, her sobbing died down and her back shook with deep breaths rather than tears.

Once she'd collected herself enough to speak, she said, "I'm sorry. I didn't mean to break down like that."

"You never have to apologize for your emotions, baby. Not to me or anyone." I lifted her chin and she looked up at me with hopeful, red-rimmed eyes. "I want a partner who isn't afraid to be honest. Who isn't afraid to be vulnerable. Thank you for trusting me. It means so much."

Carter pulled away and I let her go even though I wanted to hold her forever. She rubbed at her nose with her handkerchief. "I should've told you the whole story at Halloween. It's just. I don't know."

"What? You can tell me."

She shrugged. "I don't think I'd figured it out yet. I was trying so hard to be everything for everybody and I didn't even understand why myself."

I ran my fingers through her hair, which was adorably mussed. I winked at her, trying to bring back some of the lighthearted banter we thrived on. I was pretty sure she needed that right now. "Sometimes it takes your girlfriend nagging you to figure out that you have baggage. Keep that in mind for the future."

To my relief, she laughed and kissed my hand. "Noted." She took a deep breath. "I convinced myself I was doing it for you—taking you hiking—but I think I was doing it because I was still afraid. Afraid you'd leave if I didn't make myself indispensable."

"That's not why I'm with you, Carter."

"I know."

"It means the world to me how much you do around here, but that's not why I keep you around." She looked up into my eyes and I could see the light coming back into them. "I keep you around for sex."

Her eyes widened for a second, and then she laughed. Just like her crying, once she started laughing, she had a hard time stopping. I could tell by the way her shoulders rose and fell with each guffaw that this laughter was just as cathartic as her tears. I watched her laugh with a sense of awe. How had I gotten so lucky to find a woman like this? A woman who laughed and cried with the same abandon. How had I ever thought she was holding back?

Once the laughter faded away, Carter pulled me to her so my head was resting on her shoulder. It was a wonderful, sweet reversal of our earlier position, and I curled against her, pulling her close.

"I don't want to be afraid anymore. I want to be myself with you," Carter said.

"That's what I want, too."

I snuggled closer and we held each other for a long time in peaceful silence. Long enough for Ralph to decide the hysterics were over and it was safe for him to crawl into Carter's lap. It wasn't hard for me to slip into that daydream again. The one where we were a family, happily ensconced in our domesticity.

"So what does that mean, exactly?" I asked.

"What does what mean?"

"You said you want to be yourself. What does that look like exactly?"

I'd thought it was a question she'd have to mull over, but that was naive of me. She was a thoughtful woman, after all. A woman who spent her convalescence after breaking her ankle to sort through her emotional baggage. So it shouldn't have surprised me that she answered immediately.

"I want to eradicate the gypsy moth." After a moment, she continued, "And I can't do that selling pumpkins or growing Christmas trees."

"How can you do it?"

"I can only do it if I get a job with the National Park Service in the Shenandoah National Park."

My heart pounded so hard in my chest I had trouble catching my breath. Of course, it didn't help that our snuggling had pulled Carter's shirt tight, exposing a flash of that sexy collarbone. But the pounding had just as much to do with the gypsy moth. The Shenandoah National Park was practically on our doorstep.

"That sounds like a great plan," I said.

"I'm glad you think so because I sort of already applied. I have an interview the first week of December. Is that, um, okay?" she asked sheepishly.

I slipped my hand underneath her shirt to rest on her bare stomach. "Baby, we can make anything work together."

EPILOGUE

Thanks for choosing Carter Farms." I handed the young couple their change. "I'm impressed with how many pumpkins you could carry."

The man puffed out his chest a little as he walked away. His boyfriend leaned into him and wrapped his hands around his bicep, giving it a squeeze. There wasn't anyone else in line, so I took a sip of apple cider.

"Liar." Carter's low voice sent a shiver down my spine. Her hands settled on my hips and I leaned back into her. "He didn't carry half as many as you did last year. And that last step was awfully shaky. I wouldn't have let him get away with it."

"That's why your mom took you off the register." I pulled her arms tighter around my waist. "You're too tough. It's bad for business."

"And you're too soft. It's bad for business." Carter's lips found the spot behind my ear that made my whole body tingle.

My eyes fluttered shut. "I thought you like how soft I am."

She purred, kissing down my neck. "I do. Very much. What if we just slip off to the barn for a few minutes?"

"Absolutely not." I pulled out of her arms and turned to her, raising an eyebrow at her pout. "The barn is all set up for the Halloween festival and I'm not ruining the hay bales again. Besides, I've taken you away from work far too often this season to help decorate. Between that and your new job, it's been too much. I promised your parents we'd work the whole day to make up for it."

"But, baby." Carter stuck out her bottom lip and batted her eyelashes at me. "It's our anniversary eve."

Those big, soft eyes nearly roped me in. Not to mention the park ranger uniform she hadn't had time to change out of before starting her shift. Ever since she'd started working for the park service I'd discovered a weakness for women in uniform. I let her move closer to me and perch her hands on my hips. I came to when she dipped her head down toward me, trying to sneak in a kiss. Today was too important for me to get distracted by my girlfriend's silky voice and flirtatious eyes.

I took a step away and held her back with my hand on her chest. "You can have all of me tonight, but not before."

"It's too long to wait." She ran a hand through her hair, flexing her tattooed bicep in that way she knew would distract me. "Just a kiss?"

Somehow she was right in front of me again, the heat of her body making my brain sluggish. Before I could shake the haze, her lips brushed against mine. It wasn't even a kiss, really. Just the whisper of contact. An enticement. I mentally calculated how quickly we could make it to the tractor barn. One kiss couldn't hurt, could it? I leaned in, bringing our lips together in a much more satisfying lock.

Carter's hands had begun to wander. One followed the line of my belt around my lower back, settling just above the swell of my butt. The other stroked lower, to the outside of my thigh. My brain snapped back into focus before she could feel the contents of my jeans pocket.

I snatched her hand and used it to push her back two steps. A pout started to form on her lips again, so I knew it was time to bring out the big guns. "Doris Carter, you stop that right now."

Carter froze. She blinked once and her jaw dropped open. I bit my lip to keep from laughing and she narrowed her eyes at me.

Carter laughed and shook her head. "I can't believe you pulled out the big guns. Using my full name. That's fighting dirty."

I pushed my hip playfully against hers but made sure to back out of reach immediately after. Carter wasn't likely to give up that easily. "Nate said you would try to talk your way out of a full shift and I promised I wouldn't let you."

"I never try to talk my way out of work."

"He says you're spoiled from your dad insisting you focus on your new job instead of helping get the farm ready for pumpkin season," I said.

"He didn't say that."

"He sure did. But I smoothed it over with all my volunteering, so you're still invited to family dinner on Sunday."

Carter shook her head, but there was laughter in her voice. "You're sucking up to my useless brother, huh?"

"He's not the one who invited me to dinner. That was your dad."

"I knew he'd be the one to betray me." Carter shoved her hands into her back pockets and sighed. "He's always loved you."

"You keep telling me how lovable I am. You're really surprised they figured it out, too?"

There was a hint of pink in her cheeks. "Mom and Dad told me last week that if we break up, they're keeping you and I need to find a new family."

Now it was my turn to blush. I tried to ignore the heat and shoved my hand into my pocket, fiddling with the square box. Her dad had told me the same thing when I showed them the box now burning a hole in my pocket. I loved how much they loved me, but the idea of Carter leaving me was too terrifying to contemplate.

"I guess you better not break up with me, huh?" I said.

Carter ran her broad thumb across the line of my jaw. "Never."

I let her kiss me again. There were still a few customers around, but none of them were looking our way. Even if they had been, I needed the feel of her lips against mine. I needed the reassurance of her outdoorsy scent and the soft press of her flesh against me. I needed her. Always.

"Unless you start calling me Doris," she whispered.

"Never."

Carter gave me one last wink, then turned and walked away. I'll admit I watched her go for a little while. Okay, more than a little while.

"She does have an amazing ass," Rachel said from beside me.

"Eww, Mom!" Lily shrieked.

"Lily, don't tell anyone I said that about Aunt Nicki's girlfriend."

"Even Aunt Nicki's girlfriend?"

"Especially Aunt Nicki's girlfriend."

Lily asked, "Can I tell Aunt Nicki?"

"Well, she heard me say it, so I guess that's okay."

"Excuse me." I growled. My sister and niece looked up at me like they were noticing me for the first time. "Can you both stop talking about this?"

"Aunt Nicki, can we go carve pumpkins now?"

The farm had pretty much cleared out, and the lack of people made my stomach churn. "Not yet. I have to work until the farm closes."

Rachel pointed to her watch. "Hate to tell you, sis, but the farm is closing now."

"Oh God, are you serious?"

I yanked her wrist to glare at the watch. She yelped, but I ignored her. Sure enough, the arms of her dainty wristwatch were pointing to the scary numbers. The farm was closing in five minutes. It was time.

"Are you ready for this?" Rachel asked.

I stared up at her and suddenly I was not at all ready for this.

When I wobbled, Rachel grabbed my shoulders. "Don't freak out. You planned this. It's what you want."

I nodded but didn't trust myself to speak.

Rachel patted my cheek and gave me a watery smile, tears pooling in her eyes. "You love her, right?"

I nodded again.

"And you want to be with her?"

I nodded and squeaked out, "Forever."

"Then you're doing the right thing. And, for the record, I think it'll be great."

I nodded a final time and then I was moving, walking toward the center of the farm even though I couldn't feel my feet. Carter was standing over by the tractor barn, chatting with her mom and one of her brothers. She laughed at something her brother said and seeing that smile on her face—seeing the joy in her eyes and hearing the warmth of her voice—made my confidence return. Not only was this good and right, it was everything I had ever wanted. I gave the box in my pocket one last squeeze and snatched the two tickets wedged into the corner of my other pocket.

I held up the haunted house tickets and poked Carter in the ribs with my elbow. "I need someone to hold my hand. You free?"

Carter laughed again and turned to her mom. "What do you say, boss? Can I cut out a little early?"

"Just this once." Her mom gave me a wink. "Try not to fall down this time? Our insurance is already expensive."

"I'll try."

"I thought you hated these things," Carter said as we got in line.

"Yeah, well I like this particular one."

Before she could kiss me, the attendant took our tickets and told us to wait by the door.

Carter jerked her thumb toward the empty line behind us. "I guess we're the last ones tonight. Looks like we'll get a private tour."

"Maybe so."

I couldn't meet her eye and I knew I was fidgeting, but Carter didn't seem to notice my nerves. After all, I was nervous a lot. Although I had to admit it hadn't been so bad over the last year. I hadn't even dropped a dinner plate since Carter moved in with me last summer.

As we opened the front door, Carter said, "I still don't see why that haunted house weekend shouldn't be our official anniversary. That was when I asked you out the first time."

"Yeah, but I didn't know you asked me out. Halloween is our anniversary."

It was an ongoing discussion and Carter often teased me with it. Ever since I insisted Halloween should be our anniversary because that was when we went from casual to serious. She didn't have too much chance to argue because the lights in the foyer blinked out and the screeching and moaning soundtrack began.

Carter kept close to me throughout the first floor. They had made some minor tweaks to the haunted house this season, keeping it fresh for last year's return visitors. I hadn't been through it this year, but I knew the most important room was set up exactly the same as it had been last year.

Carter laughed into my ear as we climbed the back staircase. "Make sure you jump at the right time. Our room is coming up."

For a heartbeat, I thought she knew. That my well-laid plan had been ruined by her loose-lipped parents or my oblivious niece. But there wasn't a chance. I'd kept all the dangerous parties either in the dark or far away from Carter for the last month.

I pecked her on the cheek and stepped out of her reach as the bedroom door groaned open. "Shh. You'll ruin the jump scare."

Carter followed me into the room and the door slammed shut. It was darker than last time, but I could hear Carter breathing behind me. A light flickered near the floor and I caught a glimpse of a baby doll shoe no self-respecting zombie would wear. This was it. I took two deep breaths.

The zombie roared from the opposite corner. Carter hadn't been expecting it. She jumped, then recovered and held out her arms. I waited another heartbeat, then I went down.

"Nicki!"

The lights blazed on, blinding me momentarily. I made it down safe, though. Not landing on my forehead like last year, but on one knee.

"Nicki?"

Carter wasn't looking at me when she said my name. She was looking at all the people occupying the now fully lit room. They were pressed to the walls and furniture and their eyes were all on us.

"Carter?" I said. Her eyes turned to me then went wide. I adjusted my weight on my knee and held out my hand. It wasn't until I looked at the square box that I realized I hadn't opened it.

"Nicki?"

I peeled the box open, revealing the ring that had taken me ages to design. A broad, plain band of sterling silver because Carter hated gold. The largest diamond was set flush to the band in the center, representing our love. On either side were smaller, matched diamonds, representing our past and shared future. Her eyes welled up when she saw it.

I started again. "Carter, this past year with you has been something out of a dream. I never thought I'd ever feel anything like this. I never really believed love existed. Not until I met you."

Rachel let out a sob, which she quickly stifled. Lily stomped on her foot, which made Blake laugh. His laugh always made Carter's dad and brother laugh. Her mom slapped both of their arms. Once everyone was quiet again, her mom waved at me to continue.

Rachel whispered too loud, "Sorry. Go ahead."

"Shh," Lily hissed.

I gave them both a hard look, then turned back to Carter. She was smiling and it made me smile. That made my heart thud too loud and then I couldn't remember any of the words I'd practiced.

Carter laughed. "It's your fault. You invited all these idiots."

"Hey, I'm your father."

"Would you be quiet, Nelson? Nicki is trying to propose to our daughter."

"Is that what's going on?" Carter asked, barely holding back her laughter.

"Would everyone be quiet please?" I realized too late how loud I shouted. Still, it worked to get everyone quiet. "Where was I?" I turned back to Carter.

"You didn't know love existed until you met me."

"Right. I didn't know love—Oh shoot. Will you please marry me? My knee hurts."

Carter dropped down on both knees and cupped my face in her hands. "Of course I'll marry you."

Everyone started cheering, but I was too focused on Carter to care. She let the tears fall as she pulled me into a kiss. It was so much like our first kiss. Gentle as her breath on my skin. Sweet as a pumpkin spice latte. Warm and strong and forever.

And I would get a kiss like that every day for the rest of my life.

About the Author

Tagan Shepard (she/her) is the author of ten books of sapphic fiction, including the 2019 Goldie award winner *Bird on a Wire*. When not writing about extraordinary women loving other extraordinary women, she can be found playing video games, renovating the fixer-upper house her wife convinced her to buy, or sitting in DC metro traffic. She lives in Northern Virginia with her very patient wife and two ridiculous cats.

www.taganshepard.com

Books Available from Bold Strokes Books

Hands of the Morri by Heather K O'Malley. Discovering she is a Lost Sister and growing acquainted with her new body, Asche learns how to be a warrior and commune with the Goddess the Hands serve, the Morri. (978-1-63679-465-5)

I Know About You by Erin Kaste. With her stalker inching closer to the truth, Cary Smith is forced to face the past she's tried desperately to forget. (978-1-63679-513-3)

Mate of Her Own by Elena Abbott. When Heather McKenna finally confronts the family who cursed her, her werewolf is shocked to discover her one true mate, and that's only the beginning. (978-1-63679-481-5)

Pumpkin Spice by Tagan Shepard. For Nicki, new love is making this pumpkin spice season sweeter than expected. (978-1-63679-388-7)

Rivals for Love by Ali Vali. Brooks Boseman's brother Curtis is getting married, and Brooks needs to be at the engagement party. Only she can't possibly go, not with Curtis set to marry the secret love of her youth, Fallon Goodwin. (978-1-63679-384-9)

Sweat Equity by Aurora Rey. When cheesemaker Sy Travino takes a job in rural Vermont and hires contractor Maddie Barrow to rehab a house she buys sight unseen, they both wind up with a lot more than they bargained for. (978-1-63679-487-7)

Taking the Plunge by Amanda Radley. When Regina Avery meets model Grace Holland—the most beautiful woman she's ever seen— she doesn't have a clue how to flirt, date, or hold on to a relationship. But Regina must take the plunge with Grace and hope she manages to swim. (978-1-63679-400-6)

We Met in a Bar by Claire Forsythe. Wealthy nightclub owner Erica turns undercover bartender on a mission to catch a thief where she meets no-strings, no-commitments Charlie, who couldn't be further from Erica's type. Right? (978-1-63679-521-8)

Western Blue by Suzie Clarke. Step back in time to this historic western filled with heroism, loyalty, friendship, and love. The odds are against this unlikely group—but never underestimate women who have nothing to lose. (978-1-63679-095-4)

Windswept by Patricia Evans. The windswept shores of the Scottish Highlands weave magic for two people convinced they'd never fall in love again. (978-1-63679-382-5)

An Independent Woman by Kit Meredith. Alex and Rebecca's attraction won't stop smoldering, despite their reluctance to act on it and incompatible poly relationship styles. (978-1-63679-553-9)

Cherish by Kris Bryant. Josie and Olivia cherish the time spent together, but when the summer ends and their temporary romance melts into the real deal, reality gets complicated. (978-1-63679-567-6)

Cold Case Heat by Mary P. Burns. Sydney Hansen receives a threat in a very cold murder case that sends her to the police for help where she finds more than justice with Detective Gale Sterling. (978-1-63679-374-0)

Proximity by Jordan Meadows. Joan really likes Ellie, but being alone with her could turn deadly unless she can keep her dangerous powers under control. (978-1-63679-476-1)

Sweet Spot by Kimberly Cooper Griffin. Pro surfer Shia Turning will have to take a chance if she wants to find the sweet spot. (978-1-63679-418-1)

The Haunting of Oak Springs by Crin Claxton. Ghosts and the past haunt the supernatural detective in a race to save the lesbians of Oak Springs farm. (978-1-63679-432-7)

Transitory by J.M. Redmann. The cops blow it off as a customer surprised by what was under the dress, but PI Micky Knight knows they're wrong—she either makes it her case or lets a murderer go free to kill again. (978-1-63679-251-4)

Unexpectedly Yours by Toni Logan. A private resort on a tropical island, a feisty old chief, and a kleptomaniac pet pig bring Suzanne and Allie together for unexpected love. (978-1-63679-160-9)

Bones of Boothbay Harbor by Michelle Larkin. Small-town police chief Frankie Stone and FBI Special Agent Eve Huxley must set aside their differences and combine their skills to find a killer after a burial site is discovered in Boothbay Harbor, Maine. (978-1-63679-267-5)

Crush by Ana Hartnett Reichardt. Josie Sanchez worked for years for the opportunity to create her own wine label, and nothing will stand in her way. Not even Mac, the owner's annoyingly beautiful niece Josie's forced to hire as her harvest intern. (978-1-63679-330-6)

Decadence by Ronica Black, Renee Roman, and Piper Jordan. You are cordially invited to Decadence, Las Vegas's most talked about invitation-only Masquerade Ball. Come for the entertainment and stay for the erotic indulgence. We guarantee it'll be a party that lives up to its name. (978-1-63679-361-0)

Gimmicks and Glamour by Lauren Melissa Ellzey. Ashly has learned to hide her Sight, but as she speeds toward high school graduation she must protect the classmates she claims to hate from an evil that no one else sees. (978-1-63679-401-3)

Heart of Stone by Sam Ledel. Princess Keeva Glantor meets Maeve, a gorgon forced to live alone thanks to a decades-old lie, and together the two women battle forces they formerly thought to be good in the hopes of leading lives they can finally call their own. (978-1-63679-407-5)

Murder at the Oasis by David S. Pederson. Palm trees, sunshine, and murder await Mason Adler and his friend Walter as they travel from Phoenix to Palm Springs for what was supposed to be a relaxing vacation but ends up being a trip of mystery and intrigue. (978-1-63679-416-7)

Peaches and Cream by Georgia Beers. Adley Purcell is living her dreams owning Get the Scoop ice cream shop until national dessert chain Sweet Heaven opens less than two blocks away and Adley has to compete with the far too heavenly Sabrina James. (978-1-63679-412-9)

The Only Fish in the Sea by Angie Williams. Will love overcome years of bitter rivalry for the daughters of two crab fishing families in this queer modern-day spin on Romeo and Juliet? (978-1-63679-444-0)

Wildflower by Cathleen Collins. When a plane crash leaves eleven-year-old Lily Andrews stranded in the vast wilderness of Arkansas, will she be able to overcome the odds and make it back to civilization and the one person who holds the key to her future? (978-1-63679-621-5)

Witch Finder by Sheri Lewis Wohl. Tamsin, the Keeper of the Book of Darkness, is in terrible danger, and as a Witch Finder, Morrigan must protect her and the secrets she guards even if it costs Morrigan her life. (978-1-63679-335-1)

A Second Chance at Life by Genevieve McCluer. Vampires Dinah and Rachel reconnect, but a string of vampire killings begin and evidence seems to be pointing at Dinah. They must prove her innocence while finding out if the two of them are still compatible after all these years. (978-1-63679-459-4)

Digging for Heaven by Jenna Jarvis. Litz lives for dragons. Kella lives to kill them. The last thing they expect is to find each other attractive. (978-1-63679-453-2)

Forever's Promise by Missouri Vaun. Wesley Holden migrated west disguised as a man for the hope of a better life and with no designs to take a wife, but Charlotte Rose has other ideas. (978-1-63679-221-7)

Here For You by D. Jackson Leigh. A horse trainer must make a difficult business decision that could save her father's ranch from foreclosure but destroy her chance to win the heart of a feisty barrel racer vying for a spot in the National Rodeo Finals. (978-1-63679-299-6)

I Do, I Don't by Joy Argento. Creator of the romance algorithm, Nicole Hart doesn't expect to be starring in her own reality TV dating show, and falling for the show's executive producer Annie Jackson could ruin everything. (978-1-63679-420-4)

It's All in the Details by Dena Blake. Makeup artist Lane Donnelly and wedding planner Helen Trent can't stand each other, but they must set aside their differences to ensure Darcy gets the wedding of her dreams, and make a few of their own dreams come true. (978-1-63679-430-3)

Marigold by Melissa Brayden. Marigold Lavender vows to take down Alexis Wakefield, the harsh food critic who blasts her younger sister's restaurant. If only she wasn't as sexy as she is mean. (978-1-63679-436-5)

The Town that Built Us by Jesse J. Thoma. When her father dies, Grace Cook returns to her hometown and tries to avoid Bonnie Whitlock, the woman who pulverized her heart, only to discover her father's estate has been left to them jointly. (978-1-63679-439-6)